A town un[...]

A robber lord seeking revenge.

A band of mercenaries hired to defend . . .

The Middle of Nowhere.

The villagers sat down in orderly rows, facing Howland's motley band. Two torches blazed on either side of the Knight, the only light he would permit.

"I am Howland uth Ungen, Knight of the Order of the Rose. As you know we've come here to defend you against your enemies, Rakell and his raiders." He paused, trying to catch every farmer's eyes before he continued. "This we cannot do."

By Paul Thompson and
Tonya Cook

Preludes
Darkness and Light
Riverwind the Plainsman

The Lost Histories
The Dargonesti

The Barbarians Trilogy
Children of the Plains
Brother of the Dragon
Sister of the Sword

The Ergoth Trilogy
A Warrior's Journey

CROSSROADS

The Middle of Nowhere

Paul B. Thompson

THE MIDDLE OF NOWHERE

©2003 Wizards of the Coast, Inc.

Distributed in the United States by Holtzbrinck Publishing. Distributed in Canada by Fenn Ltd.

Distributed to the hobby, toy, and comic trade in the United States and Canada by regional distributors.

Distributed worldwide by Wizards of the Coast, Inc. and regional distributors.

Printed in the U.S.A.

The sale of this book without its cover has not been authorized by the publisher. If you purchased this book without a cover, you should be aware that neither the author nor the publisher has received payment for this "stripped book."

Cover art by Daniel Horne
First Printing: July 2003
Library of Congress Catalog Card Number: 2002114361

9 8 7 6 5 4 3 2 1

US ISBN: 0-7869-3061-6
UK ISBN: 0-7869-3062-4
620-96190-001-EN

U.S., CANADA,   EUROPEAN HEADQUARTERS
ASIA, PACIFIC, & LATIN AMERICA   Wizards of the Coast, Belgium
Wizards of the Coast, Inc.   T Hosfveld 6d
P.O. Box 707   1702 Groot-Bijgaarden
Renton, WA 98057-0707   Belgium
+ 1-800-324-6496   + 322 467 3360

Visit our web site at **www.wizards.com**

In memory of my father,
Walter B. Thompson
1920-2002

a soldier by choice

and Shimura Takashi
1905-1982

actor's actor

NOWHERE

Before,
in Nowhere

E veryone comes from somewhere, the
Elder used to say. Kender have a home,
even if they leave it once and never return from their wanderings. Soldiers and priests, merchants and monsters, all
have points of origin. A patch of ground, the shade of a
tree, a pattern of stars overhead are all parts of home.

The village of Nowhere was just that: isolated,
unknown and unremarked. A scholar could have pointed
out the larger locale on a map, but no map bore the name
of Nowhere. Unlike some hamlets kept secret and safe by
high mountains or steaming swamps, Nowhere was
nowhere simply because it was out of the way, a small spot
in a large expanse. Riches and resources they had none.
The terrain was nondescript grassland, amidst low hills
crowned with stands of willow and alder. Too scrawny for

1

lumber and too gnarled for spears or tool shafts, even the trees of Nowhere were of little use.

Despite the forgotten nature of the place, people did live there. A village had grown up around the only clear spring for two days' ride in any direction. Gray-bearded villagers called it the Eternal Spring, for in all the unbroken history of their lives, it had never run dry.

Simple huts of wattle slathered with mud daub surrounded the spring in a horseshoe plan, the open end of the shoe facing west, where the villagers kept fields planted in onions, carrots, barley, and cabbage. Constant labor was required to make anything grow. The climate was dry, and some seasons the only thing that kept the crops alive was the ever-flowing spring.

It was late summer, and the harvest was four weeks away. A minor drought had plagued the region since high summer. The usual towering thunderstorms had all passed south of Nowhere, leaving the yellow soil dry as flour. When the wind huffed down from the north, it brought with it a cloud of dust that covered everything in a drab and desiccated ochre grit.

Parched through and through from his morning's labors, Malek sought the old well. Sweat stung his eyes as he hauled up the bucket from the depths. The worn wooden pulley rattled and squeaked as the brimming bucket rose. Malek was pleased to see clear water sloshing as the container swayed upward. No matter how erratic the rains might be, the village could always rely on the ancient well.

Malek gathered in the bucket. He splashed a handful of water on the Ancestor's head, a token of appreciation of the well's steadfast bounty. The Ancestor was an upright lump of sandstone, as tall as his waist and red as the sunset, inset in the rubblestone wall around the well. Totally unlike the nondescript gray rocks found around Nowhere, the Ancestor had been brought to the village from some far-off place so long ago its exact point of origin was forgotten. In time it had become the totem of the village. Old folks in Nowhere believed it housed the spirits of every man, woman, and child who'd ever lived in the village, hence the epithet, "Ancestor." Hearth tales told on long winter nights held the Ancestor was guardian of the Eternal Spring, with ancient and recondite powers.

Looking at the bucket, Malek frowned. The wooden sides were slick with slime. Someone was not doing their job. Every family in the village took turns caring for common property like the well. In summer, the bucket had to be scraped every few days to keep the slime off. It had been so neglected green moss was beginning to grow on the bottom. Malek poured the rest of the brimming bucket into a tall waterskin and tried to remember who had care of the well this month. Willat's family? Old widow Naek? Or was it Bakar? It must be Bakar. He was known to be careless, and besides, he was unmarried and couldn't slough the job onto a wife or child.

"How goes it, Malek?"

Bakar sauntered up, a sprig of barley in his teeth. The stem was yellow-green and thin like the crop in the fields.

"It goes dry," Malek replied with a grunt. When Bakar looked alarmed, Malek quickly explained, "The weather, I mean. The well flows."

Four times Malek dropped and retrieved the bucket. He hefted the now full skin onto his shoulder. Destined for his carrot patch, it held four buckets full, a heavy load. Even Malek's sturdy knees bowed a bit under the burden. He passed his neighbor the slimy bucket without a word.

He looked out over the parchwork of gardens. It was midday, and everyone able-bodied was in the fields. Only crippled old folk and the smallest children remained in the village during the day. They kept inside, out of the sun. Nothing was stirring, not even the wind. Malek's eyes narrowed.

"What's that?" he said, puzzled.

Bakar dropped the bucket down the deep shaft. Before it hit the water he replied, "What's what?"

"That dust."

Bakar turned languidly to see what puzzled his neighbor. Though a young man, he moved more slowly than anyone else in the village, save the Elder himself.

Shading his eyes, Bakar perused the narrow column of yellow dust rising southeast of the village.

"Wind," said Bakar, unimpressed.

"Wind's out of the north," Malek replied. "That dust is coming towards us, against the wind."

As soon as he said it, both knew someone was coming. As no one ever came to Nowhere casually, visitors meant trouble.

"Sound the gong!" Malek said. "I'll go to the fields!"

Bakar loped away, almost moving quickly. On a post between the last pair of houses in the village hung a slab of bronze, green with age. As Malek sprinted past, the phlegmatic farmer picked up the wooden mallet leaning against the post and started whacking the gong. The battered metal plate rang surprisingly clearly, and the sound carried far across the open land. By the time Malek reached the edge of the communal barley field, men and women were already gathering.

His elder brother Nils was there with his sixteen-year-old son Larem, the Elder's daughter Caeta (herself the

4

oldest woman in Nowhere), the tow-headed twins Lak and Wilf, and the other adults of the village.

"Why the alarm?" demanded Caeta. Malek, out of breath, simply pointed at the column of dust, now much closer than when he first spotted it. Grim-faced, Caeta shouldered her hoe and said, "Back to your homes, everyone!"

The fields rapidly emptied of farmers, each clutching whatever tool they happened to have—rakes, hoes, dibbles. Everyone converged on the clanging gong. Trailing the crowd, Malek took the opportunity to look for Laila, his bride-to-be. He spied her in the door of her family's hut, her blind father leaning on her strong, brown arm.

The farmers collected around the bronze gong, which Bakar continued to beat until Sohn the brewer snatched the mallet from his hand. Joined by a throng of old folks and children, the villagers milled about in noisy confusion, everyone talking and no one listening.

Malek skirted the chaotic scene and hurried along the row of houses to Laila's hut. Side by side, the resemblance between father and daughter was strong. They had the same sharp chin and straight nose, and identical brown eyes. Old Marren's hair had once been honey-brown, like Laila's. There the resemblance ended. Laila was tall, straight, and strong. The same wasting disease that had stolen Marren's sight had shrunk his formerly powerful frame and turned his wispy hair white.

"It's Malek," Laila said for her father's benefit. "What's happening?"

"No one knows yet, but something's coming—"

A piercing scream filled the air. All eyes turned toward the sound, which came from the cluster of gray-haired women gathered by their houses on the south side of the

5

village. Trotting through the hot afternoon sun came a line of horsemen. The tired animals' tongues were lolling and thickly coated with dust. Riding the thirsty beasts were figures in bizarre patchwork armor: bits of iron or bronze, mail or plate, wired and tied over thickly padded suits of leather. Cuisses, helmets, and schildrons were sculpted into hideous faces, skulls, and horned monsters. War and the elements gave these hideously mismatched suits a rusty patina that resembled splashes of dried blood.

Rider after rider emerged from the swirling grit stirred up by their horses' hooves, thirty-two horsemen in all. Armed with long lances, they halted just outside the ring of village huts. Visors on their helmets were shut, lending the intruders a faceless, menacing air. It must be stifling for the men inside—if men they were.

The unknown riders were frightening enough, but on their heels came a more terrifying sight. Striding into view came a squad of towering ogres, each almost as tall as the mounted warriors ahead of them. Yellow tusks, filed sharp as daggers, protruded from the ogres' underslung jaws. Their ears were pulled down to their shoulders by heavy ornaments of brass and bone, and their nobby gray hands were smeared with dried gore. The tallest of the monsters had blue-black tattoos on their shaven pates, and dry white skulls of various victims, two-legged and four-legged, hung from loops on their tarnished armor.

The screaming became general as the villagers shrank from the monstrous new interlopers. Many threw down their tools and huddled around the old gong post.

"Ogres," Old Marren said grimly. His grip tightened on Laila's arm.

"How did you know?" she asked.

"I can smell them."

No ogres had been to the village in living memory, and Malek wondered where the old man had encountered such monsters before. He let the question go unasked, muttering instead to Marren, "Do you still have that sword?"

The old man's sightless eyes gazed into the air over Malek's head. "I do. Over the fireplace."

"I'll get it."

"Malek, no!" Laila hissed.

"Go quickly, son!" countered the blind man.

Malek dashed inside. Marren's sword was old, nicked and pitted, but he kept it well honed and oiled. Malek took it down. It felt like stone, long and heavy. He had never held a sword in his life.

Outside, the ogres ignored the cringing farmers and set about slaking their thirst at the well. Bucket after bucket of water went down the ogres' long gullets, spilling out their jutting jaws and dripping from their ivory fangs. When one ogre didn't pass the bucket fast enough, his comrades buffeted him around the head with their massive clawed hands. Slipping in the mud, the tardy ogre fell heavily against the stone wall surrounding the well. His companions hooted.

Malek counted ten ogres, each armed with a long-handled axe; burnished, well-dented bronze shields; and banded-iron armor criss-crossing their chests.

Six more horses entered the village behind the ogres. Taller and finer-bred than those the lancers rode, they bore riders in blackened three-quarter plate, much stained from long days in the saddle. One rider bore a standard pole with a short, forked oriflamme of sun-faded scarlet. When the six appeared, the lancers straightened in their saddles and the ogres ceased their frantic guzzling and sorted themselves into a semblance of a line.

The riders drew up between the well and the gong. In the center of the group, a tall horseman in streaked sable plate raised his visor and looked over the frightened farmers. Malek made out a short, wide nose and beetling brows, but the rider was undeniably human.

"Where is your headman?" he demanded.

When no dared respond, the man in black armor nodded, and the warrior beside him produced a crossbow. Knocking a thick quarrel, the bowman pointed his weapon at the crowd and loosed. To Malek's horror, Sohn the brewer collapsed, his chest pierced through.

More screaming and weeping erupted as the crowd of villagers surged away. The lancers quickly encircled them, herding the terrified farmers back to the gong. Two of the younger men tried to break free and run. Neither made it more than ten steps before they were spitted on rusty lances. Each new outpouring of blood brought fresh screams from the frightened farmers and restless growls and grunts from the ogres.

Malek had enough. He charged at the rider with the raised visor, waving Marren's old sword. He would have died for his temerity had not the invaders' leader stayed his archer's hand. Six steps from the horsemen, an ogre stuck out the handle of his axe and tripped Malek. The sword went flying, and Malek's charge ended facedown in the fresh mud.

"One of you has courage, if not brains," said the leader. The ogre who tripped Malek drove his bare foot into the villager's ribs. Shod or not, it felt like a plowshare. Malek rolled over and over from the blow. Fire and pain flashed through his side.

"Get up."

When it was clear Malek could not oblige, the leader ordered one of his ogres to get the farmer. The enormous creature, spattered with mud and smelling as if he'd rolled in the rotting carcass of a dead cow, seized Malek by the wrist and dragged him before his commander.

"Who are you?"

"Malek, Gusrav's son," he gasped.

"What place is this?"

"Nowhere . . ."

The ogre slapped Malek on the back of the head. A mild reproof by ogre standards, it rattled the teeth in Malek's jaw.

"I ask you again, what place is this?" barked the commander.

"The village of Nowhere!"

At his leader's nod, the ogre dropped him. Through tear-filled eyes, Malek watched as the invader unbuckled the chin strap of his helmet and pried the heavy headgear off. Under the sinister black helmet was a surprisingly benign countenance. Of middle age, his heavy brows and flat nose, combined with high cheekbones and deeply tanned skin, lent him an aura of refinement unusual for a bandit chief.

"I am Rakell," he declaimed loudly. "Lord Rakell. I have come to this province to bring law and order to backwaters such as this. From this moment on, I am master here. My word is your only law. Obey me, and all will be well. None shall be spared who defy my will. Is that clear?"

There was no response other than quiet weeping. Rakell ignored the muted lamentations.

"At my invitation, dwarves of the Throtian Mining Guild have established an iron mine sixteen leagues from here in the northwestern buttes of the Khalkist Mountains." Sensing geography meant little to his listeners, Rakell gave up further description. "They need able-bodied people to work the diggings. This village will provide twenty for the mine today and in thirty days' time, another twenty."

"There are only sixty-six adults here," protested one farmer weakly. "Take away forty and there won't be enough hands to harvest or plant!"

Rakell raised his hand, and three ogres waded into the crowd and dragged out the man who dared protest. While Rakell looked on impassively, they beat the poor farmer senseless with their enormous knotty fists. When blood started to flow, the bandit chief called off his thugs.

"That's enough. Cripples and corpses can do little work."

The ogres desisted. To the villagers the self-proclaimed lord of Nowhere added, "Perhaps your dialect is as backward as your wits. When I speak, it is a command, not a request!"

When the villagers persisted in clinging together in defiance of Rakell's orders, the lancers moved in, using their spears to lever men and women from the weeping throng. They cut out the first twenty they came to, ranging from Nil's teenage son to Bakar's stout aunt Yena. Torn from friends and family, the chosen villagers were shoved into line by the ogres and shackled together.

Malek managed to roll onto one knee. Catching Rakell's eye, the bandit-lord called for Malek's lost sword. An ogre complied, presenting the weapon to his commander pommel-first.

Rakell took the sword. Upon examining it, his thick brows arched up in surprise.

"How did a knightly blade get to this dustheap, I wonder?" To Malek he said, "You, farmer. Where did you get this blade?"

"My plow turned it up in the barley field," he lied.

Rakell swung the blade experimentally, testing its balance and heft. "Interesting. Pre-Cataclysm work, watered steel made by the school of Thelgaard . . . I shall keep this." He slid the old sword through his buff leather baldric.

Marren's sword! How dare he make off with it! Malek attempted to stand, but pain shot through his ribs and brought him up short. Gasping, he dropped back on his hands. Rakell's companions laughed.

"Heal up, firebrand!" Rakell said, chuckling. "Next time will be your turn. I'd take you now, but the work is hard enough with healthy ribs!"

Rakell's lieutenants ordered the huts searched. Lancers and ogres scattered, kicking down doors and dragging out women and children who'd hidden inside. Behind Caeta's hut they found her cow. A lancer looped a halter around the beast's horns and led her away. When her shaggy calf tried to follow, bawling, another lancer speared it. The sight and smell of blood inflamed the ogres beyond reason. Whooping, they fell on the still-living calf and tore it apart with their hands. Aghast, villagers watched in horror as the ogres happily ate the raw, bloody flesh with all-too-evident joy.

The human raiders filled waterskins and bottles from the well. One young warrior fetched his commander a cool drink. Rakell raised the skin to his lips, squinting against the late-day sun. The water had just begun to flow when Rakell stopped swallowing. Water coursed over his black-bearded chin.

11

"Mother of scorpions! Can it be?" he breathed. "Are there ghosts in this wasteland too?"

"My lord?" said the young man who'd given his water to Rakell.

The commander tossed the bottle to his aide and spurred his horse forward. At a slow walk, he approached the two figures standing before a rude and humble hut.

"It is you!" Rakell said. "Marren uth Aegar!"

The blind man lifted his chin. "No one has called me that for nine and twenty years," he said. "Who speaks that forgotten name?"

"I served under you as a lad, forty years ago," said Rakell. "I fought my first battle in the vale of Garnet at your side."

"Who are you?" said Laila sharply.

"Another ghost." Rakell unbuckled the gorget around his neck, revealing the base of his throat. A great livid scar stretched from under one ear all the way around to the other. Laila cried out, unable to believe anyone could survive such a wound.

"What is it, girl?" said her father.

"His throat was cut, and yet he lives!" she said, choking.

Marren breathed a single word. It might have been a name, but no one near, not even Laila, could make it out.

Rakell replaced the gorget. "It's a day for resurrections, girl, if Marren uth Aegar lives too."

To his aides he said, "These two shall come with me. Take them!"

"No!" Laila bloodied her knuckles punching a visored warrior, but it was all for naught. Her hands were pinioned, but she continued to struggle and kick. Not until a noose was hung over her father's unbowed neck did she relent.

"Leave him be!" she cried.

"He can be led or be dragged," Rakell retorted. "I can set one of my ogres to the task, or you may do it—if you behave yourself!"

Pale but furious, Laila agreed. The noose was taken off.

The lancers and ogres, with twenty enslaved villagers between them, started off at a slow shuffle, their backs to the setting sun. When Malek saw Laila and her father walking in the midst of Rakell and his lieutenants, he found the strength to stand and shout her name.

Heads turned all around. Rakell reined up, waiting to see what Malek might do. Unarmed, unskilled, the young farmer stood, trembling with rage.

"Ride on," Rakell said calmly. With his first step, his horse put a hoof through the village's well bucket, crushing it.

Lancers and ogres rampaged through the village huts, taking what trifles caught their eye. They despoiled far more than they stole. The worst loss occurred when two ogres found Wilf's pigs. With deep grunts of satisfaction, the towering monsters waded into the pen, grabbing the young farmer's fat porkers by the hindquarters. Tucking a shrilly squealing animal under each noisome arm, the ogres followed their leader out of the village.

No one moved until the raiders were just a column of dust rising from the hills again. Malek shook his fist at the drifting ochre pall.

Someone touched his shoulder. Malek spun, fists ready. It was his brother Nils.

"They took Larem!" he said. Malek saw something in his placid brother's eyes he'd never seen there before: total outrage. "He's only sixteen!"

"I know." Malek put a hand on Nils's shoulder and

coughed when the dust cloud swept over them. Every gasp felt like a knife in his ribs. Muddy streaks appeared on his face. "We must go after them!"

"Wait!" Caeta held Malek back. "You can't go. They'll kill you!"

He tore free from her grasp and stamped his feet in helpless fury. "Laila! They took Laila!"

"The Elder," said Nils, casting eyes at the windmill, sited on a low rise outside the village. There amidst the cogs and grindstones lived Nowhere's eldest resident. "Let's ask Calec. He'll know what to do!"

Old folks and children were sent back to their huts as the villagers swarmed up the hill to the mill. The airs were light, so the four vanes of the windmill quivered in place but did not turn. Without bothering to knock, Malek burst in. The others crowded in behind him.

"Aged One! Terrible news!" Malek said.

Calec raised his head from the knob of his walking stick. "I know. I saw."

No one questioned his claim. The old man couldn't see ten steps ahead, and he was nearly deaf, too. Only a deaf man could stand to live in the mill when the works were clattering. Nonetheless, for many years they'd all known the Elder could see and hear things an ordinary man could not.

"What shall we do, Papa?" asked Caeta.

"Do about what?"

"The bandits!" Malek ground his teeth. "They took our people to slave in some mine!"

The Elder's toothless jaw worked. "Take 'em back!"

Malek and the others who'd lost people today roundly cheered the old man's pronouncement, but Caeta said, "How can we? Those men are warriors. What about the ogres? How can we fight them?

"Then do nothing!" said the Elder testily. He lowered his chin to his stick and let his sunken eyes close.

"I'm going to try!" Malek declared. "Who's with me?"

Some were, and some weren't. It disgusted Malek that not all his fellow villagers would rally around him.

"Calves to the slaughter," Calec muttered. "Go now, and die."

Mentioning calves reminded everyone of the fate of Caeta's unfortunate beast. The memory of the ogre tusks biting out mouthfuls of still-living flesh was all too vivid.

Seeing the increasing number of downcast faces, Malek exclaimed, "Are we beaten, then? Do we give up our loved ones without a fight?"

"We're not warriors," Bakar said dolefully.

Malek felt as though the dirt floor of the mill was crumbling beneath his feet. "I'll go alone, if I have to!" he declared. He was almost out the door when Calec said, "Wait!"

Malek paused. "Speak your piece, old man, and be done with it."

A thousand fine wrinkles appeared when the Elder screwed his ancient face into a grimace. "Would you plow a barley field with a dibble?"

"Of course not!" A dibble was a simple hand tool, useful only in small gardens.

"But you'll fight an outlaw band alone—with your bare hands?"

"If I must," Malek replied stiffly.

"You need a plow to cultivate a field," said the Elder, wheezing a little as he shifted on his haunches. "For this great task, you need warriors to fight warriors."

"What are you saying, Papa?" asked Caeta.

"Set a wolf to eat a wolf! The world is full of spillers of blood and wielders of iron. They afflict the land as fleas torment a dog! Go and find some to fight your battle for you. Let their blood be shed, not ours!"

Everyone began babbling at once, debating the old man's notion. Nils spoke for the nay-sayers when he asked, "How will we pay warriors? They'll want steel or gold. We have nothing!"

"The granaries are full," replied Malek. "Despite the drought, the harvest will be fair. We can pay in grain."

"No mercenary will fight for barley!" scoffed Bakar.

"Some may for a full belly," countered the Elder. "Find the hungriest, and make them your champions."

After long wrangling, the farmers finally agreed. Four villagers would go forth from Nowhere to seek out warriors for hire. Malek wanted to go, and his brother Nils also volunteered. Daunted by the prospect of leaving their familiar land, no one else was quite so eager to join the expedition. Impulsively, Wilf offered to go. His twin brother Lak had been one of those taken by Rakell. Lastly Caeta announced she would go too. Someone older and more level-headed needed to go along to keep the hot-headed Malek out of trouble.

"Where should we go?" asked Wilf, scratching his rough thatch of straw-colored hair.

No one knew. None of them had ever been more than a day's walk from Nowhere in their lives.

"Go west," growled the Elder at last. "Follow the setting sun. That way lies the path of blood."

Malek clasped hands with his fellow travelers. "We'll be back in less than thirty days," he vowed.

They hastily packed a few supplies for the journey and departed before sundown. As they passed the well, Wilf noticed something strange. The Ancestor bore a large horizontal crack.

Caeta and the rest paused to examine the old stone. The sandstone pillar was broken right across.

"Must've happened when the ogre fell against it," said Nils.

"A bad sign," Caeta murmured, running worn and callused fingers over the break.

"Will the well dry up?" Wilf wondered.

Malek resumed walking. He was forty steps away before he turned back to call, "Leave that broken stone before your courage dries up!"

One by one his companions rose from the wall and joined him. Last to leave was Caeta. By the dying light of day she could see a dark stain spreading from the crack in the red stone. It spread very slowly, but when she touched the stain, her fingers were not colored or damp. The stain spreading from the broken stone did not leave a trace.

NOWHERE

Chapter One

Later, Somewhere

Seven days' journey west from Nowhere lay a border where the corners of three lands came together in one place. No country had the power to hold this shadowed spot, and none would claim it. In a way, it was another kind of nowhere, but this nowhere was well known. Many are the rogues who need a place out of the sun to heal their wounds, nurse their hates, and hatch their schemes.

The town was called Robann, a girl's name, but no one living remembered who Robann was. Bordered on two sides by forest and on the third by plain, it was a ramshackle affair of half-timbered houses, plank shanties, and squat, ominous stone towers. These last were strongholds of the town's rulers, the seven gangs of Robann.

It was a windy day, and the wind poured in the

shutterless windows. Raika kept one hand over her cup, to keep the dust out. It wasn't very good beer to start with, and a leavening of sand and dry horse dung would not improve it.

She sat with her back against the wall of the tavern. This was a firm habit of hers. She'd seen a man stabbed to death from behind in a wineshop in Kalaman once. He was a famous general, and he trusted his loyal retainers to guard his back. One of them drove an iron blade into his master's kidney. Raika had no retainers and trusted no one but herself to protect her life.

The tavern was called the Thirsty Beggar. Raika thought the name was apt after she met the owner and barkeep. Taverners were usually bluff, ruddy-faced fellows with expansive waists and red noses. The proprietor of the Thirsty Beggar looked as if he had just survived the siege of Valkinord. What a dried up, hollow reed of a man. . . .

As she thought of him, he appeared before her with a dented copper pitcher full of brown beer.

"You want more?" he rasped, hefting the pitcher in his bony hands.

"I've enough for now." She kept her hand in place on the cup.

His eyes narrowed. "This ain't a lodging house. Taverns are for drinking. You don't drink, you don't sit here."

Raika waved a hand at the nearly empty room. "Yes, a mob is clamoring for my table, isn't it?"

The barkeep curled a lip and stalked away, head hunched between his narrow shoulders. Too mean to afford a bouncer, he had no way of forcing the rawboned woman from the premises if she didn't want to go. Raika didn't. She had no place to go.

She hailed from Saifhum. Her home had been the galley *Manarca,* now at the bottom of the sea with most of her crew. All that treasure had broken the good ship's back and put her under the waves. Bags of gold and ingots of steel, row upon row, nestled between *Manarca*'s ribs. Each pair of timbers framed a prince's ransom, and Raika's share would have been a handsome sum. Then a storm came out of the great wide ocean and broke the galley in two, and down went Raika's fortune.

She'd had enough of the Beggar's cheap beer not to notice the four men when they first entered. They tiptoed in, wide-brimmed straw hats in their hands, looking distinctly out of place.

The barkeep made a beeline to the newcomers. Evidently they didn't want a drink, because the old scarecrow fell to berating them in a loud, screeching voice.

"What do you think this is, a temple? You want to warm my benches without drinking my brew? Get out, miserable fools! Get out before I take a broom to your backsides!"

"Shut up, man," Raika found herself saying.

"You can't talk to me like that! This is my place!" he shouted back at her.

"Horsedung! The Silver Circle gang owns this place. You just run it."

His gaunt face flashed more color than Raika had ever seen there. "That's a lie! I pay the Silver Circle good coin every week to stay open, but I own it."

The cause of this dispute huddled by the tavern door, listening. While the farmers cowered, a slight figure brushed past them, making for the bar.

The barkeep spied the newcomer. "You! Kender! I told you not to come back here!"

"Not me, boss. You must've told someone else. I've never been here before in my life, I swear on my granny's knickers—"

Raika laughed. This reminded the owner of her, and he turned back to say, "Mercenary trash! Get out of my tavern!"

She stood up, a study in contained power and careful lethargy. A full six feet tall with ebony skin, sun-washed sailor's togs, and a thick Saifumi turban, Raika seemed to fill the low-ceilinged room. Even the kender, seated nonchalantly on a barstool, turned to gaze at her.

Raika strode toward the barkeep. A head taller and far more robust, she backed the stooped shell of a man up against his own bar. She pushed her face to within a hair's breadth of his.

Glaring at him, she said, "What do I owe you?"

Trembling, he replied, "Nine cups of Number One brown beer, two sticks of boar jerky, let's see . . ." He counted on his fingers. "Three silvers, if you please."

Raika put two fingers in the purse tied to her wide sash belt and brought out a single large coin. It gleamed yellow in the dim light: a gold Saifhum florin. In a blur of motion, she slapped the big coin on the bar. Everyone in the Thirsty Beggar looked up, even the gray-bearded dwarf who'd been snoring in a back booth for the past hour. Before the owner could claim the gold, Raika's hand flashed back to her belt and drew a short dagger.

The men at the door, long forgotten, let out a collective gasp. Sweat trickled down the barman's face.

She raised the dagger alongside her head slowly. Three of the men at the door covered their eyes. One did not. Neither did the kender, already munching something he'd taken from behind the bar.

Paul B. Thompson

Without a word, Raika drove the dagger home. The emaciated barkeep let out a whimper and sagged to the floor.

She sauntered toward the door. The farmers made way for her. With one hand on the door, Raika looked back and said, "Keep the change."

She'd driven the dagger through the coin and into the bar. The blade was buried up to the hilt.

The kender hopped down and squatted over the unconscious man. Clucking his lips, he went around the end of the bar and filled his pockets with hard rolls, jerky, and chunks of yellow cheese. He picked up a pitcher of foamy beer. He walked back by the passed-out proprietor, stopping only to give the dagger an experimental tug. It didn't budge. Chuckling, the kender strolled out.

"Did you see that? He called her 'mercenary.' We should talk to her!" said the youngest of the men, the one with unruly yellow hair.

"She's certainly strong," agreed the lean, black-haired man, "but she won't be interested in our offer. She's has too much money."

"How do you figure that?" asked the stranger in the hood with the gray brows.

"She paid with gold and didn't take change."

The fourth man, the one with the thick shoulders and bald pate, went to the bar and tired to free the dagger. The dark, stained oak held fast to the slim blade. With so short a handle to grasp, no one but an ogre could free the dagger or the coin.

"Come on, Nils, let's try another place."

Outside, they saw Raika ambling up the street. She was easy to follow, being taller than most. She glanced back once at the four strangers, gave them a hard stare, and pushed her way into another tavern, the Boar's Tusk.

22

"What about that place?" said Malek, pointing.

Her long braid concealed by the hood, Caeta shrugged. "Any place folks gather will do."

The farmers wended their way toward the Boar's Tusk, clutching each other's cloaks. Robann was crowded by any standard, and to the innocent inhabitants of Nowhere, it was the most thickly populated place they'd ever been.

Wilf, last in line, felt a strange hand grasping the back of his woolen wrap. Over his shoulder he spied a kender, the one from the Thirsty Beggar. He was holding onto Wilf with one hand while he guzzled purloined beer with the other.

"Excuse me—?" Wilf said.

The kender lowered the pitcher and belched loudly. "You're excused, mate. I saw you fellas holding on each other, so I decided to join and up and see where you're all going."

Up front, Malek felt a tug as those behind him stopped. He spied the unwanted addition to their little group.

"What do you want?" he demanded of the kender.

"Nothing special. Just makin' my way."

"We're poor men. We've nothing to steal."

"Steal?" The kender drew himself up in mock outrage.

"You stole that beer," said Nils.

A hard roll fell from the kender's pocket.

"And that bread," added Caeta.

"Cheese and meat, too," put in Wilf.

With much affected dignity, the kender picked up the fallen roll and blew off the dirt. "I have every intention of paying!" he said. "As soon as I get some money," he added, glaring at them. Turning on one heel, he marched away.

"Wilf," Malek said, "watch your back from now on!"

The Boar's Tusk was considerably more busy than the last establishment. As soon as the farmers entered, they ran up against a wall of sights, smells, and sounds. The tavern was narrow but deep, lit by three open skylights.

"What now?" Wilf asked.

"Look for ones with swords," said Caeta. "They're the ones we need."

Keeping close together, they insinuated themselves into the noisy crowd. Malek didn't get five steps before half a flagon of wine was spilled on his shirt. It came from the hand of a sweaty fat man, who was gesticulating wildly as he related some tale to his companion, a red-bearded dwarf.

"What? Eh, sorry, friend!" said the fat man, still waving his hands. Droplets of blood-red wine flew. "Girl, fetch another pipe of this Goodlund vintage! And one for my poor, sodden friend, here!"

Malek tried to wave off the proffered drink. "I cannot repay the favor," he protested.

"Never mind!" The stout man seemed to always talk at the top of his lungs. "I don't need wine poured on me, friend, just in me!"

Caeta muttered in Malek's ear, "We'll scout the room." With that, she, Wilf, and Nils were swallowed up by the press.

A glazed clay cup of wine was thrust into Malek's hands.

"Falzen's my name," said the fat man. "This here's Gorfon, Gorfon Tattermaul." Falzen belched. "He's a dwarf!"

Malek nodded to them both with wide eyes. "Malek, Gusrav's son."

"You're not from around here," said Gorfon. He had a deep, penetrating voice that Malek found he could hear well, even through the din.

"I'm from"—he almost said "Nowhere," but he'd grown tired of explaining the village's name. "—east of here. I've never been to Robann before."

"It's a stinking sinkhole, ain't it?" Falzen said. "More so since the wars ended. Every out-of-work spear-toter north of the Newsea passes through here, seems like."

Malek drank deeply of the Goodlund wine as his mind raced ahead. Lots of soldiers looking for employment was good news.

"Are you a warrior?" he asked, looking around for his companions.

"Me? May all the forgotten gods defend me! I'm no hack-and-slasher! Steel's my line—iron and steel."

That accounted for his expansive ways. Falzen must be a wealthy man. Eyeing the dwarf, Malek said, "Are you in the metal trade as well, Master Tattermaul?"

"Aye. My brothers and I have a new concession under-way. In the east." Tattermaul let that vague remark hang in the air. "A new iron mine."

Malek almost choked. What was it Lord Rakell had said? "Dwarves of the Throtian Mining Guild had estab-lished a mine in the Khalkist Mountains?"

"Of course, the price of iron is down, thanks to the cur-rent peace," Falzen went on. His small eyes shone. "But who knows? War may break out at any time." He raised his cup to his dwarf colleague. "Here's to war and the blades it takes to fight 'em!"

Gorfon merely grunted.

As soon as he could, Malek slipped away. Loathing the callous steel merchant, he spun out an elaborate plan to waylay Falzen and the dwarf, holding them hostage against the safe return of Laila and the rest—

He gave up the idea before he'd gone five steps. Four farmers, unskilled at anything but raising crops, weren't likely to overcome a rich merchant (doubtless with his own private guards) and a thick-armed dwarf. Besides, even if they could kidnap Falzen and Gorfon, once they returned them, Rakell could raid their village again with impunity. No, the old plan was best: Find real fighters to defend Nowhere by defeating Rakell's marauders.

Malek found his companions in a boisterous crowd surrounding an incipient arm-wrestling contest. On one side was an enormous man, seemingly carved out of sinew and hard muscle. He wore a sleeveless leather vest studded with brass rings, and his coal-black hair was gathered into a single long scalplock. A narrow mustache drooped on either side of his chin. His forearms bore many thin, parallel scars.

Across from this fearsome man was an even more startling figure. Bulking larger than any human in the tavern was a great bull-headed creature, a minotaur from the islands across the Blood Sea. Naked to the waist, the minotaur presented an expanse of heavily muscled chest. His dark, bovine eyes were soft in the shadowed recesses away from the skylights. When he blinked, Malek noticed the creature had very long brown lashes.

Onlookers howled bets and waved sweaty fistfuls of coins at the combatants. In spite of the minotaur's superior size, betting was heavily in favor of the burly man. Judging by the shouts around him, his name was Durand.

"Six to four, six to four for Durand!"

Oddsmakers scratched tallies on tabletops with lumps of chalk. More money appeared in all sort of denominations—

gold coins of a dozen nations, steel rings (the common pay of soldiers), square silver plaques, uncut gems, and even a sprinkling of humble coppers. The odds rose to two to one in favor of the human. Wilf got so excited he tried to bet the buckle of his cloak, but Nils restrained him.

"All right, beef-man," said Durand with a sneer. "Shall we be about it?"

"I regret this. I really do," replied the minotaur. His voice was as low and rumbling as his physique predicted, but his intonation was surprisingly gentle.

"Enough regrets!" Durand presented his brawny right arm, palm out. "Put up your paw!"

The minotaur's great hand almost completely enclosed the human's. "Notice, please, my hand has the same form as yours," the bull-man said. "It is not a paw."

Sinews in Durand's arm leaped out as he threw his strength against the minotaur. Everyone gathered around the table began shouting, most crying "Durand! Durand!" as the man tried to force the minotaur's arm down. So far, neither contestant had budged.

Veins appeared in Durand's neck, throbbing with effort. He bared yellow teeth and bore down, bowing his head to the task. Still the minotaur's arm did not shift. Quite absently, he raised his left hand and scratched behind his short horns. Durand grunted curses at his opponent.

The minotaur had few partisans in the crowd up to now. Seeing him resist Durand so effortlessly led a few to chant, "Go, bull-man, go!"

Eyes popping, Durand let out a roar of defiance. His elbow rose until howls from the onlookers made him bring it down again.

"This is tedious," said the minotaur. "I really must go now."

Without warning, he swept his arm down to the table. Everyone heard the loud pop as Durand's forearm snapped.

After a heartbeat of silence, the crowd erupted. Those who had bet on the minotaur whooped with joy. Durand's supporters cried foul. It wasn't long before a fist was thrown, then a flurry of weighty mugs followed. Touts scrambled to recover the wagers before a riot broke out. All the while Durand writhed on the floor, grasping his broken arm.

Someone flew backward into Malek, bowling him over. Wilf received a fist in the face and spun away, stunned. Tough old Caeta picked up a stool and used it to fend off a barrage of cups and mugs while Nils frantically dodged punches thrown at his head.

Malek got to his knees. He crawled toward the only calm person in sight: the minotaur. Several men fell over him along the way, but Malek reached the bull-man's side. Liquid brown eyes regarded him impassively.

"Any shelter in a storm!" Malek said.

Just then he spied the gleam of bare bronze. A man in a soldier's tunic with a bloody nose loomed behind the minotaur, dagger drawn. Malek tried to push the minotaur out of the way, crying, "Look out!" He might as well have tried to shift Mount Estvar.

The minotaur rose and turned. Easily seven feet tall, he towered so high his attacker lost his nerve. He gaped at the bull-man, and another brawler flattened him with a bench.

"Time to go," rumbled the minotaur. He grabbed Malek by the back of his shirt.

"Hey, wait!" Malek flailed helplessly, his feet off the floor.

"You did me a good turn. I'll see you safely out of this fracas."

"But my friends—!" He pointed at Nils and the others.

"Very well."

Still holding Malek, the minotaur waded into the melee, swatting aside anyone in his way. Once Nils, Wilf, and Caeta were together, he boomed, "Follow me," and started for the door.

It was a wild trip for Malek. He kicked and struck at anyone who got in his way, but it was hard to fight while dangling in mid-air. On the way he saw Falzen cowering under a table, while Gorfon stood over him, an axe resting on his shoulder. Brawlers gave the armed dwarf wide berth.

Three men cut the minotaur off, blocking the door. "Stop, you!" one of them shouted. He carried a short sword already stained with blood. "You cost us a lot of money!"

"That's hardly my fault," answered the minotaur mildly. "It was no contest. That should have been plain."

"Shut up, beef! Pay up, or we'll take our losses out of your hide!"

His friend, armed with a broken bottle, said, "Wonder if we can make a roast of him?"

"Naw," said the sword-bearer. "By the look of him, I bet his mother was a tough old cow."

Thump! Malek hit the floor on the seat of his pants. It hurt, but it was more the indignity he resented. He forgot his small discomfort when he saw the minotaur charge. Lowering his horned head, he caught the man's sword and with a twist, tore it from his hands. Another sideways swipe, and he threw the swordsman six feet onto a table. Next he backhanded the bottle-carrier, leaving him flat on his back, out cold. The third troublemaker, seeing his armed friends undone, turned tail and fled.

Bellowing, the minotaur burst through the closed tavern door, smashing the planks to flinders. People in the street scattered at the sight of the raging bull-man. Malek and the farmers came tumbling after him. They piled up against the immobile minotaur's back.

The vast horned head snapped around, and Malek felt hot breath on his face.

"Little men, do not trouble me!"

"Don't you remember? I'm the one who warned you!" Malek replied.

Nostrils flaring, the minotaur regained his composure. "I am shamed," he said with a profound sigh. "To lose my temper over such a childish taunt! Still, no one calls my mother a c—" He bit off the hateful epithet.

"Not more than once," muttered Nils, behind his brother.

Shouts rang out from inside the Boar's Tusk. The men the minotaur had brushed aside had aroused the angry, drunken mob inside against the bull-man. They were coming, and there were two dozen of them at least.

"Time to go." The minotaur sprinted up the street, drawing stares from passersby as he ran. His long legs ate up ground at a tremendous rate, and the farmers struggled to keep up. A patrol of armed men appeared in front of him.

Someone cried, "Silver Circle guards!"

All the businesses in this part of town paid "protection" to the Silver Circle gang. News of the disturbance in the Boar's Tusk had swiftly reached the gang's stronghold, and this party of footmen had been dispatched to quell the riot and protect the gang's valuable concession.

Seeing naked swords and spears, the minotaur did a

quick about-face. The tavern mob had flooded the street. The minotaur forced his way through the angry crowd, tossing people right and left with hands and horns. The Silver Circle guards charged.

Malek waved and shouted, "This way! Follow us! Come on, this way!"

They ran down a side street, deeply shadowed by the setting sun and smelling damp. Up a narrow alley and over a fence, and they reached the rear of a large, ramshackle wooden building. Pausing for breath, the farmers and the bull-man listened for sounds of pursuit. There was noise aplenty, but it sounded as if the town guards were fighting the mob.

"I guess we escaped!" Caeta gasped, doubling over.

"Thank you for your help," said the minotaur. "I think I shall leave now. Too many hotheads in this town. Too many swords."

"Wait," Malek said. "What is your name?"

"Khorr, of the Thickhorn Clan."

"Wait, Khorr! Stay here until things calm down."

"What is this place?" The minotaur sniffed air filled with straw and horse dung. "A stable?"

"Our lodging," Wilf said wryly. "We can't afford the hostels here."

Planting his hands on his hips, Khorr surveyed the decrepit stable. "No one would look for the scion of the Thickhorn Clan in such a place!" He laughed, and the livestock within squirmed and pranced at the sound.

They went in and closed the rickety door behind them. In the loft, the farmers' meager bundles lay hidden under loose straw. As they settled in, backs against the wall, Caeta said, "How do you come to be so far from your homeland, Master Khorr?"

"It's a sad tale, long, and lacking in romance. Suffice it to say, I am exiled from the land of my clan, and I know not when I may return. Five years I've been traveling in foreign climes."

"On the run, eh?" said Nils. He rummaged through his bundle and distributed dry barley cakes to his comrades. Noting Khorr's interest, he gave the bull-man two cakes. "Kill someone, did you—if I may ask?"

"No. I chose a path for my life my clan could not accept."

Malek couldn't imagine what such a path might be. Pirate? Assassin?

"You see," said Khorr shyly, "I am a poet."

Everyone stopped chewing. "Poet?" said Wilf.

"Quite. I yearn to inscribe my name on the hearts of listeners everywhere, alongside the great bards of my race: Yagar, Kingus, Gonz . . ."

"If your people have had great bards in the past, why did your family oppose you becoming a poet?" asked Malek reasonably.

Khorr made short work of two barley cakes that would have fed a farmer for two days. "Well, the Thickhorn clan have always been seafarers," he said, licking his blunt fingers. "My grandsire, Khol, navigated the Blood Sea Maelstrom, and my Great-uncle Ghard won the Battle of Cape Balifor against the pirate fleet of Khurman the Terrible eighty-eight years ago. I wrote six hundred triplets about the battle . . ." Suddenly abashed, Khorr stopped and cleared his throat. "You see, for one of my name to remain at home in Kothas reciting verse was deemed a disgrace. They ordered me to sign on a ship, but I refused. When I defied my clan, they cast me out."

Silent lightning flickered through the gaping roof tiles.

The smell of rain was in the air. Caeta passed around a goatskin bag. It only held water, but it was all they had.

Malek explained who they were and why they'd come to Robann. "Unless we can find warriors to defeat Rakell and rescue our loved ones, our village is doomed," he finished. Thinking of Laila raised a lump in his throat all the water in the Eternal Spring could not wash down.

"There is much wickedness in the world," Khorr said solemnly.

"Where will you go next?" asked Caeta hopefully.

"South and west, I think. The lands around the New Sea are said to have a liking for the arts. Perhaps I will find a place there," said Khorr.

"Or . . ." Malek steadied himself to say aloud what he'd been thinking. "Or you could come to our village!"

"I'm not a warrior."

"You have twice the strength of any human," Malek said. "Come with us! We'll feed you well and house you. If you make a name defending us, maybe you can return to Kothas!"

Khorr stood, horns scraping the rafters. "Hmmm. I thank you for your hospitality, but I cannot accept your offer. Fighting is a brutal business. That is why I am a poet."

Thunder broke overhead, and rain poured down. The roof leaked, but the farmers moved to a dry corner. Glumly, Malek turned his face to the wall.

Heavy footsteps returned. Malek looked up.

"I'll stay as long as it rains, though, if you don't mind," Khorr said.

"Certainly! Certainly!" They made room in the dry spot for their hulking companion. Khorr drew dry straw up around his bare legs.

"It's cold here," the minotaur said. "Not like Kothas. There the sun shines hot and strong."

"You really do want to go home, don't you?" Caeta said gently.

The minotaur shook his heavy head. "A poet must experience life. Travail is the seasoning of good verse."

"If that's so, I'm a bard," Nils grunted.

Though Khorr did not say any more, Malek knew they'd found their first champion.

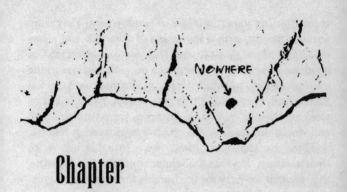

Chapter Two

Heroes for Hire

The rain continued the next day. After another scant meal of barley cakes and pickled eggs, the farmers prepared to scour Robann again. They convinced Khorr to remain behind in the stable. If Durand's friends or the irate gamblers were still after him, it would be safer for their first recruit to stay out of sight.

The powerful bull-man was not unhappy with his confinement. "It will give me time to compose," he said.

Pulling rough woolen hoods over their heads, the four villagers slipped out into the rain. To cover more ground, they decided to split into pairs: Nils and Malek would try the inns and taverns in the part of town controlled by the Red Scarf gang, while Caeta and Wilf would try their luck south of the high street, in Black Hammer territory.

Robann had a surfeit of idle warriors lingering over

cups, grousing about their lack of employment. They were humans mostly, with a leavening of dwarves, and a few woodland elves. Malek and Nils were a bit afraid of dwarves. Rakell's band was mixed up with dwarves in the mining venture, and since Malek's encounter with Gorfon Tattermaul, they couldn't be sure who a dwarf might be working for—or related to. Dwarves were very clannish and would not readily take up arms against their fellows.

Elves, on the other hand, were intimidating. With their taciturn ways and obvious contempt for humans, they seemed too lofty for the humble farmers to approach.

It was a bad morning all around for the brothers. Those fighters Malek and Nils did speak to listened until the terms of the deal were broached.

"Work for a handful of grain? What am I, a plow horse?" one mustached warrior barked with a laugh. At one hostel the soldiers were so insulted by the farmers' offer they threw Malek and Nils out in the street.

Furious, Malek picked himself up, palming mud from his face. "If I had a sword—!"

"If you had a sword, they'd take it from you and stick it where no sword should ever go," Nils said severely. "Come away!"

Steady rain washed much of the mud off the pair by the time they reached an inn called the Rusty Shield. An ancient knightly shield hung above the door, the emblem of the establishment. As the name promised, it was very rusty.

Like the Thirsty Beggar the day before, it was not a popular place. Only six customers were in the common room, each alone, each hunched over a cup. A fire crackled on the hearth, which a slender young girl was stoking when they entered. The aroma of cedar filled the gloomy room.

Malek immediately spotted the tall black woman they'd

seen yesterday. She was at the far end of the room, her back against the timber wall. She had one leg propped up on a bench, the other coiled underneath. A moment of recognition flashed across her face when she saw the farmers.

"That's her again," Malek whispered. "Let's ask her."

"All right, but watch what you say!"

They walked right up to Raika, stopping a respectful three steps away.

"What do you want?" she said slowly.

"We saw you in the Thirsty Beggar yesterday," Malek began.

"So what?"

The brothers exchanged glances. "That was quite a feat, driving a knife through a coin like that," said Nils.

"That was my last florin." She picked up her cup and tilted her head far back, draining the very last drops of beer. "I should've stuck the knife in the barkeep's skull."

"May we sit down?" asked Malek.

"What for?"

"We'd like to talk to you."

She held up her dry clay cup. "Words are dry. Are you buying?"

They had almost no money left, but Malek was determined. "Yes," he said and put a worn silver coin on the table.

Raika shouted for service, and the teen-age girl hurried over with a pitcher of beer.

"Leave it," Raika said.

The girl eyed them suspiciously then snatched the silver from the table.

Nils swallowed. That was their last piece of hard money.

She emptied one cup and filled it again. "So talk," she said.

Malek said, "We come from a small village east of here. We're in great peril there. Bandits have carried off twenty of our people, and in twenty days' time they will return for twenty more!"

"Carried off? For what?"

"To work in a mine," Nils said.

"Mine, eh?" For a moment there was no sound but the crackle of the fire and drip-drip of the farmers' sodden cloaks on the brick floor.

"What kind of mine?" asked Raika.

"Uh, iron." Malek wondered what difference that made. "We're looking for warriors, fighters, to help us get our people back and defeat the bandits."

"I'm a sailor, not a warrior."

"You're a long way from the sea," Nils countered, not unkindly. "You're obviously capable, and I think you've held a sword before."

She smiled into her cup. "A time or two."

"Will you help us?" asked Malek earnestly.

"What's in it for me?"

Here was the crucial point. Malek looked away and let his brother do the explaining.

"We're poor folk," Nils said. "We have no gold or steel. All we can do is keep your belly full and head dry for as long as you remain with us. But—but—it is a good fight."

The woman set her cup down and licked her lips. Malek tensed.

Raika threw back her head and guffawed. She clapped Nils on the shoulder and kept laughing.

"What a pair you are!" she exclaimed. Around the quiet inn, the other guests lifted their heads at the noise. "Sell you my life for three squares and a straw bed? For a good fight? Well, why not?"

Nils blinked. "You'll help us?"

"Sure. There's nothing in my purse but air and nothing in my belly but the beer I've had this morning!" She suddenly sobered. "How many brigands are there?"

"Thirty-eight horsemen, and . . ."

Malek finished for his brother. "Ten ogres."

She stared at him. "That's a lot of brawn to run an iron mine. Hmm." Raika grimaced, showing many white teeth. "I don't suppose you care if I pick up a little booty along the way?" she said. "Taken from your enemies, I mean."

If that was her only condition, the brothers were only too glad to agree. After giving her directions to the stable, Malek and Nils rose to leave.

"One of your future comrades is already there. A minotaur," said Malek. "Just so you know."

"I sailed the Blood Sea. I know minotaurs," she replied. "They fight well."

They shook hands with the Saifhumi woman and left the Rusty Shield in great excitement.

Alone again, Raika forsook her cup and hoisted the pitcher instead. Silly peasants, she mused as the brown brew slid down. Did they take her for a fool? Threadbare farmers recruiting mercenaries? Bandits operating an iron mine? What nonsense! Still, there had to be something of great value at stake. The farmers' accents and primitive garments bespoke some remote locale. If there was wealth to be had, be it gold, steel, jewels, or whatever, it shouldn't be too hard to wrest a portion for herself.

Her laughter rang out again. This time her inert fellow patrons paid her no mind, and the serving girl peeked shyly over the kitchen half-door, curious to know what made the surly stranger suddenly so merry.

* * * * *

The high street marked the limit of Black Hammer territory. More mercantile-oriented than their neighbors, the best markets were sited in their part of Robann. Fair weather or foul, the Black Hammers expected their markets to operate. Though the rain beat down all morning, the merchants unrolled their awnings and set out their wares as they did every day.

Caeta and Wilf wandered among the stalls, stomachs growling at the display of foodstuffs. Summer harvest had come in here, and tables groaned under heaps of carrots, cabbages, and dirt-caked potatoes. The aisle of butchers was even more heartbreaking as the hungry farmers walked past links of savory sausage, salt beef, smoky hams, and fresh hare. At one point Wilf staggered and sat down in the mud. Caeta dragged him to his feet.

"We must go elsewhere," she said. "I don't think we'll find any warriors here."

"Warriors?" boomed a voice. Caeta turned to see an aproned butcher standing under a dripping tarp. "We have everything at the Black Hammer market," he said, chuckling. "Even warriors!"

He waved them under his open tent. Puzzled but curious, Wilf and Caeta followed.

The butcher led them back between crates and casks to an area screened by canvas and poles. There, working on a rough table made of logs, a squat, well-muscled man with a gleaming shaved head was cutting up a cow carcass with a massive cleaver. Spattered with gore, he looked like a blood-wraith, and Wilf trembled at the sight of him. There was something vaguely inhuman about the man's features. . . .

"There's your warrior!" said the butcher, laughing. "Ain't that right, Hume?"

Thunk! The muscular man buried his cleaver in the table. Caeta and Wilf flinched at the sound.

"Yes, I am a warrior," Hume said with pride. "Misfortune has brought me to this state. Why do you mock me, Bergom?"

The butcher sneered. "Such a high and mighty fellow! You were starving until I gave you a job! I just thought I'd show these rubes how real life treats a 'real' warrior!" He chuckled deep in his barrel chest.

"Are you a trained fighter, sir?" asked Caeta.

Hume bowed stiffly. "Good lady, I am Hume nar Fanac, by birth thane to the mighty Khan of Khur."

"There is no Khan of Khur!" said Bergom the butcher.

"The throne survives, but my lord did not. So long as he lived, I was his vassal."

Caeta gripped Wilf's hand. "Master Hume, how would you like to be a warrior again instead of a butcher's apprentice?"

"In whose service, lady?"

"Ours."

"Haw, haw, haw!" Bergom slapped his pot belly, grinning from ear to ear. "This is a better joke than I thought it would be!"

Caeta stepped forward and took Hume's blood-smeared hand. "I tell you truly, sir. I and my companions have come looking for champions to defend our homes against a robber knight and his minions. We have little to offer, but our cause is just."

Hume listened and looked from the rain-soaked, somber peasants to his rude and sarcastic employer. Untying his apron, he handed it to Bergom.

"What? What do you think you're doing?" spluttered the butcher.

"Choosing the path of a warrior," said Hume. "Lady, I am at your service."

Caeta and Wilf were astounded, and the young man said, "You haven't asked for our terms!"

Hume washed his hands and face quickly from a barrel brimming with rainwater. "You say your cause is honorable?"

"It is," vowed Caeta.

"Then speak no more of terms. I am your man."

Bergom muttered dire things as Hume donned a faded leather cape and buckled on a short, wide sword.

"The Black Hammers will hear of this desertion!" the butcher growled. "Where am I gonna get another cutter on such short notice?"

"The Black Hammers understand duty," Hume replied. "What they won't understand is how much you short them on the weight of the beef you sell them. If they want to speak to me, let them find me, and I will tell."

Bergom paled. Further protests died in his throat.

Hume plopped a flat, wide-brimmed hat on his slick pate and tied it on. "Lead on, lady," he said. Dazed by their good fortune, Wilf and Caeta walked their new catch back to the stable.

* * * * *

It was a strange ensemble that gathered beneath the leaking stable roof that evening. Rations were short, but the farmers readily gave up their small portions to their newly hired fighters.

Warriors are by nature suspicious of strangers, especially

other fighters of unknown caliber or loyalty. Facing the four villagers from Nowhere, Khorr, Raika, and Hume ate in silence, scarcely acknowledging each other.

"A question," said Hume at last.

"What is it?" Caeta replied.

"Who will command us? We cannot fight alone, each with his"—he nodded to the lanky Raika, "—or her own tactics and style. Someone must command."

"Why not you? You're an experienced warrior," said Nils.

Hume rubbed his smooth scalp. "Your confidence in me is kind, but misplaced. I was but a lesser thane in Khur, one of a picked band of eight who guarded the north gate of the citadel. I've never led others into battle. I am a good follower, not a commander."

"You captained a ship, didn't you?" Malek asked Raika.

She shook her head. "I was second mate, and I'm not a soldier, I told you. I can fight, but don't ask me to lead this crazy company."

Khorr said, "We must find a captain. There must be many at loose ends in Robann."

"That'll be tricky," countered Raika. "Battle commanders will expect more than barley cakes in payment."

Wilf looked up. Stars glittered through rents in the roof.

"Rain's ended," he said. "Tomorrow we'll find a leader."

"And more fighters!" Raika said sharply. "No offense to Hume or the bull-man, but three of us won't accomplish much against forty."

"I will fight with you," Malek announced.

"All the able-bodied folk of the village will fight," Caeta added. "There's at least thirty of us. How many

43

experienced warriors will we need, do you think, to make up the difference?"

Hume drew a thick finger through the straw, calculating. "Ten, I would say. Eight at least."

"Seven's a lucky number," said Wilf, curled up and nearly asleep.

"Seven against fifty. Ha!" Raika started to think she'd made a bad bargain, treasure or no treasure.

* * * * *

Malek awoke, heart beating fast. Someone was behind him, poking about in their bags. With one eye open, he could see his friends and their three hirelings, all sleeping peacefully. With everyone accounted for, it could only be a stranger rooting through their supplies. He braced himself, grasping the walking stick he'd leaned on all the way from Nowhere.

Steady, steady, he told himself. Now!

He rolled to his feet and swung the stout staff. A fleeting glimpse of the intruder's silhouette was all Malek saw as the staff snagged on something, probably clothing, then continued on. He'd swung so hard and wildly he couldn't stop, and the force of the blow spun him around. The shadowy figure was small, close to the floor. A man on his knees, maybe? It darted away, and Malek let out a yell.

At once the stable loft exploded. Wilf and Nils jumped to their feet, totally confused. Caeta sat up and shouted, "What? What?" Hume reacted according to his training, reaching for his sword.

Raika rolled over and grunted, "Kill the rat, and go back to sleep!"

"It's not a rat! It's a thief!" Malek replied. Khorr slept on, softly snoring.

The fleeing intruder made for the ladder, but Hume reached it first. Blade bare, he shouted in a commanding voice, "Stand where you are! You can't get away!"

The shadow flitted away from him and toward Wilf. The young farmer dived for the thief's legs. His arms closed on air, and he slid six feet in the straw, piling a wave of loose fodder around his head. Nils grabbed a hayfork and charged at the elusive intruder. He missed too, the wooden tines banging hard against the wall.

"Damn the noise!" Raika said irritably, sitting up. "Can't you see I'm trying to sleep?"

"Grab him!" Malek cried.

The small gray figure ran right at her. Raika's hands moved like serpents striking, but she felt her fingers brush through hair and cloth, then the thief was past her. Surprised, she crouched and sprang. Malek clearly saw her outstretched arms gather in the diminutive visitor. She hit the floor and rolled into a ball, punching hard at the captive in her arms.

"Wake me up, will you? Middle of the filthy night! Here's another!" she said through gritted teeth.

In the meantime, Khorr had stirred. He scrubbed his wide bovine nose and propped himself up on one elbow. "What have you got there, lady?" he said sleepily.

"A dirty little thief!"

"Made of straw?"

Raika stopped punching. She thrust the object of her anger away. It was a small sheaf of hay, tied up in a bundle.

"What's this? Sorcery?" she exclaimed.

Caeta had lit a candle. Raising it high, she saw something

in the rafters shrink from the feeble circle of light thrown off by the flame.

"He's here," she said, pointing.

They gathered below. When Caeta gave the candle to Khorr, the tallest one present, they saw a pale, pointed face in the shadows. The thief clung to the beam, out of reach.

"It's a kender!"

"Should've known," Raika said.

"Come down!" Caeta said sternly. "Come down, and no one will hurt you."

"If I stay up here, no one will hurt me either."

Malek peered at the skulking thief. "Hey, you're the same kender we saw the other day in the Thirsty Beggar!"

"You're mistaken. I've never been in the Thrifty Beggar—"

"Thirsty," Raika corrected him. "I saw you too." She folded her arms, glaring. "Are you following me?"

"Why would I want to do that?"

Nils checked through their belongings. Nothing was missing.

"You see?" said the kender. "I'm not a thief. All those tales about my people stealing are vicious lies!"

Hume beckoned Khorr to bend down. The minotaur stooped, and Hume had a word in his ear.

"Very well," said Khorr. The shaven-headed swordsman lent the minotaur his weapon. Khorr stretched his long arm up, up, until the point of the Khurian's blade was below the kender's chin.

"Don't be rash!"

"Come down," Caeta repeated.

Everyone tensed as the kender gathered himself to jump. He landed lightly between them. Raika seized the back of his collar roughly.

"No," said Malek. "Let him be."

Scowling, she complied.

"What's your name?" asked Caeta.

"Carver. Carver Reedwhistle of the Balifor Reedwhistles." He stuck out a slim, rather dirty hand. "Maybe you've heard of us?"

"Nobody's heard of you, worm," Raika snapped. Carver withdrew his hand.

"We do seem to keep running into you," Malek said. He sat down on a hay bale, and the others followed his example. "What do you want? Why are you following us?"

The kender tapped the side of his sharp nose. "I listen to this," he said, smiling, "and I smell something interesting brewing. I mean, what brings a band of sodscratchers all the way to Robann? Robann, a sinkhole that collects every out-of work mercenary, hardcase, and sword-slinger for a hundred leagues around?" He pointed dramatically at Malek. "You're forming a robber band, aren't you?"

For the first time in many days, Malek and his companions laughed out loud. Carver joined in, not sensing the joke. Caeta sobered and explained their mission.

Carver's jaw worked. "Don't give me that! Hire swords for room and board only? Nobody's that desperate!"

"Some are," Hume replied. "Others like myself seek honorable service instead of menial servitude."

The kender cupped a hand to his lips and said to Raika in a loud whisper, "What did he say? Who's he calling menial?"

"Throw the runt out." She lay back in the straw, pillowing her head on her hands. "Let's get some sleep. Unless anybody wants to cut his throat first?"

"Yurk!" Carver clapped a hand to his throat. "Let's not

47

be hasty! I'm not here to spoil whatever it is you're planning. I want to join up!"

"We told you," Malek said. "We intend to save our village from marauders. It's dangerous business."

"Sure, sure. The more dangerous, the better! Let me go with you!"

"I don't think you have much to offer," Caeta said. "We need fighters, not sneak thieves."

Carver adopted a pitiful expression, but one by one they turned their backs on the kender. Malek and Nils dragged their bags of provender to where they'd been sleeping and lay down with the precious food between them. Hume stood by the ladder with the lit candle.

"Good-bye," he said.

Shaking his head, Carver went to the ladder. "Big mistake!" he muttered angrily. "Anybody'd be lucky to have a Reedwhistle in their band."

Before he turned to descend the ladder, Hume booted Carver in the rump. It was a good blow, and the kender sailed out of the loft, landing with a soft thump in the fodder below.

"Farewell!" Hume said, grinning. He snuffed the candle. For some time after, Raika could be heard snickering in the dark.

Chapter Three

The General Takes Command

Cessation of the rain brought the inhabitants of Robann outdoors in great numbers. Early in the morning, the farmers found the throngs in the streets so thick they could scarcely make any headway. Raika and Hume had come with them, leaving the too-conspicuous Khorr behind in the stable.

"Who knew—oof!—there were so many—ow!—people in the world?" Wilf said, trying to shoulder through the crowd.

The Saifhumi woman told the young farmer that none of these people lived here. They were all drifters, soldiers of fate and fortune. By winter, none of them would be in this province.

"Where will they go?" asked Nils.

"Wherever there's money or jobs," said Raika.

"Or to their graves," Hume added.

They split up once again, Raika going with Wilf and Caeta, Hume following Malek and Nils. Raika parted the mob ahead of her with ill-grace, pushing idle conversants apart and shoving dawdlers aside. Some took exception to this, but one look at the towering sailor, her large hands and taut muscles, and they sullenly let her and her companions pass.

The companions did not do so well that morning, even with Raika beside them to give weight to their purpose. They were laughed out of four taverns, three inns, and ejected bodily from a pawnbroker's warehouse. The broker was buying up arms sold by out-of-work warriors, and the presence of recruiters, even shabby ones, disturbed his business.

Hot, tired, and discouraged, Caeta and Wilf sat down by the only public work in all of Robann, the Pool of the Skymistress. This was a shallow, stone-lined basin. A very old, very worn statue of the ancient goddess of healing stood in the center, water dribbling from her open hands. Caeta cupped her hand in the pool and brought some liquid to her lips. Thirsty as she was, she quickly spat it out.

"Bad?" Wilf was thirsty himself.

"Foul." Caeta looked up at the eroded face of the goddess, feeling very old herself. "Nothing in this town is fair."

They sat down on the rim of the pool. Raika mopped her brow with a scrap of homespun. She dipped it in the water, wrung it out, and tied it around her neck for cooling.

The pool was in a small, irregular square in the northwest quarter of town. This had once been the elves' quarter, and while there were more of them about than in other parts of town, they no longer predominated. The stream of folk striding, shuffling, or sauntering past the seated trio was much the same as before—humans mostly, with the odd dwarf, goblin, or kender. The gang ruling this part of town was still made up of elves exclusively, the strangely named Brotherhood of Quen.

Across the square, the crowd stirred. Voices multiplied and grew loud. Raika stood up to see what was causing the commotion.

A pair of elves strode toward the center of the square followed by a pack of curious onlookers. At the center of the park, just a few yards from the Pool of the Sky-mistress, they halted, turned their backs to each other, and began pacing off a gap between them. Raika recognized this scene.

She said, "Stand up. This is worth seeing."

Wilf helped Caeta stand. They could only see over the crowd by standing on the moldy rim of the pool. Wilf clutched Raika's arm for support until the latter's cold glare caused him to gingerly remove his hand.

"What's happening?" Caeta asked.

"Watch."

The square was forty yards wide. The two elves stood, some thirty yards apart. Between them the ground was clear. Everyone else in the square kept back. Each elf was handed a clay flagon by one of the party that had followed them in. This they placed on top of their bare heads, holding it in place until they stood upright and steady. One of the elves was slim and fair-haired, dressed in a sky-blue tunic and wearing knee-high suede boots. He looked rich and confident. Facing him, the other elf was black-headed and swarthy, a forester of the kind who usually painted their faces with strange designs. He was garbed like a woodland hunter in a tight green leather jersey, trews, and ankle boots. His garments were well covered with stitched-up tears and patches.

A young human, dark-skinned like Raika, came out of the crowd. Like a herald, he proclaimed loudly, "Take out your slings!"

The elves produced identical slings of braided twine, with deerskin pouches for their sling-stones.

"Load one stone!"

Carefully, so as not to disturb the vessels balanced on their heads, the elves each pulled out a smooth river stone from their respective belt pouches. They loaded these into the slings.

The speaker stepped back. He cried, "Loose when you will!"

The fair elf raised his right arm and started whirling his sling, taking care not to strike the tankard poised on his head. His opponent whirled his weapon with his hand at his side, almost lazily.

The crowd erupted with partisan shouts for one elf or the other. Caeta and Wilf heard cries for "Amergin" and "Solito" in equal measure. They couldn't tell who was who.

After a long windup, the fair elf loosed his missile. The quartz pebble flew swiftly at the dark elf's head. At what seemed like the last possible moment, the forester looped his stone into the air. Incredibly, the projectiles collided in mid-air a few feet in front of the dark-haired contestant. Caroming off each other, the stones whizzed away. Wilf heard one crash into something behind him—something that broke loudly.

The mob cheered. Puzzled, Wilf muttered, "What are they trying to prove?"

"It's a duel," Raika replied. "One of them is going to die."

It didn't seem likely, given the carnival atmosphere. However the farmers noticed that while the crowd was boisterous and cheerful, the elves were utterly serious.

Without being prompted, they reloaded their slings. Again they whirled their weapons in differing styles, the swarthy elf slow and deliberate, the blond elf with eye-blurring speed. This time the forester threw first, and his missile was deflected away by a well-aimed fling by his opponent.

Money and goods changed hands in the crowd. A chant of "Three! Three!" began. Nodding slowly to each other, the elves loaded a new stone each, and quick as they did, both hurled at the same time. As close together as two events could be, both tankards exploded in a spray of red clay fragments.

The blond elf stalked to the center of the square and flung out a hand at his opponent, pointing. A hush fell over the raucous mob.

"You see!" he shouted. "I am as good as you!"

The forester combed potshards from his hair with his fingers. "No," he said coldly. "You lost."

"We broke each other's cups at the same time!"

"Mine hit first. Yours broke before mine did."

He turned to go, but the well-dressed elf charged in, caught his arm, and spun the dark-haired elf around.

"Once more then! Without cups!" he cried.

An acorn falling on the cobbles would have shattered the sudden hush. The forester looked up at his taller antagonist with wide, black eyes.

"You know what you're saying, don't you?"

"Stand to your place!" was the haughty answer. The blue-clad elf stalked back to his spot, while the forester calmly resumed his stance.

"Fifty steel on Solito!" someone yelled.

"Shut up!" A scuffle broke out to the farmers' right, quickly squelched by those watching.

Instead of stones, this time the elves loaded sling-stars, flat pieces of iron or bronze with four to six razor-sharp points. Thrown by an expert, a star point could pierce plate armor.

This time, as Solito raised his arm to spin his weapon, his opponent made a single underhand swing and let fly. Wilf and Caeta followed the glittering bronze missile in flight. One point buried itself in the center of Solito's forehead. Stricken, his own star flew wildly away. It flashed between Raika and Wilf. The Saifhumi woman stood her ground. Wilf threw himself backward into the pool to avoid the hissing projectile.

Without a sound, the blond elf fell dead.

Having been in Robann four days, the farmers expected the crowd to break into cheers for the winner. No one did. In fact, those on the outside edges of the crowd began to hurry away, eager to be gone. Before long, genuine panic seized the square, and witnesses were rushing to find every available avenue of escape.

Raika snagged a goblin hopping by. The ugly little creature squirmed and tried to bite Raika's hand, but she held him by the neck so tightly he couldn't bend down far enough to get his teeth in her.

"Leggo! Leggo!" he whined, waving his arms uselessly.

"Why all the rush?" she said. "Surely duels are common in Robann?"

"Not like this! Leggo!"

Raika shook the goblin hard. "Tell me," she said tersely.

"That one dead—he Brotherhood!"

She opened her fingers and let the goblin drop to the cobbles. Coughing, he gathered himself up and staggered away.

"What does it mean?" asked Caeta.

"The dead elf was a member of the gang that rules this part of town." Raika glanced at the blue-clad figure, left leg still bent, arms flung wide. "When the Brotherhood of Quen finds out one of their own has been killed, they may take their anger out on anyone who was here."

"We ought to go!" Wilf said. He jumped down from the pool. Algae dripped from his ears.

"Not yet. I've no desire to get trampled in some back street. Besides, we may want to talk to the winner."

Caeta's eyes widened. "You're right. He's certainly capable."

Against the thinning tide of fleeing spectators, Raika, Wilf, and Caeta reached the forester. He was standing with his head down, working beeswax into his sling to keep it supple. Wilf marveled at his coolness. The killer was the calmest person in the square.

"What do you want?" demanded the elf before Raika or the farmers could speak.

"Just a word." Raika looked at the elf's fallen foe. "That was quite a throw."

"He was a large target."

"What's your name?" asked Caeta.

"Amergin." He slurred the last syllable, Ah-mer-zheen.

"They have a proposition for you," Raika said. "You should listen."

Amergin finished working his sling. He tucked it away and recovered his blue-green cloak, left on the ground during the contest. To the farmers' amazement, they saw it was made of thousands of tiny green or blue bird feathers arranged in overlapping rows of graduated color.

"I've no time to listen to propositions," said the elf.

Caeta said, "We'll give you shelter."

"Not wise. The Quen Brotherhood will slay anyone they find at my side."

Amergin started moving. He did not run, but his movements were remarkably swift. Wilf had to jog to keep up, and even tall Raika had to hurry.

Breathlessly, the farmers gasped out their plea as they hastened through an alley toward Silver Circle territory. During the explanation Amergin said nothing, just kept moving. At the border between the Brotherhood's territory and the Silver Circle's quarter, five elves in sky-blue tunics stood watch. Amergin flattened against a wall. Raika and the farmers did likewise.

"They wasted no time!" Wilf whispered.

"The first to leave the square warned them," Amergin answered quietly. "In hopes of a reward . . . " He uncoiled his sling. "They'll not take me—at least not alive."

"Wait," Raika said. "There might be a better way."

She grabbed Wilf by the front of his rough shirt. "Play along," she murmured and shoved him out of the alley into plain view of the Brotherhood guards.

Storming out after him, she shouted, "Worthless rat of a husband! How dare you come home at this hour, reeking of drink! Where have you been? Who have you been with?"

A bit stunned, Wilf could only stammer, "None of your business!" He embellished this with a belated sneer. "Wench!"

"Wench? I'll show you who's a wench!" She threw a punch at the hapless young farmer, who closed his eyes and cringed. Raika deliberately missed him and pretended to go reeling across the street from the force of the missed blow. She collided with three of the Quen guards.

"Shameless lout, see what you made me do!" she screamed.

"Get off, human!" said one of the elves, pushing Raika away.

"Now you want to push me around, too? There's no justice in the world, no honor for a suffering wife!"

She drew back her large fist and knocked the closest elf cold. Wilf blundered into another, diverting him until Raika could knock him down as well.

The remaining three Quen gang members tried to seize them. They carried swords and batons, and though Raika was more than a match for them in terms of strength, they were agile and alert now, and she and Wilf received several punishing blows. Wilf went to his knees, arms encircling his head for protection. A Quen guard stood over him, ready to put him away, when a flat river-washed stone hit him squarely on the back of the head. It sounded like a melon being opened by a housewife.

Caeta burst out of the alley, shouting, "Sonny! What are they doing to you, dear boy?"

Distracted by the old woman's sudden appearance, one of the remaining guards mistimed his attack, and Raika tore the baton from his hands. He went for his sword, but she smashed his fingers against the hilt with his own stick. White-faced, the elf abandoned the fight. He ran up Money-lender's Street, holding his shattered hand to his chest.

Raika turned to face the last guard and saw Amergin had disposed of him already. They raced on, eager to be away before the injured guard returned with reinforcements and didn't stop until they reached the stable.

* * * * *

Inside, Khorr stood with one foot propped up on a bale of hay. One hand upraised, he declaimed,

Thus did Edzi, courageous captain, lift high his awesome ax,
To smite his former friend, now the treacher Toral,
Traitor, taunter, and terrible foe—

Sitting cross-legged at the minotaur's feet, leaning back on his splayed out hands, was Carver Reedwhistle.

"Hiya," he said, seeing them enter.

"Why are you here again?" said Raika.

Khorr lowered his arm and took his foot from the hay bale. "He was a willing audience. I was reciting *The Rage of Captain Edzi*, a famous ballad of my people."

Taking in the minotaur and kender, the elf asked, "What is this? A refuge for refuse?"

"You might say that," Caeta said, smiling. "Take your ease, Master Amergin, and we shall explain."

The elf listened in silence to the story of Rakell and the victimized village. When the woman was done, he said, "I cannot help you."

"Why?" Wilf said. "You're amazing with that sling—and you don't seem intimidated by any odds."

"I'm not a mercenary. I am a hunter. Solito bullied me into that contest. I knew it would end the way it did, but he would have slain me on the spot had I refused his challenge." He went down on one knee and ran a hand along his lean, chapped face. "There was no way out but to fight, then to flee. Your battle is not my battle."

Caeta offered him food, which he declined, and water,

which he accepted. She said, "What happens now? Won't the Brotherhood be hunting for you?" She knew the answer, but she waited for the elf's silent headshake. "If we can deliver you from the vengeful gang, will you help us?"

Amergin lowered the waterskin from his thin lips. "The Brotherhood has many blades, and if they ask it, other gangs in town will join them in tracking me down. You can't stand them all off. My fight isn't your fight either."

Caeta surveyed her comrades. Wilf was following things intently. Khorr, too, was listening, but Raika stood by the door, gazing out distractedly at the hot afternoon. Carver lay on his back with his eyes closed, one leg cocked in the air, dangling foot bobbing.

"I never offered to *fight* your enemies for you," Caeta said carefully. "Just help you elude them. We help you, so you can help us. Is that not fair?"

"Will you turn me over to the Brotherhood if I refuse?"

"No, never."

Raika looked up at the farmer's earnest reply. "They don't have much, so they can afford to be honest," she said to Amergin meaningfully. Carver chuckled.

Amergin remained kneeling. Gazing at the straw-strewn floor, he said, "The Brotherhood was supposed to send me home."

"What do you mean?"

"I come from the forest, far to the south, over the New Sea. The Brotherhood hired me as scout and tracker. I thought I was to hunt game for them, but they made me track down those who'd transgressed against them: debtors, cheats, and thieves. When I led the Brotherhood to their quarry, they did terrible things to them."

"Enough," said Khorr, speaking for the first time. "Here's your chance to be rid of them. Join us! I, too, am sought by ruffians through no fault of my own. These humans have shielded me, and I have decided to repay their sacrifice by helping them fight their enemies. Can you do any less?"

Amergin sank into a sitting position. He never said yes, but his change of posture was eloquent proof he meant to stay.

* * * * *

Half a mile away, Malek, Nils, and Hume trudged through the hot, stinking streets. Their luck had been bad all morning, and after noon word spread that the gang in charge of the northern quarter of Robann would pay good coin to find a certain malefactor who'd murdered one of their own. Taverns and inns emptied, and hundreds of tough, hungry mercenaries joined the manhunt.

The farmers entered a large establishment called the Shield and Saber. Upon entry they found the great room almost deserted. Capable of holding and serving two hundred at a time, it contained less than a dozen patrons. Eight of these were dwarves in heavy mail coats, seated at a round table and just beginning the seventh course of their noonday meal.

Hume went to the bar. His soldierly bearing and infantryman's gait marked him for what he was. He spoke briefly with the barkeep, a centaur no less, who rebuffed his queries about warriors seeking work.

"You'll hire no blades today," said the centaur, polishing the bar with a filthy cloth. "Everyone who can wield a knife, from the lordly born to the worst scum in Robann, has gone to the Brotherhood of Quen."

Malek and Nils approached. "Why have they gone?" asked Malek.

The centaur laughed, sounding not surprisingly like a horse neighing. "For gold, dirt-digger! Some fool killed the son of the gang's chief, and a price of a thousand gold pieces has been laid on the killer's head!"

"That's bad," Hume admitted.

"Word's gone 'round about you and your friends, too," added the centaur. "Farmers hiring blades for cheap." He neighed again sarcastically. "Nobody's left here but the general."

Nils looked around for a well-appointed officer, but he saw none. "General?"

"Want to meet him?"

There were no other prospects, so Malek and Nils agreed. Leathery face split in a gap-toothed grin, the centaur came out from behind the bar and beckoned the farmers to follow.

The Shield and Saber's great room was really two rooms, a large and a small, joined at right angles. In the smaller extension, which held booths and small, square tables, a few isolated souls lingered. Judging by their gray hair and bleary expressions, they were too old, too sick, or too lost in drink to take interest in a manhunt.

The centaur stopped by a back booth. He rapped his hairy knuckles on the headboard. "Hey, general! Wake up! You have visitors!"

"I can pay my bill," groaned a voice on the other side of the partition.

"That I know, or you'd be in the street now!"

Braying, the centaur left them.

"This is a fool's errand," grunted Hume.

Malek peeked around the partition.

Seated inside the booth was an older man, near Caeta's age. Gray-bearded, his long hair was lank and matted. He wore the moldering remnants of a fine uniform. Brass buttons, where not missing, had turned green from neglect.

The old soldier turned red-rimmed eyes toward Malek. "What do you want, stranger?"

"Are you a general?" asked the farmer.

"I was. Once." Three wine bottles, one lying on its side, were strewn about the table. The old man reeked of sour wine and unwashed clothes.

Malek waved Hume and his brother forward. "May we speak to you, General?"

The general shrugged.

The three slid onto the bench across from the old man. He studied them, squinting against a cloud of age and drink.

"You're not human," he said to Hume. "What are you, half-ogre?"

"That's not important," Malek said firmly. "Hume is in our employ."

"Doing what?"

"Defending these good people and their home from raiders," Hume replied stiffly.

"Huh." The general reached for the nearest bottle. Failing to find a cup, he drank directly from it.

"This is a waste of time," Hume muttered.

"Mind your tongue!" the general said. "You're in the presence of Howland uth Ungen, Order of the Rose, and Knight of Solamnia!" He missed the edge of the table with the bottle, and it fell into his lap.

"I'm in the presence of a drunken fool," snarled Hume.

"Yes, I'm drunk! I've been drunk for the past four

years! You'd be too if you'd seen what I've seen, done what I've done . . . lost what I've lost."

"We need an experienced commander," Malek pressed on, heedless. "With our people and the warriors we've hired, we have some chance against the bandits, but we need a real commander to lead us! Someone with experience in the field."

Howland's eyes fluttered and closed. He began to snore.

Hume got up, his face a mask of stone. "This one is a liar as well as a drunkard. No Knight of the Rose would sink so low."

The centaur barkeep returned. "The last coin you gave me was tainted, general! It had more lead in it than gold!" He saw Howland's head lolling and spat. "Get out, you cheat! Sleep it off somewhere else!"

He dragged the unresisting man out and stood him up against the booth wall. Rifling through the pockets and pouches in Howland's clothing, he found no more money. Cursing, he flung the old man to the floor.

"The boss will take it out of my hide if the receipts are short tonight!" Glancing into the booth, he saw a gleam of metal.

"Ah!" Nestled in the corner of the booth was a sword, scabbard, and belt. It was a fine, straight weapon, plainly finished, but it was real steel.

"I'll just keep this!" said the centaur, grinning.

"Wait." Hume's broad hand clamped down on the centaur's arm. "You can't take a man's sword. No matter how low he's fallen, a warrior's sword is his soul."

"Put it in a poem!" The barkeep tried to wrench his arm free but found Hume's grasp too strong. "You want trouble? The Iron Gang rules this inn. One word from me, and the three of you will be swinging from their parapet by sunset."

"Let go, Hume," Malek said. The proud thane did so reluctantly. The centaur was about to drag Howland out by his heels when Hume spoke again.

"How much does he owe?"

"Eh?"

"Sir Howland's bill—how much?"

The centaur's bristling brows twitched. "Two gold."

"You said only one was tainted."

"One's for my trouble—and silence."

Hume drew his short sword. Though he drew underhand, with his grip reversed so as to keep the point down, the centaur blundered back, upsetting a pair of chairs.

"Peace!" said Hume. "I was only going to offer my own blade in payment for the bill."

Cautiously, the centaur reached out to take Hume's weapon. He licked the blade and plunked it with his finger.

"Not steel," he muttered. "Wrought iron, ten years old. Worth two, maybe three gold."

He weighed the easy prize of Hume's sword against Howland's better blade. Good sense prevailed, or perhaps it was the hard glint in Hume's eye. The centaur flung Howland's sword to Malek.

"Take it, and begone! Cheaters are not welcome in the Shield and Saber!"

Boosting the unconscious man between them, Malek and Nils carried Howland out. Hume preceded them, carrying the general's sword with reverence.

Back at the stable, there was much explaining to be done. Caeta told her comrades about Amergin and the duel. Malek told them about the manhunt.

"He killed the son of the chief of the gang!" Malek said worriedly. "If he's found here, our lives won't be worth a field of rocks!"

"Calm yourself," Caeta urged. "Amergin is fantastic with his sling, and a cooler head I've never seen. He's agreed to help us if we get him out of town safely. Will you forsake a bargain already struck?"

Malek was tempted, but fourteen days had passed already. Sixteen more, and Rakell would return to Nowhere for another twenty villagers. Worse, there was no way to know how the farmers already taken, including Laila, were faring.

"Very well. We'll keep your bargain, Caeta."

Carver squatted by the still-snoring Howland. He sniffed and made a face. "Who's the rosebud?"

"His name's Howland uth Ungen. He's a Knight of Solamnia and a general."

"He needs a bath," Carver observed.

Malek frowned. "Why is that kender still here?"

"Because I haven't killed him yet," Raika said. Carver thought she was joking.

Caeta knelt by Howland. She turned his head this way and that then lifted his hands one by one, examining them with care. She felt his legs and kneaded his belly a few times.

"What's she doing?" asked Khorr.

"Caeta's the best stock breeder in the village," Nils replied. "I've seen her do that to calves. She's checking to see if he's sound."

"He is," she said, arranging Howland's arms at his side. "He's not been on the bottle too long." Rising, she added, "You say he was a general? We need a general. We can't be too choosy."

"We know nothing about him," sputtered Wilf. "For all we know, he could be a former cobbler or a tailor."

"Scars."

The male farmers looked puzzled. "What scars?"

"His arms have many scars, like so." She made parallel slashes with her hand up one arm. "Sword cuts, old ones. He has healed wounds on the front of both legs."

"Lance wounds received by a man on horseback," Hume said admiringly.

"He's got almost all his teeth, too."

"Which means what?" said Raika. Seated with her back against the stable wall, she watched them intently as they clustered around the sleeping Howland.

"He's eaten well all his life. That and his recovered injuries means he's had a healer's care. I would also wager he's worn a helmet most of his life, as his teeth are not broken out, and his face isn't marred."

"Splendid!" Carver cried, clapping his hands. He flopped on the straw. "Do me next. Tell me what my life has been!"

Caeta ignored him. "Shall we keep this old dog? He's worn out, but a wise old hound is a better hunter than the spryest pup."

It was getting dark. Out in the streets of Robann, armed mobs were searching for Amergin. Other, smaller bands were hunting Khorr. Time and the scant welcome the town afforded was running out.

"Put the question to him when he wakes," said Malek. "That's all we can do."

NOWHERE

Chapter Four
Exit, Pursued

N o one slept that night. The farmers and their hired fighters kept to the stable, but there were periodic alarms as bands of bounty hunters stormed in, searching for Amergin. Khorr was still being sought by vengeance-seekers too. Since it would arouse suspicion for all of them to hide, Hume, Raika, and the farmers concentrated on keeping the Kagonesti and the minotaur out of sight. But how to hide a seven foot tall bull-man?

Amergin they secreted under the floor of the loft. While they wrangled about burying Khorr in dung or under a heap of hay, Carver solved the problem neatly. He took the hulking poet by the hand and led him to a stall between two cows.

"Kneel down," said the kender.

Khorr went down on his knees. The kender filled the stall around the minotaur's lower body with loose hay, then stood back to admire the effect.

"Not a word," he cautioned, "no matter what you hear! Keep your eyes down. Yes, like that. Perfect!"

He swaggered back to the arguing companions. Sir Howland, the drunken Knight, was snoring, but the others (save Amergin) stood in circle, loudly debating various schemes.

"Cut a hole in the wall, and have Khorr put his head through it," Raika suggested. "If anybody asks, we tell 'em he's a trophy."

"No, no!" said Nils. "Anyone can tell the difference between a stuffed head and a live one!"

"Have you a better idea?" said the Saifhumi woman belligerently.

"Hello! Hello!" called Carver. "I've solved the problem."

Just then (for the fourth time that night) a party of vigilantes burst into the barn. Seeing Malek and the rest, the leader of the gang said, "Who are you? What are you doing here?"

Before the frightened farmers could speak, Hume growled, "Same as you: hunting for the one who killed the Quen chief's son."

"It's been half a day, and nobody's found him yet," the vigilantes' leader replied. He was a coarse, sallow-looking fellow with lank brown hair. Behind him was a mixed band of goblins and similarly seedy humans.

"Maybe he's left Robann," said Wilf.

"Ain't possible. The Brotherhood's got trackers out in all directions. They ain't picked up nothing." Shifting his torch to his left hand and lowering his right to the hilt of his sword, he added, "The rat must still be here."

Raika said, "Well, we haven't got him. If we did, we wouldn't be standing here jawing with you, sunshine."

The gang leader's eyes narrowed. "Then you won't mind if we search the place ourselves?"

Raika all but yawned. "Suit yourself, boys."

Malek and the farmers looked alarmed, but Raika, Hume, and Carver all managed a disinterested facade. One of the goblins stood over Sir Howland, prodding him with the handle of his pitchfork.

"Who's this?"

"Not an elf. Ears not pointy, see?" Raika leaned against a post and clasped her hands behind her head. "Don't you even know what a Kagonesti looks like?"

The vigilantes poked and prodded around the big barn, finding nothing but a few random chickens nesting in the straw. Two of the goblins fell to chasing a fat white hen until their boss stormed over and cracked them on the head with his knout.

The humans in his group climbed into the loft. Hume and Raika exchanged a look. Carver lay on his back and made moo-ing noises.

Malek could hear the men clomping around, thrusting spears into the loose hay. He prayed the board covering Amergin's hiding place would not be dislodged by their probing.

A scraggly fellow with stringy hair and a wisp of a beard stuck his head over the loft rail and said, "Nothing up here, Nub."

"Then get down! We got plenty more places to check!"

Men and goblins filed out. The leader, Nub, was the last. Screwing up his face as though he smelled something bad, he swept the barn with his eyes one last time before departing then ducked out.

Caeta sighed deeply. "Where's Khorr?"

Carver made more cattle sounds then laughed. Arching his back, he sprang to his feet like an acrobat.

"As my old Uncle Trapspringer used to say, the best place to hide something is under the seeker's nose!"

He strolled to the cow stalls and stood in front of one, gesturing to the horned head above him. "Speak, Khorr!"

"What shall I say?" The minotaur opened the stall door and stepped out.

The kender had missed Khorr by two stalls. He covered his error with a high-pitched laugh.

"I'm so clever I even fool myself!"

Malek nodded. "Maybe the kender will turn out to be useful after all."

Howland uth Ungen snorted, choked, and sat up. "Wine!" he croaked. "Give me wine!"

Malek, Nils, Caeta, and Wilf slowly circled around him. Holding his head in his hands, the fallen knight repeated his plea.

Malek squatted and offered him the neck of his waterskin. Howland seized it in both hands and drank greedily.

"Is this old souse really any good to us?" Wilf murmured.

Lowering the leather bag with a gasp, Howland said, "Good enough even to whip you clod-hoppers into fighting shape!"

Malek said, "Do you remember us?"

"I remember," Howland said gruffly. He wiped his crusted lip with the back of his hand. "How many warriors have you got, so far?"

"Five, counting you."

"Six!" Carver said brightly. "Don't forget me!"

Malek grimaced. "Six, it seems."

"Help me up." Howland held out his hands to Nils and Malek. They dragged him upright. "All right, all right. Might as well get down to business. All of you, line up."

No one moved.

"I said *line up!* Better you learn one thing first—when I give an order, you do it!"

Awkwardly, they sorted themselves into a single line facing the Knight. With Khorr at one end and Carver at the other, they made a strange-looking company.

"Tcha!" Howland snapped. "What a command!" He stood in front of the minotaur, fists on his hips. "You're big enough, I'll grant. Have you any skills?"

"I've memorized all six thousand lines of *The Rage of Captain Edzi*," said Khorr.

Howland squeezed his bloodshot eyes shut. "Any *fighting* skills?"

"I'm a good wrestler."

"A wrestler. I see. We'll just have to ask the brigands to come close enough for you to hug them, won't we?"

Howland moved down the line to Hume. "You look like a soldier."

"Yes, sir. I am Hume nar Fanac, by birth thane to the mighty Khan of Khur."

"In what were you trained?"

"Pike and halberd, sir."

Howland nodded. "Any archery?"

"No, sir."

The knight moved on to Raika.

"Before you ask, I'm a sailor, not a warrior," she said dryly.

"You're no stranger to swords, I fancy."

She shrugged. "The sea is a dangerous place."

Howland walked off a short way. A rake and a pitchfork

leaned against one of the inner stalls. Taking one in each hand, he went back to Raika. Without warning, he flung the pitchfork sideways at her. She caught it, glaring.

"Are we going to pitch hay?" she said.

"You pose too much, woman, and you're too free with your mouth. Let's see what you can do."

Raika grinned. "Any time, old man."

Caeta stepped out of line to protest. Howland was hung-over, dehydrated, thirty years older than Raika, and six inches shorter. "I don't want our new general injured before he has the chance to train us."

"Get back in your place!" Howland snapped.

He drew back a few steps and beckoned Raika toward him. As she advanced, he swiftly thrust the handle of his rake between her ankles, tripping her. Before Raika knew it, she was flat on her belly, and Howland had the head of the rake pressed against the back of her neck.

"Got you," he said.

"Yeah, quite a coup for you, old man. Trip me when I'm not looking!"

"Do you think war has polite rules?"

He let her up. She crouched low, the tines of her pitchfork level with Howland's chest. His grimy brigandine would not keep out those sharp iron points.

"Ha!" Raika jabbed hard.

Howland's feet never shifted. He parried, catching the tines with the rake handle and flipping the pitchfork back over Raika's shoulder. It stuck quivering in the floor, and Howland administered a stinging blow across her back with the other end of the rake.

"Twice," he said, coughing a little.

Raika kept her temper in check. She retrieved the pitchfork and held it in both hands in front of her like a quarterstaff. Howland made a few elementary attacks with the rake, which she easily warded off. Then the attacks came faster. Left-right-left-left-right came the blows. Raika gave ground. Right-left-right-right-left. Sweat sheened her face and arms.

Howland circled away, coughing more. "I'd shave my head for a draught of wine," he muttered. Carver heard him, grinned, and scurried up the ladder into the loft.

"You're strong and quick," the old Knight told Raika, "but you must learn to anticipate the enemy's next move. Only that way can you hope to defeat him."

He started toward her, pivoted, and came from the other direction. The gray rake handle blurred.

Left-right-left-left—

"Ha!" said Raika. She moved to block a blow from the right, and met only air. The blunt end of the rake handle hurtled at her face. Raika flinched, but Howland stopped it a hair's breadth from her cheek.

"And three times," he said. "You thought you had my moves figured out, but only because I pointed out the pattern to you. Another lesson: Don't listen to what an opponent tells you. Your enemy wants to hurt you, not help you."

Malek grabbed his brother happily. They'd found a real leader at last!

The rake clattered to the floor. Close behind it came Howland. Sick and exhausted, he fainted dead away.

Raika caught him. Though he was filthy, she held on to him, lowering him gently to the straw.

"You surprise me," said Khorr. "You have a heart after all."

"He's not my enemy," she snapped. "He's my commander."

Paul B. Thompson

Carver returned with Amergin. The kender descended the ladder nimbly, even though he was hampered by having a squat bottle of Goodlund wine in one hand and a folded straight razor in the other. Seeing Howland stretched out on the floor, Carver sighed.

"And here I was going to shave his head!"

* * * * *

If the gods had still dwelt in the world, they might have granted the farmers a boon. Since history and the teachings of the wise held otherwise, the heavy fog enshrouding Robann the next morning could only have been luck.

It crept in, loose airy tendrils of white seeping through the cracks in the stable walls and roof. No one got any rest all night, save for Sir Howland, who was all but dead to the world, and Amergin, who slept soundly in his hiding place. Wilf grumbled quietly about the hunted sleeping better than his protectors, but his friends were just grateful to see the dawn.

Hume drew back the wide door. Damp coils of mist flowed in.

"This is good," he said. "Fog will shield us from pursuit."

They packed hurriedly. Caeta woke Howland, shaking the old Knight's shoulder until he stirred.

"What is it?" he asked too loudly.

"Quiet," she whispered. "Enemies are all around us!"

He opened one eye, squinting at the dull gray dawn as if it were the unbridled glare of the desert at noon. He coughed and groaned.

"Time to go, sir," said Hume.

Howland got to his hands and knees but seemed unable to rise further. Caeta cajoled, but any attempt to stand brought on a noisy fit of coughing.

"Wonderful!" Raika said. "A commander who can't stand!"

Hume laid Howland's sword and scabbard on the floor a few feet in front of him. "Sir, I saved your weapon," he said. "Rise and take it."

"Pick it up, or I shall," Raika added.

The old man coughed. "No one," he rasped, "carries my sword but me!"

With a supreme effort, he pushed himself up. Reeling, he clung to Wilf and Nils for support. Hume took up the sword and held it out to Howland. With dignity, the Knight hung the belt around his shrunken waist and closed the clasp.

Amergin walked out first, a lethal star in his sling. To prevent any telltale glints from giving them away in the fog, he'd coated all their faces with candle soot.

Raika and Hume went out next, keeping the Kagonesti in view. Nils, Wilf, and Sir Howland went next, followed by Khorr, Carver, and Caeta. Finally came Malek. He put the last of their paltry valuables, a rough nugget of garnet, on the stall for the landlord to find. That done, he soundlessly swung the door shut.

The town was strangely quiet. The usual bustle and chaos was absent this morning. Practically everyone in town had passed the night hunting for Amergin, and most were abed now, dreaming of the blood money dangled over their heads by the Brotherhood of Quen.

"Go east out of town," was the only directions the farmers had given, so Amergin walked toward the brightest patch of fog, trusting that was where the sun was rising. Tension within the party ran high.

Carver said, "This reminds me of—"

"If you say 'Uncle Trapspringer,' I'll kick you," Raika's voice drifted back.

"I was going to say, 'the waterfront at Sanction,' thank you very much."

"Shh!" Caeta held a finger to her lips.

They had to cross the High Street to get out of town. Amergin halted and pressed himself against a wall. The others stopped.

They heard voices in the fog ahead. Sounds of horses, and wheels turning.

The characteristic whistle of drovers, punctuated by the crack of whips, told them they were near the main thoroughfare. Fog or no fog, morning market goods had to be moved.

Amergin flipped the hood up on his cloak. The dark, forest-colored feathers would not hide him in the mist, but the hood did obscure his elven features.

He strode into the street. Fog closed around him.

Hume started to follow, but Raika held him back. They waited, and when no alarm arose she nodded, and they moved on.

They had no trouble until Khorr crossed. A two-horse dray rumbled up, and the horses faltered and reared at the unfamiliar shape of the minotaur looming over them in the fog. The driver worked his whip, trying to get the team moving.

"Look, Shay—a minotaur!" said the other man on the wagon's seat.

"So what? Ain't you ever seen one? Get out of the way, bull-man!" yelled the driver.

"Weren't those soldiers huntin' a minotaur last night?"

"Nah, it was an elf. Wasn't it?"

"No," the man said in a low voice that carried. "I heard some say they was looking for a minotaur. Killed a man in a bar fight, he did."

Khorr could have moved on, but instead he turned back to say politely, "I didn't kill Durand. I only broke his arm."

The wagoneers did not hear him over the neighing of the agitated horses. Seeing the seven-foot Khorr coming closer, the men panicked. The driver lashed out with his bullwhip. His companion stood on the seat and shouted, "Help! Help! The murdering minotaur's here!"

Malek rushed out of the fog. "For goodness sake, Khorr! Quiet them!"

The bull-man raised his powerful arms and snorted menacingly. The men paid no attention, but the horses did, straining against their harness, rearing and backing away. The rolling wagon pitched the standing man into the cargo, a bunch of half-grown pigs. Outraged, the pigs squealed and plunged about loudly.

The driver dropped his whip and tried to quiet the horses, but they were too distressed. Pushed back against the ridge of cobbles along the gutter, the wagon teetered then crashed over on its side. Pigs spilled out and ran squealing into the mist. Driver and companion were thrown to the street.

"Come on!" Malek snapped, grabbing the mild-mannered minotaur by the hand. The farmer hated to think what Khorr would do when he tried to cause trouble!

The rest were waiting for them in a narrow lane cut between two houses. The dark bulk of a gang's tower was visible off to their left. If they'd judged things right, it was the seat of the Silver Circle.

They reached a curving avenue Raika said was called Sawbones Street because so many surgeons lived there.

Amergin slipped ahead again. He hadn't gone five steps
before a flurry of arrows fell around him. Iron broadheads
struck sparks on the cobbles. The Kagonesti whirled and
flung his star-loaded sling at the rooftops behind him.

"Stand where you are!" Hume said roughly, holding
Nils back with an outstretched arm. Everyone behind the
Khur soldier hugged the wall of the near house and waited.

Having loosed one star, Amergin sprinted for the nearest cover. Directly across from him was a corral full of
horses, ringed by a split-rail fence. He vaulted easily over
the waist-high barrier, somersaulted into the corral, and
vanished.

Without preliminary explanation, Hume cried loudly,
"There he goes, men! After him!" He charged out, heedless of the unseen archers. Reluctantly, Raika and the rest
followed. Hume waved them on.

"Keep moving," he said in a low voice. "They won't
shoot if they think we're chasing him."

Malek, last in line, stooped to pick up one of the arrows
that had been aimed at Amergin. The shaft had splintered,
but the pale blue fletching was intact.

Raika glanced back and saw what he was holding. "Sky
blue is the color of the Brotherhood of Quen," she said.

Malek peered up through the mist. He could see the
ragged roofline of houses behind them but no sign of
movement. Where had the archers gone?

They raced on, barely keeping the Kagonesti in sight.
The sky was brightening all the time. When the sun got
well up, the fog wouldn't last long.

Skirting the corral, Caeta saw dim figures dashing
through the mist off to her right. Alarmed, she looked left
and saw more shadows flickering between the houses on
that side.

"They're all around us!" she said.

"Hounds to the hare," Howland said, wheezing. "They're using us to trail their quarry."

A bowstring twanged. Almost immediately they heard the hum of Amergin's sling and a short, sharp scream.

They trampled through a muddy garden plot, almost stumbling over the body of a slain elf. One of Amergin's smoked stars was imbedded under the dead elf's left ear.

Carver busied himself over the fallen Quen Brother, helping himself to the contents of the elf's pockets and pouch.

At the far end of the garden was a rubble-stone wall. Amergin was crouched behind it, sling held loosely in his hand. One by one they dropped beside him. Khorr had to practically flatten himself to keep his great head down.

The mist was breaking up. Through tattered shreds of fog, they could see a phalanx of armed gang members blocking the way. Their pale blue cloaks hung limply in the still air.

"Amergin!" called one. "Give yourself up! The rest of you, this is not your fight!"

The Kagonesti uttered a single syllable of his native dialect. No one had to translate his private rejoinder.

"All right, commander," Raika said to Howland. "Here's a military problem. What do we do now?"

The old Knight peeked over the long cairn. "In an orthodox battle, I'd called for archers to dislodge them then charge with sword and lance."

Raika sniffed. "I left my prancing steed at home with my bow."

"Give up, Amergin! Come quietly, and I promise you a quick death!"

"Who could resist generous terms like that?" said Carver.

Khorr gripped the wall with both hands. "Sir Howland, we have no bows but stones aplenty," he said. "Will that do?"

"Why not?" Hume said, taking a stone in each hand. "Warriors must learn to fight with ready means." He hurled them both at the elves barring their way.

Khorr joined in, and the young farmers too. They popped up, lobbed their stones, then ducked down again, expecting arrows to come winging back.

The first stones hit in front of the elves, caroming off the pavement. Startled, the Quenites backed up a bit, then nocked arrows and loosed. Hume got one through the armpit of his tunic before he threw himself down with alacrity.

Raika joined the bombardment. After two of their number were knocked down, the gang officer drew his sword and shouted, "Enough of this nonsense! Let's charge!"

The archers parted ranks, revealing a dozen sword-armed comrades, but when they rushed the garden wall, Amergin rose up with his sling.

Three Quenites went down, clutching their legs. Amergin had thrown three stars at once. He reloaded and hurled again, bring down two more. The remainder hesitated and inched back.

"Volley!" Howland cried. The stone-throwers hurled their missiles, pelting the wavering gang with more stones. More elves went down with cracked heads and bleeding scalps. The survivors backed away.

"Now's the moment! Charge!"

Hume, Howland, Khorr, and Raika scrambled over the wall and ran yelling at the elves. Carried away in the fervor of the moment, Malek, Nils, and Wilf followed.

Carver stood on the wall and whooped encouragingly while Caeta hurled stones over their heads.

Raika had almost reached the retreating elves when she suddenly realized she was unarmed. The elves didn't seem to notice. They ran up the street, away from the yelping band attacking them. Amergin flung sharp bronze stars by their ears until they gave way and fled farther.

The only person to actually close with the elves was Hume. He grabbed one gang member who'd taken a stone to the head and sat dazed on the ground. Lacking a blade, he head-butted the unhappy elf then relieved him of his sword.

In moments the battle was done. The fleeing elves' footfalls faded up the hill, and the street was theirs.

"Ha! We did it!" Wilf crowed.

"We were lucky," Raika said cheerfully. "They weren't expecting a crowd of crazy humans, just a lone forester."

Hume stuck the slim elf sword through the sash at his waist. "Help yourself to their weapons before they come back with reinforcements," he said. Seven members of the Quen gang lay unmoving on the street. Two were dead, slain by Amergin, and the remainder were insensible. Malek, Nils, Wilf, and Raika gathered up all the weapons they could carry.

Howland, author of their tiny victory, stood with his hands braced on his knees, retching. Caeta came up behind him and comforted him.

Amergin waited a few yards away, fog swirling around him. Wilf came to him, arms laden with swords and daggers.

"You're an amazing fighter," Wilf said. "I've never seen anyone use a sling like you!"

The Kagonesti coiled the thong around his hand. "Among my own, I'm counted a mediocre marksman."

There was a trace of a smile on the dour elf's face.

Hume urged speed, and they quickly fled the scene. Once past a final row of shanties and storehouses, they beheld open country at last.

"Where to now?" Amergin asked.

"East. Our village is seven days' journey from here," Malek said.

Amergin nodded briefly. He ran down the weedy hillside to a ravine, headed roughly in the right direction.

"How are you feeling, general?" Raika asked.

Howland wiped his mouth with the back of his hand. Though pale, he looked a little stronger than before. Leaving Robann was like a tonic to him.

"The Brotherhood isn't done with us yet," he said. He glanced over his shoulder at the weathered rooftops of Robann. "Follow the elf. He'll keep to the low ground, and so should we."

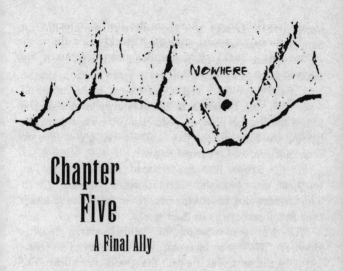

NOWHERE

Chapter Five

A Final Ally

Fifteen days had passed since Rakell came to Nowhere and stole Laila away. Fifteen days.

That time hammered in Malek's brain with every step he made. Half the time was gone before the raiders would return to enslave twenty more of his friends and neighbors, and they were still four long days' walk from home!

It didn't help that summer showed no sign of fading. Every step seemed a struggle in the heat. A haze covered the blue of the sky, leaving it a dull white, the color of steam. The sun hung low over their heads, glowing like hot iron through the haze. Since leaving Robann, the party had kept to sweltering airless ravines and gullies. Light breezes stirred the trees atop the hills, rattling the dry leaves, but the farmers and their hired champions did not dare show themselves against the light sky.

They were being followed—even Wilf could tell. By night, distant campfires lit up the western horizon. On the first night there were eight, the second night four, and since then, one. Howland assumed bounty hunters in the pay of the Brotherhood of Quen had come after them but finding the fugitives too fleet and elusive, a few gave up each morning and returned to town.

Yet the danger had not lessened, he told them. The toughest, most persistent hunters were the ones to fear. The farmers took to looking over their shoulders so much they developed cricks in their necks.

"There's worse to watch for," said Howland, glancing skyward. "We'll soon be crossing the territory of an Overlord." In the past year, he told the group, a red dragon of fearful power had claimed much of this land as his own. The dragon exacted stinging tribute from every caravan or trading party crossing his domain. Still, a small band of empty-handed travelers like them probably would not attract the dragon's notice, or so Howland prayed. So far the farmers had seen no sign of the dragon on their journey to Robann.

Four days out of Robann their path took them across a well-marked dirt road, passing northeast to southwest. Amergin approached the road cautiously. There was no one in sight, but he felt the flour-soft dust on the path with his fingers, bringing them to his nose to sniff.

Howland halted the group behind a stand of bracken. He and Hume ventured out to confer with the Kagonesti.

Howland looked as if he'd regained ten years of his life since leaving Robann. His complexion and carriage had improved, his eyes had lost their fevered look, and he even allowed Carver to crop his matted hair.

"I could do a very artistic trim," the kender said, scissors poised.

"Cut it all off," replied the Knight. "Let me start this venture clean."

With a shrug, Carver cut Howland's hair down the scalp, leaving only a fine, brushy nap on the old man's head. Without his lank, gray locks Howland's sunken eyes and broad forehead lent him an air of perpetual sorrow. He now resembled a priest more than a fighting man.

Knight and soldier stood on either side of the pensive elf.

"What can you see?" asked Howland.

"Many people came this way, two or three days ago."

"How many?" said Hume.

"More than twenty on foot. They were walking quickly, pulling a two-wheel cart." He stood up, dusting his hands. "No pony."

"Soldiers?"

Amergin shook his head. "Ordinary folk—farmers, herders. Men, women. Most barefoot."

"Where did they go?"

The elf pointed down the road, southwest.

"Probably just peasants on their way to market," said Howland. He turned to his hidden companions and waved them forward.

"What's wrong?" Malek asked upon joining them.

"Nothing. All is well."

"I never said that," said Amergin tersely.

Exasperated, Howland said, "Is there any obvious danger?"

"Perhaps. Something is strange." Without a word of explanation, he started down the road. The farmers were appalled. For days they'd taken great pains to conceal their tracks. Now the elf was leaving clear footprints in the soft dust.

Howland and Hume shouldered their gear and hurried after him. When no one else moved, the Knight barked, "Don't just stand there gawping! Move!"

"The heat's gone to the elf's head," Raika said.

Khorr, who wore an old apron draped across his horns to keep the sun off, said, "It's some clever forester ploy, do you think?"

"What I think is, I need a drink," she replied.

The road curved to the left until it led due east. Heavy, gnarled trees crowded in on both sides. The shade was welcome. Years of traffic had worn the path into the earth, and before long they were traversing a sunken road, bounded on either side by near-vertical hillsides.

"Feels like a trap!" Raika said, looking around nervously.

"I wouldn't want to be caught here by cavalry," Howland said. Ahead, Amergin continued his tireless lope.

The hills flattened out again, and Amergin stopped. Off to his left, a sandy path led away from the road to a copse of maples. He held out one hand, palm down, his signal to halt. Howland reined in the hot, tired party.

"Wait here," said Amergin. He dropped the sling to his fingers, loaded it, and moved on stealthily toward the maple grove.

Raika flopped heavily to the ground. "Who's got water?" she said loudly. Howland shushed her.

Caeta unslung her waterskin and handed it to the Saifhumi woman. Carver squatted by the roadside, and the farmers followed suit. Khorr found a spot in the shade, pulled up some wild onions, and set to munching.

After a brief foray, Amergin returned, looking adrift.

"I don't understand," he said. "Come and see."

One by one they trailed after the Kagonesti, who urged them all to silence. When only halfway to the maples, it became clear a sizable crowd of people were ahead in the grove, standing perfectly still and not making a sound. The effect was so strange Howland, Hume, and Raika drew their swords.

Amergin paused by a lordly maple, peering in puzzled fashion around the stout trunk. Howland, Hume, and Raika glided past him. When they were close enough, Raika grabbed hold of the nearest onlooker, a scruffy peasant in a dark brown jerkin. He didn't move at all despite her straining limbs. The fellow seemed rooted to the spot.

She uttered a sailor's curse and tugged again, harder. Seams of his coarse shirt tore, but the fellow was as immovable as a marble statue.

Howland spoke sharply to another. No response. Unaccustomed to being ignored, he swatted the man's backside with the flat of his blade. Not the slightest protest escaped the man's lips.

Hume walked around the frozen people to see their faces.

"Great Khan!" he exclaimed. "Sir Howland, look!"

Every one of the unresponsive onlookers, all humans, stood with their eyes open, staring straight ahead. Their faces were scorched red by the sun, and their lips were cracked and peeling. Howland felt for a pulse in the young man he'd struck.

"This one seems alive," he said, perplexed.

"So's this one," said Raika.

"These, too. What ails them?"

They moved through the crowd and found everyone in

the grove in identical condition. Twenty-two people in all, standing rigid, eyes open, gazing at . . . what?

Beneath the largest maple in the copse was a two-wheeled cart of the sort used by woodsmen, little more than an oversized wheelbarrow. Standing in the cart was a strangely dressed man with a noose around his neck.

"Oh, ho!" said Raika. "A lynching!"

She, Howland, and Hume gathered by the cart. Four peasants gripped the sides of the cart, ready to drag it out from under the unfortunate fellow, but they were paralyzed as well, mouths agape, as if they had been struck rigid in mid-motion.

"This beats all," Raika said. "If the gods still lived, I'd call this magic!"

Howland regarded the benoosed man thoughtfully. "I wonder what his crime was?"

The lynching candidate appeared to be near Raika's age, thirty or so. His skin was olive brown, an unfamiliar hue in these parts, and his hair was glossy black, cut bowl-style, straight across on his forehead. His neck was shaved behind his ears. His nose was flat and his face round. No trace of a beard sprouted from his chin. Both his hands and feet were tightly bound with rope.

"A foreigner," Hume remarked.

"Yes, but from where?" answered Howland.

"That's a nice pearl in his ear," said Raika. The bright white gem was pinned by a gold stud through the condemned man's right earlobe.

She climbed into the cart. "I think I'll fetch it off him—"

Her weight made the small cart shift on its wheels. Howland and Hume were about to protest when Raika saw the foreigner's black eyes blink.

She let out a yell and fell backward to the ground. In

an instant Amergin was at her side, sling twirling. Seeing the elf enter the grove, Khorr, Carver, and the farmers came running.

"He's alive!" Raika shouted, pointing.

"I am," said the man in a pleasant, cultivated voice, "and I'd like to stay that way."

Hume cut the halter loose from the tree with a single swing of his newfound sword. Freed from the danger of strangling, the stranger's knees promptly folded. He sat down hard in the cart.

Malek, Nils, Wilf and Caeta got no further than the ring of motionless watchers.

"Come away now!" Malek called to Howland.

"Wait." To the stranger he said, "Who are you?"

"My name is Ezu. Will one of you kindly untie me?"

No one moved to help him. Raika got up, looking as if she wanted to restore the noose to the tree and kick the cart away.

Ezu sighed. "People of this land are so inhospitable! This hapless traveler needs your help!"

"Cut him free," said Howland. Hume obeyed, despite Raika's protests.

"We know nothing about him," she said. "He could be the worst criminal in the world!"

"Oh, I'm not *him*," Ezu said, as Hume sawed through the ropes that bound his wrists.

"Who?" asked Hume, pausing.

"The Worst Criminal in the World. I met him once. Fascinating fellow—"

Once free, Ezu climbed out of the cart. His gait was very unsteady. "I've been standing for three whole days," he explained with a disarming smile. "I didn't dare move, lest I end up dangling."

"What happened here?" asked Howland.

Ezu ignored the question and said, "Can we move to different ground? These unhappy folk wished to kill me, so you'll understand that I find their company disagreeable."

Howland, for once, deferred to the others. "What do you think?"

"Seems like a decent enough chap," said Hume.

"He could be anybody!" Raika complained.

Amergin's sling remained in his hand. "Let him come," the elf said. Opinion delivered, he turned on his heel and walked away.

They hastily left the maple grove, though not before Carver made his rounds, "finding" odds and ends in the lynch mob's pockets. He did not get much, but for once Caeta did not criticize his pilfering.

"I despise mobs," she muttered to Malek.

Ezu limped along, surrounded by Nowhere's hired warriors. Malek gave him water, which the stranger drank gratefully.

"I imagine you want some explanation," he said, once his thirst was slaked.

"And damn quick," Raika muttered.

"As I said, I am Ezu, a traveler. I've been in this country many days."

Howland said, "Doing what?"

Again the easy smile. "As I said, traveling. It is my pleasure to visit distant lands and see places I've never been."

"You just travel? How do you live?" asked Wilf.

"By my wits, mostly." Seeing this did not satisfy his companions, he added, "When necessary, I apply myself to any odd task that needs doing. After I'm paid, I can continue my journey. It is my goal—my dream—to travel completely around the world."

"You sure talk funny," said Carver.

"Madman," was Raika's verdict.

"Why were those people trying to hang you?" asked Hume.

The charming stranger looked pained. "They blamed me for their misfortune. Some bandits came through the district shortly after I arrived. They carried off many of the locals. I believe they intended to force them to labor. Since I am a stranger in their country, they thought me in league with the bandits."

The farmers stopped dead in their tracks. "It must be Rakell!" Malek raged. "Rounding up more captives!"

"Maybe he needs more slaves to replace the ones who've died," blurted Wilf. He regretted saying this when saw the anguish on his friend's face.

"You know the situation then?" said Ezu casually. "Good. The folks back there decided I was some kind of magical spy, divining where their villages and secreted food supplies were and betraying them to the bandits. The mob seized me, declared me guilty, and marched me down the road to hang me.

"Bandit scouts often use this road," Ezu added. "The peasants meant to leave my body where the bandits would find it." In spite of the grim topic, Ezu managed a grin. "My death was to be a warning to others."

"Folks here seem made of sterner stuff than you," Raika mused to Malek.

"They are many, we are few," the farmer replied defensively.

"All this is fascinating," Howland said, "but what happened to the lynch mob? How did they end up so stricken?"

Ezu cupped a hand to the back of his head, looking embarrassed. "My doing, I fear."

"Magic!" declared Carver.

"Not at all. I used Piroquey's Powder on them."

"What powder?"

"Piroquey's Powder," Ezu explained. "It is a rare substance I picked up in my wanderings. Sprayed in the air and inhaled, it causes a waking paralysis."

"Why did you use it?" asked Howland.

The genial stranger said, "I thought once I'd stopped the hanging, I could wriggle out of my bonds, but they tied me too well. When you came along, I was wondering if I would get loose before the mob woke up."

Malek grunted. "I wish you hadn't used all the powder. A substance like that would have been invaluable against Rakell."

Carver had ideas of his own about Piroquey's Powder. "How long will they be asleep?"

"They could awake at any time."

All the more reason to leave as soon as possible. Howland gathered everyone together and signaled Amergin they were going. The elf set off due east again, skirting the grove of silent vigilantes.

"Begging your pardon," Ezu said, trotting after Caeta and Khorr. "This one would like to know if he might accompany you? At least to safer surroundings?"

"It's not at all safe where we're going," Caeta replied, "but you're welcome to join us for as long as you like."

"Splendid!" Ezu bowed again. He ran back to the grove and returned, bearing an ornate satchel. It was made of strips of shiny black wood, jointed with twine. A woven handle on top allowed him to carry it.

"All my worldly goods," he said, patting the box. "Couldn't leave that behind!"

The Middle of Nowhere

* * * * *

The march continued long after sundown. Time was short, and the farmers pressed Howland to hurry. The old Knight kept the party going until darkness was well upon them then called a halt. They had reached the edge of the high plain. The dull, steamy sky at last dissolved into the deep azure of dusk. Hills were fewer and lower, and trees stood out like isolated sentinels against the darkening sky.

"Cold camp, remember," Howland said. "No fire."

Carver shinnied up a chestnut tree for a look around. He slid back down and reported he could see a single campfire in the near distance, glowing against the velvet sky.

"How far?" asked Howland.

"Two miles, maybe."

"I tire of being chased," Raika said.

"So do I," said Hume.

"Want to do something about it?" asked Howland.

The Saifhumi woman nodded.

"Take Amergin with you, and see if you can't discourage them from following us. Hume and I will stay here. We need to guard our own camp. Just because a fire is burning nearby, that doesn't mean the fire-builder is beside it.

"It's an old wilderness trick," added the Knight. "A fire draws trouble, like moths. While we send a force out to deal with our pursuer, they may choose the same time to attack. We must be vigilant."

They camped in a shallow ravine lined with windblown leaves. Worn out by the journey, Wilf, Nils, and Caeta were soon asleep. Malek, brooding, could not succumb to slumber. All sorts of awful images crowded his thoughts: his friends and neighbors slaving in a black pit under the whips of cruel overseers. Weak ones, too feeble to work, being given to the ogres . . . Laila, sleek as a yearling doe, at the mercy of Rakell and his cronies—

The odd stranger, Ezu, loomed over him. "Greetings," he said. "May this one join you?"

Malek grunted, shifting to one side. Ezu dropped beside him. He opened his satchel and took out a sheaf of waxed paper. Unrolled, Malek saw it held strips of dried fish of some kind. Ezu offered some to him.

He was tempted. Malek had eaten nothing but barley cake and water for days, and now that was running out. He and his comrades had privately agreed all the food would go to the warriors. His belly was like the sky overhead—black and empty.

"Thank you," he said, warily taking just one strip. The fish jerky was actually quite tender and fiercely salty. Malek's jaw clenched from the powerful taste.

"So," said Ezu, "you seek to fight the bandits, all of you?"

Malek tried to look innocent and failed.

The stranger shrugged broadly. "When I see farmers and soldiers traveling together, I wonder . . . you do not bear their baggage, so you're not porters. You and Sir Howland—" He held his hands up, palms down and parallel. "He listens to you. You're his equal, yes?"

Malek bit off more fish. "We hired them to fight for us."

"I would like to observe your struggle."

Malek eyed Ezu uncertainly. "Our fight is not a show."

"This one has been to many lands and seen many battles," Ezu said. "My knowledge is yours for the asking. It may prove handy."

The fish strip gone, Malek licked salt from his fingers.

He didn't trust the odd visitor, not at all. Maybe the lynching party was onto something. Maybe Ezu was a spy for Rakell.

"I am not a spy for anyone," said Ezu, as if listening to Malek's thoughts. His precision was so great Malek jumped to his feet.

"I'll have to talk it over with my friends," he said, unnerved. "Then you'll have our answer."

"Right-right." Ezu rose. "Use this one how you can. You will not regret it."

Malek already did.

* * * * *

Flat on their bellies, Raika and Amergin crawled toward the flickering fire. Burning windfall branches crackled loudly in the night, silencing nearby crickets and frogs.

"Anybody there?" she whispered. The elf shook his head ever so slightly.

Raika studied the scene. The campfire had been laid in the center of a triangle of oak trees. A single bedroll lay on the ground close by, along with a wicker basket equipped with carrying straps. It looked as though the fire-builder had stepped away, and might return at any moment.

Amergin said softly in Raika's ear, "Trap. I'll go round." His breath, like his manner, was cool. Noiselessly he slid away. The last she saw of him was the blackened soles of his bare feet merging into the shadows.

Something with many legs crawled across her neck. She flicked it off without bothering to look at it.

The longer she studied the camp scene, the more Raika

was convinced someone was actually in the bedroll. At casual glance, the blanket appeared open and empty, but staring at the firelight playing over its contours, Raika thought someone was moving under the blanket. There was even a sideways lump where the sleeper's foot would be, turned outward at the heel.

No sign of Amergin. That meant nothing. The Kagonesti would not be seen unless he wanted to be. How could she let him know her suspicions about the bedroll? There might be other enemies lurking in the night.

Time passed with such slowness Raika felt her fingers and toes tingle. She drew in her hands and slowly pushed up on her knees. No responding movement from the bedroll.

Using her fingers to keep the blade from scraping on the scabbard, Raika drew her sword, one of the ones taken from the Quen guards in Robann. Raising the hilt to eye level, she sprang from the shadows and ran at the sleeping figure. Her long legs covered ground quickly—three, four, five long strides, and she was standing over the bedroll. The only part of the sleeper not covered by the blanket was a short shock of brown hair.

She used both hands to drive her blade into the supine figure. Raika felt fleeting resistance, then the sword point dug into the hard earth.

A man impaled thus would die swiftly, but he would also cry out, scream, or writhe in agony. Her victim did none of that, nor did he bleed. Instead the sleeper turned his head and opened his eyes, gazing steadily at her. Horrified, Raika whipped back the blanket.

Under the blanket was a small pit, carefully hollowed out. Her 'victim' sat in this hole with a sword across his knees. The rest of the body she'd recognized under the blanket was a dummy, stuffed with rags and tied to a thick plank. Her sword tip was buried in the piece of lumber.

The bounty hunter brought his sword up, presenting the point under Raika's chin. Though his hair was cropped close like a human's, he had distinctly elven features.

"Yield," he said calmly.

Raika let out a snarl and threw herself backward to escape his poised blade. She reeled away, off balance, and tripped. Falling hard, she felt rope beneath her fingers. A net!

The bounty hunter was out of his hole and had pulled hard on a cord lying just beneath the dirt. Somewhere a bent tree limb unbowed, and Raika snapped off the ground, completely enfolded in a heavy net.

"Let me down! Let me down!" she stormed.

"Can't. You're the catch of the day," said the elf. Judging by his coloring, he was Kagonesti, but his clothing and sword were human-style, the kind worn far to the south.

"If you know what's good for you, you'll let me down!" Raika raged.

"I don't think so." He shoved his sword in its sheath. "You have friends about. How many came with you? Where are they now?"

She called him most of the filthy names she knew. Ignoring her, he slipped away into the darkness.

Raika was a good six feet off the ground, bent double so tightly she could not get a hand through the tight mesh. She struggled until something bright whizzed by the campfire, striking an oak tree with a loud thump. Raika saw it was one of Amergin's polished bronze stars. Hope surging, she groped for the Quen knife tucked in her sash.

There was a crashing in the underbrush. A heartbeat later Amergin burst into the clearing. His sling had been sliced in two. He wore no sword.

Close behind him came the bounty hunter. He stepped into the circle of firelight and barked a short sentence in Elvish. Amergin did not reply.

"My sword! In the plank!" Raika cried. Amergin spotted the bedroll decoy. He ran to it, planted one foot on the board, and wrenched the blade free. To Raika's surprise, the bounty hunter made no effort to stop him.

"*Ko'aq ketay*," he said in Elvish. "Do your best."

The Kagonesti crept toward each other, each one sidling to his right. As a result, they circled the clearing, the campfire and Raika between them. She struggled to free her knife, but blood was beginning to thunder in her head. If she was hung up like this much longer, her wits would founder.

The bounty hunter vaulted over the campfire and alit within arm's reach of Amergin. They traded a few quick cuts, nothing fancy. Raika was relieved to see that Amergin knew something about using a sword. He thrust at the bounty hunter, who threw himself backward to avoid Amergin's point. In so doing, he collided with Raika, setting her swinging. Blades flashed perilously close to her helpless backside.

"You've got a whole clearing! Fight somewhere else!" she cried. Suddenly, Raika realized that the collision had loosened the knife from her belt. It fell below her left hip. Straining hard, she worked her right hand across to grasp it.

The bounty hunter made a whirling overhand attack, moving his sword so quickly all Amergin could do was hold his weapon over his head to ward off the blows. He countered only once, a short thrust aimed at the bounty hunter's face. The crop-haired elf slapped the blade away with his hand.

"You're done," he said in Common. "Give up."

"You're not taking me back to Robann," Amergin said. You know what the Brotherhood will do to me?"

The hunter nodded curtly. "Too bad. My fee would be double if I delivered you alive."

Amergin drew away, keeping his back to the dark woods. "How much are they paying you?" he asked. "Whatever it is, I'll pay you more."

"I can't do that. A contract is a contract. I've never failed to bring in my quarry."

A fast flurry of slashes and thrusts drove Amergin to the foot of one of the oaks. The hunter caught up his foe's blade and with a flick of his wrist sent Amergin's sword flying into the night.

"*Malo takhi*," said the hunter. The benediction meant, "Enter darkness."

He extended his arm for the final lunge but never completed it. With a resounding thud, Raika broke a plank over the bounty hunter's head, and he collapsed.

Moments later, Howland, Hume, and Carver raced in, ready for a fight. They'd heard the clatter of swordplay and come running.

Raika tossed the broken board aside and rolled the unconscious elf over with her toe. She took the knife from her teeth and put it to his throat.

"Wait!" said Howland. He picked up a brand from the fire and held it up to light the bounty hunter's face. "By my Oath! Do you know who this is?"

"A tricky little wretch about to meet his ancestors!" Raika snarled.

"It's Robien! Robien the Tireless!"

Hume said, "Really? The very one?"

"I'm sure of it!" said Howland. "Twenty years ago we tracked down the murderer Valneer together. Chased him to the Icewall, we did. He's a fine fellow!"

Carver hunted through the bounty hunter's bag and found a weighty purse. "Here's the blood money!" he said as he slipped the sack into his shirt.

Amergin stood over Raika and his enemy. "So, the one and only Robien. I should not be surprised. Solito was the chief's son."

Still with her knife at his throat, Raika said, "Who's this Robien, anyway?"

"The most famous tracker and bounty hunter in six nations," said Howland. "They say he's never failed in a mission and brought a hundred malefactors to justice."

"He's certainly failed tonight!" Raika declared with a laugh. She drew back her hand. Amergin caught it.

"No," he said.

"Why? He would have killed you!"

"He is an honorable brother of the forest. He does not deserve to have his throat cut like a wayward bandit."

Raika rocked back on her haunches. "What a bunch of noble fools you all are! What are we going to do when we fight Rakell and his gang? Spare them because they're honorable brigands?"

"If we let him go, he'll simply come after Amergin again," Hume said.

Howland tossed the burning branch back in the fire. Putting his sword away, he pondered. Finally he turned to Amergin.

"It's your life. What do you say?"

The Kagonesti's long face was a mask. "Let's bring him along."

"Bring him?" Raika, Hume, and Carver said in unison. The Saifhumi woman said, "That's crazy!"

"He's wields a fine sword. Why not invite him to join us against the raiders?"

"He's been paid to find or kill you! Why would a hunter of his reputation go back on his word?"

Howland went to Carver and held out his hand. "The bounty. Give it to me."

"I'm the one who found it," said the kender, sulking. Reluctantly he gave the purse to the Knight.

"Amergin is right. We might use him," said Howland. "Leave the how and why to me. Until then, tie him up. Khorr can easily carry him awhile."

They obliterated all traces of Robien's camp and carried off every scrap from the site. The farmers were more than a little worried by this new way of gaining a recruit, but by now they trusted Sir Howland's judgment. Every sword was crucial. So was every passing moment.

The journey resumed before dawn.

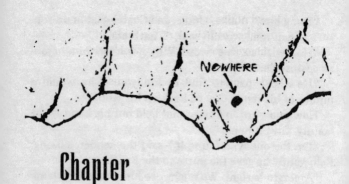

NOWHERE

Chapter Six

Fearful Charges

There it is—Nowhere."

Malek stood with Howland uth Ungen on the highest prominence for miles around, a round-topped hill the farmers called Caper Mountain. Mountain it was not. It rose only forty feet or so above the surrounding plain, but that made it mountain enough for these parts.

Spread out below them were a patchwork of fields and gardens, diligently tended throughout the growing season. Barley covered the most ground, and the green stalks were browning as much from lack of rain as from the coming harvest. Here and there swatches of dark green stood out among the brown lakes of grain. Garden plots were watered daily. Tender vegetables needed more sustenance than hardy grain.

Sir Howland noticed none of this. All he could see was the rude horseshoe of houses in the midst of a flat plain. Tiny figures moved around the gray dot Malek indicated was the village's sole well.

How could anyone defend such a defenseless spot? Was it even possible?

The Knight palmed the sweat from the stubble growing out of his scalp. Hot and tired though he was, he felt good and strong. The journey on foot had purged the toxins from his body, cleansing him of much bad wine and self-pity. The farmers' cause had paid him more that a full belly—it had revived Howland's honor. For him, duty was an appetite no less sharp than hunger or thirst. Now, though, when he first beheld the ground he was asked to defend, his spirits sank into his dusty boots.

On the rearward slope, the rest of the hired swords lolled, watching kites and crows wheeling through the cloudless sky. Nils, Wilf, and Caeta chafed at the delay. They were near enough home to smell the barley growing, but Howland had insisted on this stop. He would not rush his troops into an unknown situation, he said firmly.

Ezu amused Khorr and Carver with tales of distant lands. When the story called for it, he pulled out some artifact from his satchel. Most were inconsequential—a string of beads, a thick disk of glass, a cup with a needle floating inside—but backed by Ezu's strange charm they became wondrous relics.

"And this," he said, brandishing the glass disk, "was made by the glassmasters of Oe. A fantastic place, Oe. Every house, grand or mean, is made of glass."

"Let me see!" said Carver. Ezu placed the disk on his small palm. It didn't seem so special as he examined it. It was just a round lump of clear glass, not even a pretty color.

"Hold it by the edge and look through it," said Ezu.

The kender did, and exclaimed, "Khorr! Your eyes are huge!"

The minotaur felt along his massive brow. "They're no bigger than usual."

Carver lowered the glass. "Heh! So they are." He peered through Ezu's toy again, and once more Khorr's face swelled to monstrous proportions.

The kender laughed.

Khorr said, "Let me see." He looked through the glass, first at Carver, then Ezu. "It makes things look bigger," the minotaur said.

"Right-right!" Ezu replied. "That is what it does. In Oe, they call this a 'lens.'"

Carver snatched the disk from Khorr's thick fingers. He looked at everything through the glass—grass, pebbles, Ezu, and a frowning Raika, sitting ten feet away with her sword bare, guarding the quiescent bounty hunter.

"Ho, she's even bigger," he said. A new target occurred to him. "My foot!" He bent down, resting his chin on one knee, and gazed at his bare brown toes through Ezu's lens.

The sun was behind him. Rays gathered by the glass came to a point in the center of Carver's big toenail.

"*Yow!*"

The kender leaped into the air, arms and legs flailing. Ezu's disk went flying, but the smiling traveler caught it with surprising deftness before it was lost in the grass.

"I'm burned!" Carver yelled, clutching his foot.

"What's all the row?" muttered Howland, glancing down the hill. "The kender. Should've known."

"Well, can it be done?" asked Malek urgently.

"On my word as a Knight, I don't think so. No." Howland swept a hand across the distant vista. "The terrain has no more relief than a plate. There's nothing here to impede horsemen. Even if we could ambush part of Rakell's force, there's aren't enough of us to stop him from overrunning the village."

Malek's eyes burned. "It is hopeless then!"

Howland put a hand on the young farmer's shoulder. "Nothing's hopeless, lad. What's needed is another way. I came here thinking like a Knight, ready to defend a regular town. That's not what we have. Your village is more like . . ." He groped for a metaphor. "Like an island in a sea of grass. Islands can be defended."

"Perhaps Raika will have some ideas. She's a sailor."

"Hmmm. She might, if we can get her to forget about Robien for a moment."

Since capturing the ranger, Raika had not left Robien's side. She was plainly proud to have taken so famed a bounty hunter, and she treated him as her personal prize. Robien, for his part, seemed strangely content to be a prisoner. When the situation in Nowhere was explained to him, he neither agreed nor refused to join the defenders. He merely watched and listened to all that went on around him, as Raika watched him in turn.

Hume climbed Caper Mountain and took his place at Howland's side. As the only other trained soldier in the band, he'd become Howland's lieutenant.

"There's our castle," Howland said ironically. "What do you think?"

"It has walls of air." Hume shaded his eyes with one hand. "How far is it to Rakell's camp?"

Malek looked stricken. "No one knows."

Howland nodded vigorously. "We must find out where it is. It's always better to carry the fight to the enemy's stronghold. Good thinking, Hume."

They descended the hill and roused their comrades. Carver limped into line alongside Khorr, eyes shooting darts at the bland Ezu.

"We're going to the village," Howland said. "It's vital at this point that the enemy not know we're here. For this reason I'm dividing us into four groups, each to be lead in by one of the farmers. Hume and I will follow you, Malek. Caeta leads Khorr and Carver. Nils, you take Raika and the traveler—"

"I'll not go without him," Raika replied, nodding at Robien.

Howland sighed. "Very well. Raika and Robien will go with Nils. That leaves Wilf to guide Ezu and Amergin. Remember, quiet and calm are vital. No unnecessary displays or tomfoolery." He stared meaningfully at Carver. "We'll meet at Malek's house."

Howland, Hume, and Malek departed. By the time they disappeared into the head-high grass at the foot of Caper Mountain, Nils started out with his strange pair, Raika with sword bared and Robien with his hands tied behind his back.

Wilf led his two down the north side of the hill, intending to swing wide around the fields and enter Nowhere from the north. That left Caeta with Khorr and Carver alone on the hill.

"So," said the kender, rubbing his hands. "Where's the gold mine around here?"

"There is no gold mine."

"Beg your pardon. I meant silver mine."

"No silver, either."

"Jewels?"

Caeta shouldered the threadbare sack she carried her traveling gear in. "You've been told, kender, time and time again. There's no treasure! We brought back fighters to free us from Rakell's raiders. That's all!"

She stalked down the slope. Khorr gave Carver a mildly reproachful look and followed her.

"Yeah, right!" Carver muttered. "No treasure? Ha! You just don't want to share it fair and square!" He stamped his foot, wincing from the burn he gave himself with Ezu's lens. "Think I'll give up and go home? Not me! Not Carver Reedwhistle, master of adventure!" Realizing no one was listening, he hurried after Caeta and the minotaur. "Wait for me!" he shouted. When they didn't, he repeated his call louder and louder each time.

Not half an hour had passed since Howland had demanded stealth from his followers. Already the warriors' quiet entry into Nowhere had been shattered by the irrepressible kender.

* * * * *

Wind raised eddies of dust around the silent huts. Malek stopped at the well to offer Howland and Hume fresh water. The old bucket, broken the day Rakell kidnapped Laila, Larem, and the others, had been replaced by a flimsy container made of woven grass. It leaked copiously as Howland raised it to his lips.

"Where is everybody?" Malek wondered out loud. "It's strange. No one working in the fields, no children playing in the shade . . . "

"Perhaps Rakell came back sooner than expected and took them," said Hume.

"No, they must be here." Howland lowered the grass bucket. "We saw them from the hill. They're hiding from us. They're afraid."

Malek reddened. "Fools! They can see I'm with you!"

"They fear strangers," the Knight said. "Can you blame them after all that has happened?"

Malek ran to the nearest house and rattled the door. "Come out! Come out, Vank! You too, Dora! Bakar, Fayn, Luki, where are you?"

He ran to the next house, calling his neighbors' names. Howland and Hume remained at the well, embarrassed but outwardly stoic.

Malek fell to kicking at doors and cursing his fellow villagers. No one emerged until the others arrived. Not until Nils, Wilf, and especially Caeta returned were the farmers reassured by familiar faces. Slowly, one house at a time, they opened their doors and peeked out.

"Come out, you damned rabbits!" Malek raged. "Greet our guests! They've come here to fight for you. Can you not show them some gratitude?"

Gradually the people of Nowhere collected on the common ground between their homes. Mothers hugged children close to them, while husbands nervously flexed work-worn hands around their garden tools.

An aged villager appeared in a gap in the crowd. Caeta gave a little cry and rushed forward to greet her father. Not waiting for an invitation, Howland also went to meet him. Hume stayed by the well with the recruits.

Caeta wiped happy tears from her eyes. "Papa, this is Sir Howland, a Knight who's come to help us."

"Greetings, my lord," the old man said. "Thank you for seeing my daughter safely home. I never thought to see her or the boys again."

"We've come a long way," Howland replied briskly. "There is much to do. Where can I quarter my people?"

After a brief consultation between elder and daughter,

Caeta said, "Marren's hut is empty. The raiders took him and his girl Laila. You may sleep there."

"I shall want to meet with every able-bodied man and woman in the village. We've come to fight your enemies, but we will need plenty of help."

"I will call a village gathering after sunset," said the elder. He grasped Howland's hand with his bony one. Aged or not, his grip was hard.

"We are determined to fight," rasped the elder. "To the death."

Howland managed to smile. "A true warrior doesn't fight to the death," he countered. "He fights until his enemies are defeated—or dead."

Breaking away from the elder and his daughter, Howland signaled the others to join him. He led them across the dusty square to the hut they were told to occupy. Frightened, curious farmers openly stared at their would-be saviors. Few of them had ever been more than a day's walk from home, and an ebony-skinned woman, two elves, a minotaur, a kender, and Ezu with his exotic features filled them with wonder. At one point a small boy darted out from behind his mother and ran up to Khorr. With exaggerated care, he lightly touched the minotaur's brawny flank.

"Yes?" asked Khorr in his cavern-deep voice.

With a yelp, the child fled back to his mother.

"They're scared," said Robien. "Scared because we're different."

"I hardly know what I'm doing here," the Saifhumi woman muttered.

"A noble thing."

She snorted. "You think so?"

The bounty hunter halted to look over the wide-eyed

crowd watching them. "Until this moment I didn't believe Sir Howland's story about oppressed farmers. Now I see it's true."

"Move along." She gave him a shove.

Ezu, trailing the rest, paused to examine a group of villagers clustered in front of a pair of joined huts. Smiling and speaking in a soothing voice, he fingered the women's bone hair clasps and the men's tools.

"There is little metal here," he observed to one of the inhabitants. "Perhaps a trade—a hair clasp for—"

Amergin came back and took him in tow.

Marren's hut was a single room, with a pounded clay floor and central hearth. Because Marren was blind, what few pieces of furniture he and Laila had were fastened securely in place. Raika promptly claimed the bed, a simple wooden frame filled with moss and straw.

"Ah!" She reclined and for the first time in days took her eyes off Robien.

Howland entered. "Listen, all. We're to meet with the village elder and his people tonight. Before then, I have tasks for you."

"Fire away, captain." Raika cupped her hands behind her head and closed her eyes.

He ignored her. "To my eye, this village appears indefensible. If Rakell is half the soldier I imagine he is, he thinks so too. That may give us an advantage. An enemy is most vulnerable when he believes he has the upper hand."

"What shall we do?" asked Hume.

"For now, we've got to whip these villagers into fighting shape. Malek says there are twenty-five or so capable of fighting, but they must be properly led. Otherwise, they'll just be sheep driven before wolves."

Carver made baa-baaing noises. Howland ignored him.

"Each of us who is able will take six or eight farmers in hand and teach them how to move and fight together," he said.

"Are we not all able?" asked Khorr.

"Ezu is not a warrior. Neither is Carver. As for Robien—I'd be glad to have you with us, but as a prisoner, you're under no obligation to fight for your captors," said the knight.

The Kagonesti ranger, kneeling with his hands still tied, looked thoughtful. "I don't know what fate is planned for me," he said, "but I would rather fight free than stay bound. Captivity is death for a freeborn elf like me. I will not try to escape."

"That's good enough for me." Howland ordered Robien cut free.

Raika protested. "What's to stop him from fleeing in the night and betraying the lot of us to the Quen Bortherhood?"

"The choice is his." Howland's tone was clear. The matter was not open for debate.

"What about Amergin? Has he no say?"

The barefoot forester was leaning against the doorway, watching but not speaking, as usual. When Raika invoked him he said, "If Robien gives up his contract to return me to Robann, I have no objection to his fighting with us."

"A contract is a contract," the bounty hunter replied tersely.

Raika pointed triumphantly at the stubborn elf.

"You're making this difficult," said Hume.

"Honor has a way of making life difficult. It also gives life meaning." Robien shrugged his pinioned shoulders. "On the other hand, the Brotherhood did not specify *when* I was to bring my quarry in. Given the circumstances, I believe it could be a long time before I return Amergin to them."

Howland said, "Cut him loose."

Hume hacked through the rawhide lacing. Robien stood, rubbing his raw, chafed wrists. "Thank you," he said to Howland.

Howland was somber. "Don't thank me. You may have agreed to your own death."

They discussed arming the farmers with makeshift weapons. At last Carver spoke up.

"I can make whippiks for the villagers and teach them how to use them. Anyone can use a whippik, even human children."

"True," Hume said thoughtfully. "Many of the village children are no bigger than kender."

Carver made a face. "Size isn't everything, you know."

Khorr raised a meaty hand shyly. "What's a whippik?"

Carver strode to the hearth. "A whippik," he explained, "is a throwing stick with loop of gut or twine on one end. By sitting a stone or dart in the loop, a whippik can propel the missile almost as far as a bow. They're simple to make. All we need is a piece of straight wood as long as the thrower's arm. And projectiles, of course."

"All right," said Howland. "Carver, you're in charge of the village children old enough to use a whippik."

Grinning fiercely, the kender swaggered back to his spot between Ezu and Khorr and squatted on the floor.

"What other weapons can we make?" asked the Knight.

"Spears," said Hume.

"Lash a stone to a handle and you have a mace," said Raika.

"Slings," said Robien, glancing at Amergin.

"Our friend is deadly with one," Howland agreed, "but can you teach simple-minded farmers to sling?"

"In a year of practice, yes."

Howland nodded. "You have twelve days."

"They'd be better off throwing rocks with their bare hands," protested Amergin.

Howland sighed. "Try to train them anyway."

"While you're working the villagers, Hume and I, with Malek and his brother, are going to look for Rakell's stronghold and scout it out. If we can, we'll free some of the captives he's holding, while thinning his ranks as much as we can."

"What about defenses for the village?" asked Raika. "Once you attack Rakell, he'll know we're around. He may strike back before we're ready to stand up to him."

Ezu stood. Smiling as always, he said, "Hello? This one has ideas along those lines."

Everyone looked at the stranger skeptically. Not intimidated, Ezu continued.

"I've been to many places, in many lands. I've seen all sorts of fortifications, from high stone walls to the permanent rings of fire around the citadel of Kamkorah . . ." Temporarily lost in his memories, his voice trailed off.

Howland cleared his throat, and Ezu snapped back to the present. "I may be able to recall some feature we can use to shield these poor people from their tormentors."

Tired from the long, hot journey, Howland was in no mood to listen to the foreigner's odd, elliptical speech. "Fine. Study the matter and try to come up with a physical defense for Nowhere." To Hume he muttered, "At least it will keep the fellow busy and out of our way."

Howland dismissed his troops until sunset, when they would gather in full conclave with the villagers. "You're

113

free till then," he said. "Keep to the village, but stay out of sight! Rakell may have sentinels watching everything that happens here."

The defenders of Nowhere drifted out until only Howland, Hume, and Raika were left. The old Knight wanted to draw up a sketch-map of the vicinity. He and Hume discussed the lay of the land and ways to defend it. Raika seemed asleep.

"You'd better keep an eye on our world traveler," she said, her voice flat with fatigue. "I don't trust him."

"Seems like a harmless fool to me," Hume replied.

"Those people were going to hang him for a spy."

"Which he freely told us," Howland pointed out.

Raika opened one eye. "The best way to disguise a lie is by telling the truth."

Howland nodded grudgingly. "Since you don't have Robien to watch any longer, maybe you want the job?"

She never heard his jest. Raika, her back to both men, was already snoring loudly.

Chapter Seven
The Measure of a Knight

The grand meeting of the inhabitants of Nowhere and their new defenders took place after dark. To avoid being seen by Rakell's scouts, the conclave was held in a barley field west of the settlement. Aside from a few boys left behind to keep watch, everyone trekked silently into the night to meet the warriors come to help them. Hope was in the air. The foreigners and their strange ways seemed full of portent for success.

The villagers sat down in orderly rows, facing Howland's motley band. Two torches blazed on either side of the Knight, the only light he would permit. When Caeta entered the clearing with her father, Elder Calec, on her arm, Howland bade them sit up front. Once the elder was seated, he began.

"I am Howland uth Ungen, Knight of the Order of the Rose. As you know, we've come here to defend you against your enemies, Rakell and his raiders." He paused, trying to catch every farmer's eyes before he continued. "This we cannot do."

The stunned silence that followed extended to his comrades. Hume looked the most stricken of all.

"We cannot do it with the forces we have on hand. I therefore recommend you abandon this village and move elsewhere."

Howland folded his arms across his chest and waited. For a time the only sound was the crackled of the burning torches. At last Calec coughed a little and raised his creaking voice.

"What deceit is this?" he rasped. "Are you admitting defeat before the fight has begun?"

"I tell what I know to be true," Howland replied. "This place is indefensible."

Old Calec struggled to his feet, disdaining his daughter's supporting hand. "You did not come here to tell us that! Why say it now?"

Howland met the elder's knowing gaze. "Because the alternative is very hard."

"I have lived here eighty-eight years," said Calec. "My father and mother lived here before me, and their parents before them." He waved a gnarled hand at the folk behind him. "We're farmers. We know hardship. Every day we draw breath is a battle against drought, disease, and death. What can be harder than that?"

"Just this: To win, to survive, everyone must fight. *Everyone.*"

The elder spat in the dust. "Give me a stick or a stone, and I'll fight."

The farmers and families behind him were not so sure. A loud murmur rippled through their ranks. Their unease was voiced by Bakar. "Why did we seek warriors, if we're expected to fight anyway? We could have done that all along and saved food and water!"

"Will you not fight for your homes and families?" asked Hume.

Raika snapped, "You'd be slaughtered without us!"

Voices grew louder as accusations of bad faith and cowardice flew back and forth. Khorr had to restrain Raika from punching a farmer who called her craven. Fearing violence, some villagers tried to creep away unnoticed in the dark.

A high, warbling whistle cut through the heated words. It grew in intensity until many had to clap hands over their ears to bear it. Everyone turned to the source of the sound, standing in the rear ranks of the newcomers.

Ezu removed the metal pipe from his lips. The piercing note ceased. Far away, nightbirds screeched, and a rare wolf of the plains howled in lonesome protest.

"What is that?" asked Howland.

"A whistle, as used by the sailors of Ladosh." He tucked it away in his baggy trousers. "Effective, isn't it?"

"Unbearable!" said the minotaur. "I thought my head would split!"

"Many animals find it intolerable. Wolves and dogs, for example." The howls of the wild creatures could still be heard. "And horses."

"Horses?" Howland understood. "Will your whistle upset Rakell's cavalry?"

The amiable traveler shrugged.

"May I see it?"

Ezu handed Howland the device. It was brass, about as

117

thick as a woman's little finger, and eight inches long. The walls of the tube were thick, and two slots were cut in the upper surface, one about a third of the length from the mouth end, the other halfway along. Howland put the whistle to his lips and blew. No sound emerged.

He blew until his face purpled. Ezu gently took the whistle back. "Perhaps it's not so useful after all," he said to the mystified Howland.

Now that calm had been restored, Amergin spoke up. "I'm not a soldier," he began, "but I have fought mounted foes before. There are no walls around my home forest, but no marauder dares enter it."

"Trees are a good fence against cavalry," said Hume.

"I speak not of fences or trees," said the Kagonesti. "Fences can be broken down and trees burned. What my people do to deter attack is lay traps. Many, many traps. Our settlements are ringed with them."

"Trenches!" offered Hume. "My khan once defended the whole of the Khurman Peninsula with a line of trenches. The land there is desert, loose sand and gravel, with no trees of any kind. We dug two lines of trenches across the peninsula and turned back the horde of ogre warlord Shagrah-de."

Howland pulled out the goatskin parchment he'd procured that afternoon and examined the simple map he'd drawn of Nowhere. He beckoned Malek, Nils, and Caeta to look at it with him. Though blind, Calec joined them.

"These are useful ideas." He ran a finger across the drawing. "Where did the raiders come from before?"

Malek pointed. "They approached from the south." He tapped the parchment at the open end of the horseshoe of houses. "When they were nearer, they circled around and rode in from the west."

It made sense. Ogres and horses need room to maneuver, and it was easier to funnel them into the open end of the village than to squeeze them between huts.

"We might be able to close this open ground with a trench," Howland said.

"Add a barrier of sharpened stakes to fend off horses," suggested Robien.

Howland studied his map, frowning. "Once the bandits find they can't just ride in as they did before, they'll try to break through the ring of houses. The huts are too flimsy to stop ogres," he muttered.

"Fill them with dirt," said Khorr.

The leaders, clustered around the map, looked up at the hulking poet.

"Fill the huts with the dirt left over from digging the trench," the minotaur said. "It has to go somewhere. If the houses are full of dirt, no one can break through them."

One or two villagers sent up a wail, at the idea of filling their homes with dirt.

Howland grinned a little. "This affair is beginning to intrigue me!"

"Then you'll stay and fight, after all?" asked the elder.

"If your people stand with us, we'll stay," the Knight declared.

Many of the younger farmers cheered, and their cries were echoed by Howland's motley troop. Some older villagers still seemed unsure.

"If we resist, Lord Rakell will kill everyone of us," one said.

"Those who do not fight do not deserve to live!" old Calec growled.

He seized Sir Howland's hand in rough but fervent fellowship. The Knight shifted the aged farmer's grip from the downward, country folks' grip to the upright warrior style.

"Now we are sworn to the task. Time is short. Let's begin," said Howland.

The outline of the trench was scratched in the earth that night. By dawn, digging was underway. Baskets were filled with dry earth and hauled to the farthest houses. The villagers cleared their belongings from the huts and dumped the dirt inside. When full, each hut would hide a mound of earth nine feet high.

According to Howland's instructions, each member of his band took five or six villagers to train. Carver gained an instant following among the Nowhere children, eleven of whom eagerly lined up to learn the secrets of the whippik. Raika showed the best weavers in the village How to lash round stones onto rake handles to serve as maces. Khorr stripped to the waist and joined in digging, where he did the work of four men. A small contingent worked alongside him, and he recited the minotaur war epic *Six Axes for King Banu* as they labored on the trench. Amergin and Robien took their bands of followers into the fields to learn how to lay forester traps. Elderly villagers were set to converting garden tools to spears.

Howland, Hume, Malek, and Nils looked on as the preparations began.

Malek said, "Sir Howland, did you mean what you said? Is Nowhere really doomed?"

"I would not be here still if I thought so."

Thus reassured, Malek and Nils picked up their packs and walking sticks and set out to scout Rakell's camp.

Alone with his leader, Hume said, "You made them believe it, sir."

Grim-faced, Howland accepted his comrade's judgment.

"I did what I had to. People too afraid to greet their defenders stand no chance against ogres and mounted brigands. I had to stir them up, find the rams among the lambs."

They started after the brothers, down a path through the waving lake of grain.

"Tell me truly, Sir Howland, can we win?" Hume asked.

"No honest commander ever knows that," was the Knight's sober reply.

* * * * *

Where the farmed land ended, the wild land took over. Stiffer than barley, plains grass did not bow with the evening wind. It stood against the breeze, sighing and shivering. The well-marked path from Nowhere soon faded into the undergrowth. Hume drew his sword and took the lead, cutting a path for the others.

A hundred paces beyond the cultivated field all traces of settled life vanished. The change was profound. In the standing barley, men were the masters, and the wild creatures of the plain were interlopers. Just a few steps away from the growing grain, roles were reversed. Farmer or warrior, in the wilderness everyone was alone.

Nils related that as a boy he'd hunted rabbits here, creeping through the high weeds with a crude, two-pronged spear. Half a day's walk south of Nowhere there was a stream, he said, a brook that flowed from the east a few miles before vanishing.

"The westernmost spur of the mountains lies more than forty miles from here," Howland told Malek. "If my memory and the maps of my old master, Garab uth Dreher, can be trusted, that is."

"Forty miles! Are we going that far?" asked Malek.

"We can't spare the time. If we don't find any trace of Rakell's force by noon tomorrow, we'll return to Nowhere."

Stars appeared in the purple sky, lighting up one by one like lanterns hung in distant windows. The party rested under a wind-tortured elm tree, drinking from the same flask and eating from a common bag of parched corn.

"How long have you been a soldier, Sir Howland?" asked Nils.

"All my life. I was born to it."

"Did you always serve this Lord Garab?"

"No." The Knight took a long swig of cider. "My first liege was the noble Harbard uth Farnan, may he rest forever in the company of fallen heroes."

Hume rubbed his bare dome. "I know that name. Lord Harbard was a great Knight?"

"A great Knight and a gallant warrior," said Howland. "From the time I could walk I served his house. I would have—should have—died for him."

Awkward silence engulfed the lonely elm. Hume and the farmers remembered the state Howland had been in when they found him in Robann. Was his fall into degradation and despair linked to the fate of Lord Harbard?

Malek screwed up his courage and began to ask, but Howland replied before the questoin was complete. Night shielded the Knight's long face, so only his voice transmitted the pain of his long-ago memories.

"I was but six and twenty when the end came. It was a terrible time, the Chaos War. The Order gave Lord Harbard the task of defending the city of Fangoth from the Knights of Takhisis. He had an army of five thousand, which seemed like more than enough to do the job. Four thousand were yeoman infantry, free men trained in arms and called up in time of war to defend our country. Backing up the yeomen were four hundred mounted knights and six hundred archers, who were elves from the old Qualinesti realm. With this force, Lord Harbard was confident he could defeat treble his number in Nerakan levies."

Nils and Malek were ignorant of politics outside their land, but the deep sorrow in Howland's tone forestalled them from asking for details.

"Fangoth is ringed on three sides by heavy forest. Only the east lay open, and from the east the enemy came, three thousand five hundred of them. In command was Burnond Everride, the Hammer of Nordmaar, the plunderer of Throt and Estwilde. Ah, what a bold and dangerous man! Had he known more honor, he could have been a gracious foe, but Highlord Burnond was too ruthless and cruel.

"His army seemed a joke to us. A thousand mercenary halberdiers from Saifhum—"

"Raika's home?" said Hume.

Howland grunted an affirmative. "Rugged fighters, but their only loyalty was to their paymaster. Burnond had five hundred Knight-lancers of the Dark Order, but the bulk of his force was two thousand goblins, armed with pike and shield. Goblins! Can you imagine taking the field against Lord Harbard and free yeomen with a mob of stinking goblins?" The old Knight's voice had risen almost to a shout. He mastered his anger and continued.

"Harbard arrayed the army in an arc to protect Fangoth. The archers were twenty paces to the fore, and the yeomen were drawn up shield to shield to withstand any charge of Burnond's horsemen. We Knights sat under the walls of the city, in reserve. Lord Harbard told us we wouldn't have much to do! A few volleys of arrows, and the goblins would run away—that's what he said.

"Burnond formed his goblin infantry into a solid phalanx six ranks deep. They were armed with long pikes, twelve feet long. The rear ranks laid their pikes on the shoulders of those in front of them, making a moving hedgehog of steel points. To motivate the goblins, Burnond placed young fanatics of the Dark Order at their backs with whips, to scourge the goblins if they faltered. Can you see it? Vile vermin, driven like pigs to slaughter by blows of a rawhide whip! Where is the glory in such warfare?"

Crickets chirped in the deep shadows. A rich tapestry of stars covered the sky from horizon to horizon. Somehow the faint glitter of a million stars made the night seem darker rather than light.

Howland wrung the last drops from the cider flask. It was mild stuff, not like the rotgut sold in Robann taverns.

"A veil of archers could not stop two thousand pikemen propelled forward by whiplash," he said dully. "The elves loosed and loosed, finally aiming over their knuckles at the black wall of spear points coming at them. In the last moment Lord Harbard gave them leave to withdraw. The elves wore no armor. No one expected them to fight infantry of the line.

"The goblins pushed on, driving deep into the yeomen. Their pikes were so long, our men couldn't reach the enemy with their swords. Hundreds of yeomen were slain without striking a blow! When the curved lined began to bow backward under the press, Lord Harbard ordered his Knights forward. We rode around the right end of our own line, thinking to take the goblins in the flank.

Burnond had foreseen this move, curse him. The Saifhumi were waiting for us. Lord Harbard thought they would scatter if charged with sword and lance, but they had been trained by Lord Burnond to stand before cavalry. Harbard, Harbard, you should have ignored the halberdiers and gone after the goblins!"

"What happened, Sir Howland?" said Malek.

"We were cut to pieces. The Saifhumi had hooks on the ends of their bills, and they dragged our men from the saddle and hacked them to bits. They cut off Lord Harbard's head then his arms and legs. . . . His bloody limbs were thrown back to us! I was unhorsed, and trampled. When I awoke, I was a prisoner of the Knights of Takhisis."

The balance of the battle went just as badly for Harbard's army. The yeomen fought and fought until horsemen of the Dark Order threatened to cut them off from the city. Then they broke. The city, unprepared for a long siege, surrendered to Burnond Everride six days later.

"Defeat wasn't the worst of it. My ruin had just begun. After the battle of Fangoth Field I served the man who murdered my liege," Howland said, whispering. He acknowledged Hume's shocked expression. "Shocked? Garab uth Dreher was Lord Burnond's cavalry chief, and I lent my sword to his service. We captured men were given that choice—service or mutilation. Warriors who refused to serve the Knights of Takhisis had their eyes put out, or had a hand or foot chopped off. Then they were turned loose, to wander as beggars, object warnings to anyone who would resist Takhisis's rule.

"I was young and vain, and like most young men, I valued my body more than my soul. I could not bear the thought of being maimed and useless. I told myself, if I stayed whole, I could one day fight to bring down

Burnond Everride and his kind. I joined them and fought battles against my former companions.

"When Chaos raged loose on Krynn, the Knights of Takhisis joined the Knights of Solamnia. I tried to rejoin my comrades, but they rejected me, calling me a turncoat. After the war, that reputation stayed with me.

"You'd think that sort of reputation would be good for a hired warrior, but it's not. It's death. Keeping faith with your companions is the only virtue a mercenary understands, and they demand it above all. For decades I scratched the barest living from my skill at arms."

Howland stood and drew a deep breath. "Now I'm no good to anyone any more as a warrior, except to dirt-poor farmers from Nowhere."

Hume hung his head, unable to speak. Malek burst out, "Your past doesn't matter here, Sir Howland! Save my betrothed and my brother's son, and you'll always have a place of honor in our village!"

Howland said nothing to this promise but stood by the slumped Hume. "What say you, soldier? Do you think me worth following now?"

Hume raised his heavy head. His broad, bald brow glistened with sweat.

"I am one-quarter ogre," he said, choking. "Do you know what that means? Not human. Not ogre. Used for my strength and steadfastness and despised for my broken ancestry. Do you think me worth having as a follower?"

Howland laid his hand on Hume's shoulder. "No child chooses his ancestors. If you are true, you have nothing to be ashamed of."

Hume stood and met his leader's gaze. "If you keep faith with your soldiers today and tomorrow, then yesterday means nothing."

Truth breaks many strong bonds, but sometimes it also forges them.

* * * * *

They found Nils's stream before dawn and followed it eastward. Howland reasoned a mounted outfit like Rakell's would need plenty of water in a dry region like this. Sure enough, they found a spot where the clay bank had been churned up by many shod horses' hooves.

"How old would you say these tracks are?" Howland asked.

Nils felt the yielding clay with his fingertips. Ferns just above the creek bank had been trodden down, but the leaves were still green and pliable.

"No more than day," said the farmer.

"I agree. What does that imply?"

Hume said, "They water here often!"

Howland nodded. He waded through the shallow stream to the opposite shore. "There's nothing like twenty or thirty horses' tracks here. More like six or seven."

"A patrol!"

"Yes. Rakell is careful. He sends out patrols every day to sweep the plain for signs of trouble."

"Or useful prisoners," Malek added bitterly.

"We'll set our trap here," the old Knight assured him. "Four men can ambush six right enough. We won't pick a fight with Rakell's entire force, just whittle him down a bit and take some prisoners, maybe."

The watering spot had little obvious cover from which to stage an ambush. Both banks were gentle, grassy slopes without big trees or boulders. Greenery on the banks was lush enough to hide in, but men on horseback might see them lying on their bellies in the weeds.

Nils wandered away from the others, probing the bottom of the stream with his walking stick.

"Look here!" he called. "The water's deep enough here to hide us!" He demonstrated by sitting down in the stream a few steps west of the ford. He drew his knees up to his chest, and all but the crown of his head disappeared beneath the silvery water. He popped up again, gasping.

Howland said, "That's a start. We'll need more than two feet of water to make this work." Gathering his comrades to him, he explained his ideas.

* * * * *

Like a silent furnace, the sun came up. The steam-colored sky returned, and the air was heavy with unbroken sweat. A line of riders appeared, shimmering in the morning heat. Seven horsemen, lean and alert, rode slowly down the path to the creek, four on the left, three on the right. Marching disconsolately between the lines of horses were eight prisoners, bearing balks of timber across their shoulders. Long leather buckets hung from both ends of these timbers. The daily water detail was near its destination.

Chatting idly as they meandered along, the riders were equipped with a mix of arms and armor. All had breastplates of some description, ranging from a fluted southern pattern to a heavy, riveted relic of old Nordmaar. Each warrior carried a sword and shield (slung on his back), but for herding sluggish captives they also carried light spears, which could be cast or carried.

Leading the water detail was a hard-faced veteran with the insignia of a corporal on his helmet. He rode into the flowing stream and let his horse drink his fill. Twisting on his thin, worn saddle, he said, "Men on the left, water your animals. Those of you on the right, watch the prisoners."

The last of the four men on the left side of the column steered his horse into the water. Near the center of the stream, the animal balked, bobbing its head many times and nodding.

"What is it? A snake?" asked the corporal.

The rider reined back his horse. "Don't know, corp. Something's got old Dodger spooked."

In the water three dark objects rested on the bottom. They resembled logs, driven into the sandy creek bed. The trooper was about to poke at them with his spear when his comrades on shore, still unwatered, loudly complained about the delay.

"All right, you lot. Let your animals drink."

The last three riders waded in with their horses, none of which shied from the unknown objects. When their mounts were slaked, the corporal ordered the prisoners to fill their buckets. The captives filed in, dipping first one side of their carriers, then the other. The corporal moved out of their way, riding up higher on the north bank.

He spotted something startling in the grass, a man's limp arm, fingers slack. Hand on his sword, he guided his horse toward the motionless limb. It proved to be attached to a squat, powerfully built man with a shaven head. Purplish red stains covered the man's face.

"Dugun! Fetz!" he said loudly. "I found someone!"

Work stopped. The prisoners stood in water up to their knees. The two named men rode across to their corporal.

"Ugly brute!" said the one called Fetz. "Is he human?"

"Looks like your brother," quipped Dugun.

"Shut up and check him," snapped the corporal. Dugun dismounted and kicked the body, none too gently.

"Hey! Hey!" When he got no response, the brigand squatted beside the unmoving body to see if the man was still breathing.

He never got the chance to find out. In the blink of an eye, the "dead" man drove a slim iron dagger into Dugun's chest.

"He's alive! Watch out!"

The corporal's warning was too late. Hume rolled to his feet, snatched the sword he'd been lying on, and thrust upward. His point caught the corporal below the hip guard of his breastplate, driving deep into the man's side. Blood spurted from the corporal's lips. With an incoherent cry, he toppled from his horse.

Screaming, the captives threw down their buckets and fled to the south bank. One of the riders in the stream put a ram's horn to his lips and sounded a long, wavering blast. The stream around him erupted, and the three sunken "logs" burst from the water. Malek, Nils, and Howland had plastered themselves with gray mud, leaves, and waited on the creek bed, breathing through hollowed-out cattail stems.

Malek cupped both hands under the horn blower's heel and levered him off his horse. When he hit the water Howland gave a quick stab of his sword. The flowing stream gushed red.

Chaos became general as the captives scattered and the remaining riders rode into the creek to attack their unknown foes. Nils swung his walking stick like a club, rapping a horse on the nose. The startled animal reared and plunged, but the rider skillfully kept his seat.

Roaring a battle cry, Hume waved his sword over his

head and charged toward the melee in the creek. One horseman cast his javelin at him. Hume batted it aside and slogged on, kicking up sheets of spray with his feet. He made for the still-bucking horse. On its next rise, Hume got under the flailing hooves and planted his hands on the animal's chest. A man of ordinary size and strength would have been crushed into the stream, but Hume planted his feet and pushed horse and rider over backwards.

Malek leaped onto the rump of another horse, grappling with the man in the saddle. They struggled briefly, but Malek was powered by rage long suppressed, and he hurled the brigand into the water.

An arrow flicked by his face. One of the men had strung a short bow and was taking shots at the four attackers.

Malek slid off the horse. He'd couldn't ride well anyway, and the beast's side was good cover against arrows. When he raised his head to see if he could pinpoint the archer, he saw something that made his heart split in two.

Laila.

She was one of the prisoners fetching water. Malek saw her helping a fellow slave, a dazed old man, out of the water. He screamed her name.

"Malek?" she cried. "Malek, is that you?"

Shouting madly, he tore through the shallow stream, making for the south bank. Arrows hummed by him. but he neither heeded nor feared them. Laila got her aged companion onto dry land then started across the creek to meet Malek.

Howland dueled desperately with a fully roused warrior, fending off his spear thrusts with his sword. The rider was skilled and turned away each time Howland attacked, using his greater mobility and reach to put the gray-haired Knight on the defensive.

Now Nils saw Laila. Heedlessly he crossed in front of a brigand, who threw his lance. It struck Nils in the thigh. He collapsed in the water. Blinded with pain, he got to his knees and yanked the iron spear head from his flesh.

Drawn by the rider's horn, more mounted men converged on the creek. Howland heard the rumble of many horse coming.

"Withdraw!" he shouted.

Malek was too close to Laila to turn back. She was almost close enough to touch. Hardship had lined her face, and her formerly spotless homespun was torn and dirty, but she was his Laila nonetheless.

A prancing roan horse cut off his beloved from him. The rider struck her down with the butt of his spear. Enraged, Malek flung his stick at the man and shouted, "Butcher, leave her be!"

Coolly the man turned, couching his spear under his arm like a lance. He dug in his spurs, twisting his horse's head in a half circle to get at Malek. The young farmer backed frantically, but the water was knee deep, and it slowed him. Malek clearly saw the square-shaped spearhead plunging at his chest.

From nowhere Hume appeared, sword at maximum reach. He ran it right through the charging rider's leg and into his horse. Men and beast fell together in tremendous fountain of spray.

Saved by his comrade's rush, Malek tried to pull Hume from his tangle with the fallen horse and rider. The burly warrior rose, spewing creek water from both nostrils.

"Rally to Sir Howland!" he gasped. "Back to shore!"

"But Laila! It's Laila!" Malek cried, trying to get around Hume.

Hume shuddered suddenly. To his horror, Malek saw an arrow sprouting from Hume's broad back. Before he could even react, two more struck. Hume groaned deeply. His knees buckled.

"Get to shore!" he said through bloody, gritted teeth.

A hand seized the back of his shirt and pulled him away. Malek saw the Khurish warrior fall facedown in the stream.

Nils was dragging him. Malek tried to fight his way free, but his older brother held on. "Laila's back there!" he screamed.

"I saw," Nils replied. "We can't reach her! Hume's done for! We must get away!"

More horsemen appeared on the path, galloping to the fray. Gasping from his wound and spitting water, Nils let Howland take hold of his brother and drag him onto dry land.

Stumbling and staggering, the three men fled into the high grass. Had the horsemen been bolder, they might have caught them all, but without a leader to take charge, the riders gathered up the prisoners, the killed, and the wounded and beat a retreat.

Enough time passed to convinced Howland they would not be back soon. He marched Nils and Malek back to the water's edge.

Two dead horses floated in the stream. Rakell's men had dragged Hume's body ashore and chopped off his head.

"They took it back to their warlord to prove they fought," said Howland. Anger, like sparks falling on tinder, slowly ignited inside him. "How did he die? What happened?"

"It was my fault," Malek admitted. "I saw my betrothed among the captives. When I tried to reach her, a bandit almost got me. Hume saved my life, but they put three arrows in him . . ."

Howland stalked to Malek and struck him in the face with the back of his hand. Delivered by a lifelong soldier like Howland, it knocked the farmer to the ground.

"Hothead! You nearly killed us all!"

"We got five of them!" Malek countered. "I thought I could save her!"

"Hume was worth more than any five cutthroats! He was vital to us! What will we do without him?"

Nils stepped between them. "Rakell knows he has armed foes about, but he may not realize we are from Nowhere, not yet. We must go back and ready ourselves!"

Howland said nothing but waded across to where Hume's body lay. He pried the sword from the man's stiffening fingers and returned. He offered the Quen blade to Nils.

"No more mistakes!" he said through clenched teeth. "We have no margin for misfortune left! Tell your miserable brother to harden his heart. I won't let him sacrifice our lives or the village for the sake of a single woman. Is that clear?"

Deeply ashamed, Malek slunk away. Nils, looking burdened by his new weapon, trudged after him.

It was a while before Howland uth Ungen followed his charges. It took a long time for him to dig a decent grave.

NOWHERE

Chapter Eight

Nowhere to Run

"'mon, you clods! Straighten that line! And yell when you attack—yell like you mean it! Yell your guts out!"

Eight farmers, five men and three women, rushed headlong across the dusty village common, screeching as loudly as they could. They gripped makeshift wooden spears and wore ragged cloth turbans on their heads. This last detail was Raika's special contribution. The rolled cloth would provide some protection against raps on the head.

"Besides," she said, "turbans make you look civilized."

As shock troops, the farmers had a long way to go. Because they were different heights and strengths, they couldn't maintain an even line once they started moving. The long-legged quickly outpaced the short, and over a distance the strong moved faster than the weak.

All morning Raika stormed up and down, waving her hands and shouting at anyone out of place. When she finally let her inept troops rest, Raika went to the well to rinse dust and disgust from her mouth. Robien sat there, watching the maneuvers. He perched on the surrounding wall, feet dangling on either side of the Ancestor. The lower half of the broken sandstone block had almost changed from red to blue, owing to the stain spreading down from the crack.

"Traps all laid?" she said, dropping the bucket into the cool, stone-lined shaft.

"Not all," replied the elf. "Some must be done after dark."

She hauled on the rope to bring the bucket back up. "Why after dark?"

"Some of the triggers must be set in darkness. After they're in place, a single miscast shadow can set them off."

The Saifhumi woman regarded him skeptically. Unlike most mainlanders, she had never stood in awe of elves. All the ones she ever met were clever and cultured, but they didn't seem any wiser than anyone else.

"Your troops are shaping up," Robien said politely.

"Shaping up to be killed." Raika hoisted the full bucket over her head and dumped the water over her. She spat grit, and added, "They don't stand together, they don't think together, and they don't fight together. The bandits will have them for supper."

"Maybe you're not going about it the right way."

"Oh? How would you train these yokels?"

"Having them run around charging is pointless. Not one of them has the fortitude to attack mounted men. That's as well. All they need to do is defend, not attack."

"I had no idea you were such a general," Raika said, wiping her face with her turban.

"I've lived a long time and done many things. Many years ago, I was a soldier."

Raika slouched against the well wall. "Then you teach them, master!"

Robien did not reply but strolled out into the hot sun. Raika's villagers were marching in circles inside the row of houses, shoulder to shoulder. Robien stood in front of them and waited. When the farmers came abreast of him, he held up a hand to stop them.

"Hold," he said mildly. He took the spear from the nearest man, Malek's cousin Fayn. He was a rangy fellow five years' Malek's senior, with rusty red hair all over his body and a multitude of freckles.

"Any of you ever speared a man before?"

The farmers shook their heads.

"How about a horse?"

No again.

Robien nodded. "Follow me," he said.

They looked to their nominal commander for guidance. Raika shrugged and waved them away. Let the elf drill the fools if he wants, her gestures seemed to say.

Robien shouldered the borrowed spear and led the farmers to a gap between two of the houses. Both huts had been filled with dirt, and the rattan fence between them, meant only to keep chickens out of the root cellars beneath each house, had been reinforced with concealed piles of cordwood and stones. It was no real impediment to a determined attacker, but the strength of the fence would certainly surprise and perhaps unhorse unwary riders.

"Here," said Robien, halting. "Five of you defending this

gap ought to be able to hold off any number of horsemen."

"How?" asked Fayn.

Robien took the three biggest men and arrayed them between the huts. Two women knelt between them, spears braced against their feet.

"You must keep your nerve above all," Robien told them. "If you break, the riders will slaughter you, but if you hold your line and keep points out, the enemy will turn away, I promise."

One of the women laughed nervously. "Why should they break before us?"

"No one wants to get speared," Robien replied dryly. "They'll ride at you, screaming dire threats, but they won't charge home. What they really want is to scare you into running."

Robien held out his arms. The huts were far enough apart that he couldn't quite touch them.

"Only one horse can get through here at a time," he said. "Two, in a pinch. If you see two or more riders bearing down on you, stand fast! They'll turn away or else collide trying to fit between the houses. When they do, you'll have them."

A shower of short arrows fell on Robien and the farmers, followed by gales of childish laughter. The elf picked up one of the missiles. It was blunt and fletched with stiff green leaves.

"You must also beware of enemy archers," the bounty hunter said.

More laughter from above, and Carver appeared on the roof of the left-hand hut, surrounded by a gang of scruffy, bright-eyed children.

"You are all victims of the Nowhere Whippik Corps!" Carver said.

"I hope you'll use sharper ones on the raiders," Robien replied.

"To be sure! They're being made even now."

Robien nodded. "It is a sound tactic to put missile-throwers on the high ground."

Thinking of missile-throwers reminded him of Amergin, his sling-toting quarry.

"Has anyone seen Amergin today?"

"Not since he left with you this morning," said Fayn.

"He was supposed to be laying traps in the northeast approaches," Robien mused. "I wonder if he's come back?" He dismissed the farmers and made for the west end of the village where Khorr and some men still labored hard on the trench.

The open end of Nowhere was abuzz with activity. Outside the growing trench, pairs of village men and women pounded heavy stakes into the ground. Good-sized trees were hard to come by on the high plains, so these stakes were rafters or center posts taken from their houses. Once the posts were driven in half their length, a farmer with a hatchet whittled the ends to a formidable point.

Behind the row of stakes, the trench cut into the soil like a fresh wound. Beneath the yellow topsoil was clay, thick gray earth too heavy in which to grow crops. Elderly villagers hauled the clay away in baskets to fill emptied houses. The trench already stretched across the open end of Nowhere. Now Khorr and his diggers were hurrying to deepen it.

The minotaur made a tremendous impression as he stood hip deep in the earth, his broad shoulders sheened with sweat, his naturally bronze skin gone copper in the hot sun. He'd broken two ordinary mattocks before Wilf made him a tool worthy of his size, lashing three ordinary handles to the only iron-headed pick in the village.

Robien stood to one side, keeping clear of the urgent bustle. He called out to Khorr.

The sweat-soaked poet leaned on his implement and palmed his face dry with a colorful kerchief.

"What is it?"

"Have you seen Amergin?"

"Not since yesterday. Is he missing?"

Robien felt his jaw tighten. "No. I just need to find him."

"Perhaps you should engage the services of a good tracker!"

The minotaur was wittier than he looked. Robien ruefully waved his thanks. Khorr called for water and downed an entire bucket fetched by two village women. The bounty hunter moved on.

He crossed on a plank laid over the open trench and slipped between the slanting stakes. From there he looked back over the entire village. Carver and the children clambered over the thatched rooftops, launching blunt darts at each other. Raika's hoarse shouting rose over the cloud of dust where her spearmen were still drilling. Sir Howland and Hume were out on reconnaissance. The strange Ezu had spent the past two days collecting rocks and plants from the countryside, but it was unclear if he was doing anything of real value. Khorr slaved away, digging by day and reciting minotaur epics to his crew at night.

That left the missing Amergin. Robien didn't believe his fellow Kagonesti would have run away. Howland's odd company had gotten Amergin out of Robann, and saved him from the Brotherhood of Quen. He would not abandon those to whom he owed a debt. So where was he?

Out of sight of the working villagers, Robien put his head down and ran. He was fleet of foot, but his speed was an asset he chose not to share with the farmers or the mercenaries. To survive, everyone needed an edge. Robien had several he kept close to his heart. The time might soon come when he would need every advantage he could wrest.

At Howland's request, both elves agreed not to set up any traps on the open ground between the village proper and the fields. Once inside the sea of barley, or past the green garden plots, anything was fair game.

Robien neared a stand of corn. Aside from some indistinct noises coming from the village, all seemed calm. He put a hand to his mouth. "Amergin!" he called, not too loudly. He continued in Elvish, "Where are you, brother?"

A crow rose squawking from the corn rows. Robien watched it depart, protesting loudly in the manner of all crows. It fluttered away, becoming a black wrinkle against the dull, hazy sky.

He slipped between the closely growing stalks. Sunlight filtered between the curled-up leaves, dappling the ground. This was a perfect place for a trip-line. Robien dropped to one knee and removed his belt. Made of hardwood pegs strung together on a rawhide core, the belt was normally flexible unless the pegs were twisted a certain way. Robien ran them through his hands, deftly rotating the segments until his belt had been transformed into a rigid rod. He leaned forward, probing between the corn stalks. Almost immediately he snagged a horizontal filament. Palomino horsehairs, gleaned by Amergin from the grassland around them, braided together into a strong, thin twine, invisible under ordinary circumstances. Here was a trigger all right. Where was the trap?

He sidled sideways through the corn until the horse-hair zigged away from him. Following the line, Robien found Amergin's trap. Amid the green corn, a double line of green canes stuck in the dirt were bent back at a severe angle. The trigger line ran back and forth among the bent stalks. When tripped, the canes would fly up in a rippling wave, flailing anything within reach. Amergin had studded the cane stalks with whatever sharp objects he could find—flakes of flint, chicken bones carved to points, beef shoulder blades made keen by the Kagonesti's knife, and inch-long thorns from the plains gorse bushes. None of these were lethal (unless poisoned), but they could put out an eye or spook a horse with ease. Robien was impressed. Amergin knew his business.

He moved on, finding three layers of intertwined traps. Beyond the corn field, Amergin had hollowed out a mossy bank of earth. It looked solid enough to walk or ride over, but the slightest weight would cause the shell of moss to collapse. Underneath was a hole six inches deep and over twelve feet long, deep enough to hobble a horse or break a man's ankle. Amergin had done all this without leaving any trace.

Next the bounty hunter found a series of snags—hidden or disguised lengths of thorny creeper, more horse-hair twine, and rawhide thong. The snags were linked so that anyone struggling to get out of one would make the others tighter. Not lethal, again, but troublesome to foes.

The outermost line of traps was the deadly one. Robien was intrigued by Amergin's cool cunning. By putting the worst traps first, he would convince the enemy that succeeding ones would be as bad or worse. If Rakell's men were quick to anger, they might bull on through, heedless of any danger, anxious to avenge their hurts. That would surely give away their position. In any case, the defenders would reap a benefit.

The outer trap was clearly marked. Amergin had set up four widely spaced scarecrows, made of tree limbs, leaves, and mud. He modeled them to resemble foot soldiers in armor. If the light were poor enough, the enemy might be fooled at first. Each figure was a trigger. Sunk in the ground around the scarecrows were four hinged stakes, each a good two feet long, made of green wood. Anyone striking or otherwise disturbing a scarecrow would cause a heavy stone to fall from the figure's head into a deep, narrow hole. The falling stone caused the stakes to rise and snap shut on the scarecrow. With luck, Amergin could impale three or four of the enemy with each one.

Robien stood close to one scarecrow, admiring the delicate system of notches and lines that made it work. A voice behind him said, "What a lot of foolishness."

Amergin's voice. He turned quickly but saw no one. Robien said in Elvish, "You are a master of trap-craft. I salute you."

In Common, Amergin replied, "Don't try to cozen me by using the old tongue."

"As you wish." Robien reverted to the language of humans. His eyes darted from side to side, trying to spot the hidden forester. They were in the open, surrounded by grass, but Robien couldn't see his quarry at all.

"Your camouflage is excellent," said the bounty hunter.

"You've been among the sky-folk too long," Amergin said, using the Kagonesti term for those who did not live in the woods—whether human, kender, dwarf, or elf.

"Not so long that I couldn't find your traps," Robien said.

"How many?"

"Four sets."

"There are six."

Robien moved away from the scarecrow, careful not to jar it. "Your skill is greater than mine. Is that what you wanted to hear?"

A hunched figure emerged from the chest-high grass. Amergin had encased himself in a large grass drape so he melted into the surrounding growth.

"I want you to understand. When we fought in your camp, you bested me because the woman interfered. In the wild, you would never find me, much less catch me."

Robien nodded. "I let her take me—you know that, don't you?"

The grass-figure shifted. "Robien the Tireless taken from behind by a human? Not in a year of springtimes."

Amergin pulled the grass hood off his head. His dark eyes were rimmed with red. He'd apparently not slept these past two days.

"I'm tired, bounty hunter. I don't want to go on wondering if in the end you intend to sell me to the Brotherhood."

"Sell? What I do, I do honorably. Service rendered for money paid."

"I am a person, not a service!" Amergin exclaimed.

"We can settle this afterward. The villagers—"

"Let's settle it now!" Amergin drew his knife. "Renounce the Brotherhood's contract, or I'll water the weeds with your blood!"

As Robien's hand closed around the handle of his sword, the rumble of moving horses reached them both. Hunter and hunted's eyes met.

The forester pulled his hood down and vanished into the grass. Robien ran, hunched over, to a small sour apple tree on the crest of a slight slope. To the east he saw eleven riders cantering through the grass. The lead horseman raised his hand, and the riders reined to a stop.

"It's beyond those fields, yonder? See the green? That's it," said the leader.

"Should we spread out, Keph?" asked one of the men.

"It doesn't matter. There's not a sword in the place." He laughed shortly. "Nor a man to wield one!"

Two riders detached themselves from the rest and took up positions not twenty feet from Robien.

"Keep an eye out," the leader, Keph, told them. "We'll be back in two days to relieve you."

"Bring wine!" said one of the scouts.

"And meat!" said the other.

Keph laughed. "I'll bring you a feast deluxe."

Something brushed against Robien's elbow. Amergin was lying on his belly close enough to touch him.

"Let's take them," he whispered.

"What, now? Wait till the others are gone!"

"Now. Quietly. It will disturb the rest."

With a mild rustle, Amergin was gone. The remaining nine horsemen trotted away, heading southeast.

The two scouts sat slouched on their animals, facing the unseen village. As Robien watched, he noticed the scout on the left's horse shying a little, as though the beast had detected a serpent near its feet. A snake would be less dangerous, the bounty hunter thought.

Robien crept forward as fast as he dared, knees bent, hands brushing the ground. He left his sword in its scabbard and took out his hunting knife, a single-edged weapon as long as his hand. Teeth clamped on the blade, he worked his way closer to the unwary men.

One scout's horse stirred a little. The rider patted his animal. "Steady, steady," he crooned.

"He wants to go back to camp too," said the other man.

Robien was behind them, no more than six feet away, when Amergin rose up like a ghost and grabbed both men by their mantles, jerking them backward off the rumps of their mounts. The horses took off, neighing and tossing their heads.

Amergin threw himself over one of the men, covering him with his grassy cape. The other man struggled to rise and draw his sword. Robien took him from behind, clamping a hand over the man's mouth and burying his blade in the small of his back.

The grass flowed away, revealing the second rider dead.

"Now what?" asked Robien, breathing hard.

Amergin gripped the dead man's collar. "Bring him."

They dragged the bodies over the hill. Amergin proceeded confidently, leading Robien to a small depression in the hillside. This hollow was full of brambles. Amergin shoved the dead man in then took Robien's victim and pushed him in, too. Robien thought they were done, but Amergin retraced their path, plucking up bent grass and wiping away any bloodstains. When he was done, only the most expert tracker could have detected where the bodies had been taken.

By now the frightened horses had overtaken their comrades, causing consternation among the other riders. They came galloping back. Robien made ready to retire, but Amergin gripped his wrist hard. He spread his grass cape over the bounty hunter.

"Watch. Listen."

The brigands circled the spot where their companions had disappeared, prodding the grass with their lances.

"Juric! Vago!" the leader called.

More than once the men passed within spitting distance of the Kagonesti but failed to detect them.

"Keph, where are they?" one man cried.

"Hiding. They must be!"

"Vago wouldn't do that!"

"Neither would Juric!"

Keph said, "Then they've deserted, the scum."

The dead men's friends protested vigorously. Keph cursed them into silence. "If they didn't desert, what happened to them? Did they disappear into thin air?"

A gaunt, hawk-faced rider pushed the helmet back on his head and fearfully scanned the sky. "Something took them," he intoned.

His leader scoffed. "What? A dragon? Don't you think we would've seen anything big enough to carry off two armed men?"

Hawk-face would not be talked down. "There's a reason why this land is deserted. There are wild spirits, malign powers abroad here!"

"You're mad, Botha! The gods are dead, and all the ghosts died with them ages ago!" Keph circled his nervous horse. "Besides, this land isn't empty. Farmers live here."

"Maybe they have a pact with the dark spirits—"

Keph struck Botha with a mailed fist. The blow rocked him, but the hard-riding warrior kept his seat.

"That's enough!" Keph snapped. "There are no spirits! There's no power here greater than our Lord Rakell, understand?" He circled again. "Juric and Vago have deserted, I tell you. You heard 'em. They didn't want picket duty, so they ran off. They're hiding in the grass out there, somewhere. If I had time, I'd set a fireline and smoke 'em out, but Lord Rakell's on the move and expects us back before sundown. So be men, not children! Let's go!"

The bandits rode away. Once they were out of sight, Robien threw back the grass mat and sat up, drawing deep breaths. It was nearly airless under there.

"Seeds are planted," Amergin said, shucking off his camouflage hood and gauntlets. "Now we will let them grow a little." He started back to the bramble gully.

"What are you going to do now?" Robien called after him.

Amergin didn't answer.

Robien followed, curious. Amergin dragged the bodies out and lashed their wrists together then draped the dead raiders on two of his scarecrows, looping their arms around his figures' necks. It was a macabre scene, two corpses each hugging a scarecrow as if they were long-lost comrades. Rakell's men were sure to be frightened or infuriated when they found them. Seeing Amergin's macabre ploy, Robien wasn't sure which he felt himself.

Chapter Nine

Gifts and Secrets

It was dark when Robien and Amergin returned. Robien made a wide circuit of the isolated village, checking the traps. When all was done, the two Kagonesti walked back to the village through the barley, tossing lightly in the night wind. Neither elf spoke to the other.

A bonfire blazed in the center of the village common. The bright fire startled the elves, and fearing trouble, they separated. Each entered Nowhere at a different point between the darkened huts. Yet all was calm. There were no signs of a raid.

Howland had returned. Malek and Nils were also present, but Amergin didn't spot Hume. Curious, the elf made his way to the old Knight.

Caeta accosted him. "One of your comrades has been

killed," she said sadly. Amergin didn't need to be told which.

Robien approached the bonfire from the other side. The villagers huddled around the flames, grass mats and blankets spread on the ground. With their homes filled with dirt, they would be sleeping in the open for a while.

Raika rose from her haunches when she spied the bounty hunter. "First blood to Rakell," she said. "They got Hume."

"We got two of them today," Robien replied. He described the killing of the two bandits.

News that the Kagonesti had encountered Rakell's scouts so near the village sent a spasm of terror through the assembled farmers. Howland summoned Amergin and Robien, asking for every detail of their fight.

The laconic Amergin had little to say, so Robien, no big talker himself, had to supply most of the details.

"It was a small band, eleven men on horses, armed with sword and lance. Only nine rode away."

"We slew four at the ford but lost Hume." Howland's grim face looked gray by firelight. "Young Malek saw his bride among the slaves fetching water. Seeing her unhinged him. Hume went to his aid, and that's when he fell."

The Knight looked over his downcast troops and the dispirited villagers. Something had to be done to stop this slide into despair. If it went on unchecked, Rakell could win without striking another blow.

A speech praising Hume's humility and courage might help, but Howland never got the chance to deliver it. The somber air around the bonfire was invaded by the weird, unnatural keen of Ezu's whistle. Heads turned.

Into the ring of firelight strolled the traveler. He looked even more bizarre than usual. Over his baggy trousers and loose tunic Ezu had pinned scores of flowering plants, all different. There was thistle, dandelion, red and white clover, tiny climbing roses, tufts of corn silk, bean flowers, violets—all the common blossoms found on the northern plain. By firelight, the paler blooms took on a rosy glow, like cat's eyes by a blazing hearth. In addition, Ezu wore a pair of deer antlers, cast off long ago and whitened by the elements, fastened to a thick leather strap he wore tied around his forehead. He cut an eerie figure, part-human, part-animal, part flowering field.

Coming into view with his whistle at his lips, Ezu had his eyes shut. A few feet from Howland and the mercenaries, he halted.

"Good people!" he said, taking the brass stem away and opening his eyes. "I compliment you on the richness of your domain."

Somehow the whistle disappeared from his hand. Ezu cupped his hands together and blew lightly into the hollow they made. When he flung his hands apart, a pearl-gray dove fluttered into the air.

Chuckles all around.

"He's a petty conjurer!" Raika said with an amused grunt.

The villager children—and Carver—rushed forward, surrounding Ezu. While they clamored for more tricks, he extended a finger, almost touching the tip of the kender's sharp nose. Carver stared at it, going cross-eyed in the process. The children giggled.

Ezu suddenly inverted his hand, and there under Carver's nose appeared a small golden sphere, about the size of an acorn.

"Take it," said Ezu pleasantly. "It is yours."

The kender took the small ball. He sniffed it, brow

furrowed, and hastily peeled off the outer wrapping of gold foil. Inside was a stark white pellet. Impulsively, Carver popped the white pill in his mouth. He gasped a little then grinned.

"Spice candy, just like Auntie Fastswitcher used to make!"

The children pleaded for treats of their own. Ezu stood back a half step and spread his hands wide. Golden globes rained from his fingertips—or were they really coming from his voluminous sleeves?

Boys and girls scrambled in the dirt, retrieving every last morsel. While this happy chaos continued, Howland, Raika, and Khorr came forward.

"You didn't tell us you were a juggler," growled Howland, folding his arms.

"I have many talents," Ezu replied. "Lady, would you assist me?"

Raika looked doubtful. "I don't hold with this sleight-of-hand rubbish."

"It's magic, not sleight-of-hand. Please."

Khorr gave the Saifhumi woman a playful nudge, which was enough to send her staggering into Ezu's arms. He steadied her as she slapped his helpful hands away. Those watching laughed, even Howland.

"I heard magic had gone away," Ezu said. "In my own small way, I've tried to bring a little back."

He passed one hand over another. "I once visited your homeland, the island of Saifhum," Ezu said softly, keeping Raika's eyes on his darting hands. "What from there do you miss the most?"

Her answer was quick and firm: "My lover, Enjollah!"

The village women behind Raika cheered her sentiment.

Ezu stroked his beardless chin. "Sadly I cannot produce Enjollah for you, so what else? A favorite trinket perhaps, food, or drink?"

"Thornapple," she said, smirking. "I haven't seen Saifhumi fruit since coming to the mainland."

Undaunted, Ezu began making distracting hand gestures again.

"No, wait! I've changed my mind. Thornapple *wine*." She grinned.

Ezu looked perplexed but only for a instant. "Very well, though it may take longer . . . for what is wine, but fruit grown old and gone awry?"

He thrust his right hand high into the air, fingers spread. Everyone followed his broad, dramatic motion, paying no heed to his left hand, which went behind his head. When it returned, he held a small pot-bellied bottle.

The crowd gasped. Ezu presented the bottle to Raika.

Her mouth worked, but no barbs issued forth. She looked helplessly at Howland.

"What is it?" he asked, amused.

"I know these bottles," she said. "They're only made in Saifhum!"

"Open it!" Khorr urged.

She pulled the cork with her knife tip. A strong, sweet aroma overcame the smoky smell of the bonfire. Raika took a fast swig. Coughing, she said, "Thornapple wine! And strong!"

Howland took the bottle and sniffed the neck. "Thornapple brandy," he suggested.

Raika grabbed the little jug back and gulped a second mouthful.

More of the crowd surged around Ezu, some laughing, some clapping, and not a few demanding he produce some long-ago delicacy they remembered. Ezu silenced them with a whirl of his hand. The brass whistle appeared. He didn't need to blow it. The mere sight of the piercing instrument calmed the excited farmers.

He looked up at the minotaur. "My robust friend," he said, "inside that spreading torso beats the heart of an artist. What gift may I give you?"

The great horned head shook slowly from side to side. "There is nothing you can do for me. The understanding of my clan cannot be accomplished with a wave of your hand."

Ezu rolled the whistle across the back of his hand. It vanished once more. He sighed. "I fear you are right. If I could make your people revere you as a poet, I would, but an artist must earn acceptance. He cannot demand it." He tugged one of his fat earlobes. "Still, even poets need inspiration."

He tucked his hands into his sleeves, rolling them around his arms a few times. When Ezu took them out again, they were empty. The audience murmured with disappointment.

"Give Khorr a treat!" cried Carver, cheek bulging with candy.

Several people in the crowd, including Caeta, echoed the kender's cry.

Ezu said, "But he already has his treat!"

Khorr looked down at his callused and blistered hands. Nestled in the palm of his left hand was what looked like a painted block of wood five or six inches long. Brown eyes wide, the minotaur held up the strange object.

"Is this—?"

Ezu nodded sagely.

Raika, slightly tipsy from her thornapple brandy, thrust

her face close to Khorr's prize. "Whatsit?" she said loudly.

"A *ronto*," the minotaur said. The reverence in his voice was obvious. He held the block out for all to see. Pushing on one edge, the block fanned open, becoming a collection of thin wooden slats held together by a pin driven vertically through the end of each piece. The slats were covered with elaborate, colorful pictures, painted in neat lines.

"It's a book!" said Carver.

"A recitative," Khorr corrected. "The pictures help the poet recite the story."

"What poem is it?" asked Howland.

Khorr's liquid brown eyes glistened. "*The Saga of the Nine Captains*! The greatest sea-epic known to my race!" He turned back to Ezu, who was standing quietly, examining some of the flowers pinned to his trouser leg. "My ancestor, Kozh the One-Horned, was one of the Nine Captains! Did you know this?"

Ezu, distracted, looked up and said, "Why, no. How could I?"

Raika put her arm around the traveler's neck, a friendly headlock that brought blood to his face. "Rascal! You're all right! But what about Sir Howland? What does he get?"

"Sir Howland will get what he wants, soon," Ezu replied. His tone was devoid of playful banter or double meaning. Raika released him. "But it is not I who will give it to him."

The Knight bowed his head slightly, accepting Ezu's pronouncement—or was it a prediction?

Khorr strode back to the bonfire, now reduced to a pair of lesser fires divided by a pool of glowing coals. He spread the wooden leaves of the *ronto* and began to recite:

Nine captains commanded, nine ships should sail,
To all corners claimed by the horned-folk's king.
Who will wander? Who will wager their lives?
Said Kruz, conqueror of the kingdom. . . .

Fascinated farmfolk crowded around the declaiming minotaur. Children crawled into their fathers' and mothers' laps, still sucking on Ezu's wonderful treats. Their breath reeked of spice, mingled sage and mint, and they listened wide-eyed as Khorr related the adventures of the nine minotaur captains.

Raika pushed through the crowd, claiming a prime spot at Khorr's feet. Carver joined her.

No longer the focus of attention, Ezu turned to go. Howland called out, "Master Ezu—a word, if you please."

The genial traveler paused. "Yes?"

Howland waited until he was nose to nose before saying in guarded tones, "I wonder: Who are you? What are you up to?"

"I told you, Sir Howland. I'm a mere traveler."

"But no ordinary man."

Ezu bowed. "You're very kind—"

Howland caught him by the arm. "How could you have these things? Kender spice candy? Brandy from Saifhum? A book of minotaur poetry? By my Oath, do not tell me these were souvenirs of your sojourns!"

"I can only tell you the truth, good Knight. This one has been to Saifhum, Mithas and Kothas, and Hylo where the kender dwell. All my little gifts tonight could have come from there to here with me."

" 'Could have'?"

"A good juggler leaves his audience guessing, doesn't he?"

Without any effort, Ezu freed himself from Howland's grasp and walked away. The old warrior's fingers closed on air. He blinked in astonishment.

"Ezu! Ezu, your prediction: What is it I shall get?" he cried.

Ezu's voice drifted back, like the fading notes of his pipe: "Honor. Honor . . . " His silhouette merged with the black outline of the old well.

Howland ran a few yards after him. In the deep shadows away from the dying bonfire the flower-bedecked, horn-headed stranger was nowhere to be seen.

* * * * *

Work on the defenses came to an abrupt end the next day. The first gilded grains began to fall from the drooping barley stalks. All other considerations were ignored as the ageless signal was seen. It was time to harvest the crop. Amergin and Robien had to disable their many traps in the field. All other work stopped as the villagers devoted themselves to the task. Raika grumbled about the villagers abandoning their drills, but Howland was not displeased.

"It's sound for them to harvest," he said. "The food is needed, and it would look suspicious to Rakell's scouts if they found the crop moldering in the fields. Surprise is still an important element of our success."

"How can there be any surprise?" Khorr said. "Two of their men disappeared, thanks to Amergin and Robien, and you fought them at the watering ford. Surely Rakell knows armed strangers are in the area?"

"He may, but I'm counting on him not linking the incidents to Nowhere. He must lose men all the time to desertion and small, local skirmishes."

While the farmers labored over their crop, Howland conducted a tour of their defenses. The trench barred the open end of the village. It was deep enough to stop any charge by mounted men, and the road leading to it was strewn with sharpened stakes and mounded earth. Khorr and thirteen villagers would defend the trench.

"You'll be the first to fight," Howland told the minotaur. "Rakell has no respect for the farmers, and the best way to break an enemy's resistance is to crush them at their strongest point."

"He will not pass," vowed Khorr.

"That's the spirit! Once he realizes your position is strong, he'll turn away to spare his troops casualties." Howland put the trench at his back and surveyed the rest of the village. "Next, he'll try to filter his horsemen in between the houses."

"And we'll sting them from above with our whippiks!" cried Carver eagerly. "We've made over four hundred darts!"

"That's good, but take some other missiles to the rooftops with you—stones, wood, baskets of dirt—anything weighty. Understand?"

The kender gave the Knight a sloppy salute.

"Carver and the children will punish them, though they won't be stopped by youngsters with whippiks," Howland went on. "The filled huts and disguised fences will confuse them, but if Rakell is any leader at all, they'll eventually break through."

"Next we meet them with our spearmen," said Raika.

"Yes. Each of us will lead a band of villagers to counterattack any raiders who get through."

"Where do you want me?" asked Robien.

Howland sighed. "With Hume gone, I will need a second-in-command. Will you take the job?"

No one objected, so Robien agreed.

"Stay by me, then. I may have to send you to the others with instructions from time to time."

"How will it end, Sir Howland? When will we know we've won?" Raika asked.

Gripping his sword hilt, the Knight replied, "When there are no more enemies to kill."

*   *   *   *   *

Two peaceful days passed, then three. The barley crop slowly accumulated by the threshing pits, where teams of farmers beat the brown stalks to liberate the grain. Women and old folks tied the battered straw into sheaves, which they returned to the fields in neat, orderly rows. Seeing the bundles of straw gave Howland an idea.

"Make some of the sheaves hollow," he told Malek. "We can post lookouts inside them to keep watch for the bandits." Grunting agreement, Malek did as Howland asked.

Since seeing his beloved at the stream, Malek had fallen into a black gloom. At first his brother Nils believed Malek was upset by seeing his bride in servitude, but Raika offered her opinion.

"He's not sad. He's furious," she said sagely. "All he can think about now is burying his blade in Rakell's chest!"

In four days, all the barley was cut. The formerly lush fields were now patches of stubble, dotted with standing sheaves. Green garden plots, once bounded on all sides by brown grain, now stood out like islands of fertility on the barren plain. The corn would stay green another four weeks, the beans and other small crops only two.

"It's amazing Rakell hasn't struck yet," Howland mused. "How many days left of the thirty he mentioned until his return?"

"Today is the thirtieth day," Caeta answered.

Howland gave swift orders. "No one is to leave the village alone, or travel more than an hour's walk away. I don't want the brigands picking up fresh prisoners they can interrogate."

"That means no hunting," Nils said. "No fresh meat."

Howland was adamant. The enemy was due at any time, and they couldn't afford to loose a single villager, either as a fighter or an informant.

Amergin, who came and went like a ghost, offered to go on an extended reconnaissance and restore his ring of traps. Howland agreed.

"Don't get caught!" he said in jest. The idea that Rakell's idle troopers could catch the elusive Kagonesti seemed ridiculous.

With a new sling made for him by Caeta and a sackful of stones and stars, Amergin slipped away.

The sun was setting. Farmers carried on their threshing by torchlight, and the womenfolk prepared special harvest cakes for everyone. Howland and his little troop sat in a half-circle by the village well, eating hot barley cakes smeared with wild honey and fresh butter.

Raika said, "If I ate like this every day, I wouldn't mind the low pay!"

"If you ate like this every day, you'd be bigger than Khorr," Carver quipped.

Raika aimed a kick at the kender, who scooted out of reach. When he made a few more unkind remarks about Raika's increasing girth, she got up to give him a real blow.

She never delivered it. The half-eaten cake fell from her fingers.

"Hey, don't waste good food!" Carver protested.

Raika pointed to the horizon. Howland jumped up, shading his eyes against the setting sun.

The low rise south of Nowhere was two miles distant, separated by fields stripped clean by the harvest. Sitting along the ridge were a line of horsemen. By the setting sun's ruddy light, Howland could see the gleam of steel.

One of the village women saw the horsemen too and let out a shriek. People ran back and forth, snatching up children and dashing to their huts, only to remember they were filled to the rafters with earth.

Someone beat the bronze gong by the well. Howland barked, "Stop that noise! Stop it, I say! It's only a scouting party!"

Robien cracked the joints of his long fingers and said, "Shall we go after them?"

"No. There's no point. We can't stop Rakell from returning. If we reveal ourselves now, it'll only makes things harder for us later."

They stood to arms all night. Villagers sent to take up spy positions in the hollow barley sheaves reported small bands of horsemen riding around the village all night, but none closed in. This might have been because of the Kagonesti traps they blundered upon. Many were found sprung, and several marauders were killed. Men and horses were also injured, and the brigands evidently spooked. By the next morning, all the village's spies, Amergin included, reported the enemy had ridden away. There were none in sight.

It seemed like a miracle. Was their fear of Rakell's band exaggerated? Had the enemy been repelled by a few forester tricks and traps? Many thought so. Raika and Carver loudly proclaimed victory, and more than a few villagers rejoiced.

Two men did not celebrate. Malek still burned to free Laila from Rakell's thrall, and Howland uth Ungen remained at his post by the well, carefully honing his sword.

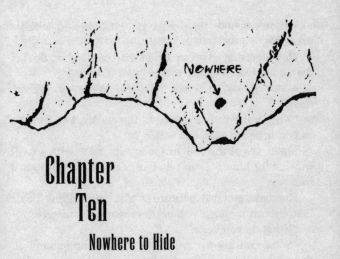

Chapter Ten

Nowhere to Hide

The army of robber lord Rakell did not appear that day or the next. When they were three days past the deadline Rakell had set for his return, the people of Nowhere grew confident they had escaped another brutal invasion. Amergin ranged farther and farther out from Nowhere, seeking Rakell's riders, and found none. He scoured the land as far south and east as the stream where Hume was killed but could find no fresh signs of the enemy.

Caeta spread the news, and the farmers wept with joy. Even those who'd lost loved ones to Rakell's first visit were vastly relieved.

Amidst a growing mood of celebration, Malek sought out Howland. He found the Knight at the edge of the south barley field, alone, whittling a gnarled stick.

"I don't believe the danger is past," he said without preamble.

Howland shaved off a curling wisp of wood no thicker than a feather. "I agree."

Malek looked relieved. "You do? What can we do, then?"

"The initiative has passed to the enemy. For now we can do little but wait and watch."

Malek swept the Knight's judgment aside with a swift wave of his hand. "I can't do that! Laila lives, and I must find her!"

Howland stopped whittling. "Are you willing to do that, even if it means you never return to Nowhere?"

"What do you mean?"

"Some unforeseen event has thrown the bandits off their schedule, something more serious than Amergin's traps. Rakell may have encountered the dragon overlord. He may have been defeated by another, superior force. He may have gone away to ravage another province. We won't be safe until we know for sure. Are you willing to track him down wherever he went?"

Malek didn't hesitate. "Yes!"

Howland nodded. "What about your brother? Will he go after his captive son?"

The young farmer looked over his shoulder at the cluster of weather-worn huts that was his home. "Larem is his only boy. He'll go, too."

"Make sure, then bring him to the well at sundown."

Come dusk, Malek and Nils presented themselves to Howland. With Howland was Robien.

"Welcome," Howland said to the brothers. "I asked Robien to lend us his counsel." He lowered his voice. "I'll be as straight as I can with you: Far from being safe, as everyone thinks, I believe we're stll in danger. Rakell is on the move with his entire force, however large that may be, and I'm sure he'll show up here sooner or later."

"Why do you think so?" asked Malek.

"I've turned events over and over in my mind all day. The bandit chief is doing exactly what I would do in his place. I'm convinced Rakell's gone on a wide sweep north or south of us, and he'll turn around and strike when it suits him. He knows something's amiss in Nowhere, and he's trying to draw us out."

"How could he know?" said Nils.

Howland scowled. "In many ways, I'm sorry to say. It's my fault. We made ourselves too well known at the stream crossing, digging the trench and with the elves' traps. Add these things together and you get one answer—armed resistance, centered on the village."

Four farmers, well-soaked with homemade beer, lurched past with Carver, singing loudly. They hailed Howland as they went by.

"Poor fools," Robien said. "They'll be shocked when the enemy reappears on their doorstep."

Malek said, "Tell us what to do, and we'll do it!"

"Find your bride."

Malek flushed with excitement. He was about to swear his life to the task, but Howland cut him off.

"Save the heroic declarations," he said. "What's needed now is resolve, not posturing. I want you two—" he nodded at Malek and Nils—"to strike out on your own. One of you go northwest, the other southwest of the village. Search out Rakell's force."

"Why can't you go?"

"I don't dare send my people," Howland explained. "I need locals who know the land and who won't look out of place if they get spotted. Go as far as four days' journey from Nowhere," he told them, "and circle back to cover as much ground as possible.

"Know this: You may not find anything," added Howland. "You're tracking men on horseback and a pack of ogres, but they are skilled at moving with speed and stealth. But we must try to find where the enemy is. Will you do this?"

"We will," Nils said for both of them.

They collected food and water for eight days' travel. Before crossing the plank laid over the trench, Robien stopped Malek and pulled the sword from his scabbard.

"What are you doing?" Malek exclaimed.

"No farmer carries a sword. If you're caught, the enemy will know you've been away from the village to buy arms."

"He's right," said Howland. "Leave the weapon."

"You can't send me out unarmed!" Malek cried. "That blade has Rakell's name on it!"

"You can have a knife and a staff," said the Knight. "No more. Your purpose is to find the enemy, not attack him."

Grudgingly, Malek unbuckled the Quen sword belt and gave it to Robien. He and Nils crossed the trench and walked away from Nowhere, heading due west. They would stay together three or four days, and if they didn't find Rakell they would split up.

Watching the brothers recede in the distance, Robien said, "How can such foolish farmers find the foe?"

"Perhaps they won't. Perhaps the battle will be over by the time they return."

For once the cool-headed Kagonesti was nonplussed. "You want them to miss the battle?"

Howland nodded. "Rakell will strike in two days, maybe less. He'll come out of the south or north, not the west. By the time Nils and Malek return, we'll have conquered, or been conquered. Either way they'll be reunited with their loved ones."

"Why send them away then?"

"I owed them this. They've given me a chance to restore my honor. I give them this chance to preserve their lives."

Howland returned to the village, leaving the astonished Robien staring after him.

* * * * *

Raika picked her way along the line of silent huts. It was dark, and even the stars were cloaked by clouds. Each hut had been filled to the roofline with dirt, so there was no one inside. Raika wasn't looking for a villager anyway.

"Ezu?" she called softly. "Ezu, where are you?"

She'd been searching for him for a while all around the sleeping village. He didn't keep company with anyone after dark but habitually disappeared until morning. Raika wanted to know where the traveler spent his nights, and how. Was he just an eccentric foreigner or a devious spy?

She hoped he was honest. His gift of thornapple brandy had touched her deeply. It was the first taste of home she'd had in a long time. If Ezu was a spy, she'd profoundly regret burying a sword in his guts.

"Ezu? Ezu?"

The only sound she heard was the chirpping of crickets. She called the traveler's name again a little louder. Still no answer. Feeling parched, Raika crossed to the village well. She felt the stillness all around her. At the well, she leaned into the open pit to draw up the bucket. When she straightened, someone stood directly across from her, a blank black outline looming by the well wall.

"Who's there?" she hissed, drawing her sword.

The clouds parted, and starlight found Ezu's face amid the shadows. He looked odd in the darkness. A greenish yellow glow lit his face and neck.

Raika circled the well cautiously. "What's that light?" she whispered loudly.

"This?" He waved his hand below his chin, and the glow fragmented into many tiny points of light, flying away. "Fireflies."

She scoffed, lowering her sword. "How do you get fireflies to light on you and glow?"

"I acquired a certain scented oil in Sancrist. It doesn't smell like much, but it draws fireflies from miles around. "

The last insects flew away, leaving Ezu's head in darkness.

"They cling to anything anointed with the oil, and glow until dispersed," he said. "It makes a handy lamp."

Raika shook her head, bemused. "You're certainly the strangest man I've ever met!"

Ezu bowed as though he'd received a compliment.

"You've been calling me," he said. "What do you want?"

"I want to know, where do you spend your nights?" Raika asked bluntly.

"I study the land and its denizens. I am a contemplative man."

"You're an elusive man," she replied, "and maybe a spy!"

"Ah!" Ezu seemed more pleased than offended. "So

you came to catch this one in the act, did you? I told you from the start—I'm a traveler. Because I'm only passing through, this one tries to keep aloof from local events. I don't want to interfere."

"The peasants who tried to lynch you must have had a reason."

He shrugged. "Mobs don't need a reason, just an opportunity." Ezu smiled again. "And a rope." He put a hand to his throat, rubbing it.

She would've laughed, but a strange feeling quickly came over her. Her head swam, and her arms and legs seemed to belong to someone else. They would not obey her will to move.

Ezu stepped closer and extended his right index finger, as he had the night he gave Carver the spice candy. Instead of making a sweet appear, Ezu pressed the tip of his finger to the center of Raika's forehead.

"You will dream tonight of home," he said softly. "Dream of your lover—what was his name?"

"Enjollah." She heard her own voice but had no sensation she was speaking.

"Yes. Dream well of Enjollah."

When he lifted his finger, the feeling ended. Raika braced herself against the well wall.

"Sink me, I must be tired!"

"You are tired. Why don't you go to sleep?"

"I think I'll go to sleep."

"Good night, lady. May all your dreams be happy ones."

Raika's head stopped heaving like an argosy's deck in a cyclone. She walked past Ezu, vaguely aware of him leaning against the low stone wall.

And he was gone.

Fog and cobwebs evaporated from Raika's head. She

doubled back and circled the well. The field stone wall was waist high, and Ezu was nowhere to be found. He was not crouching low, trying to deceive her. He was gone. The only place he coud have gone was down the well. . . . She leaned far over the wall and peered into the inky depths. Below the Eternal Spring glimmered. She couldn't see the mossy walls of the shaft, but there was no sign of Ezu in the well either.

Shaken, she retreated to her bedroll near the village gong. Carver was nearby, lying sprawled on his back, mouth agape, wheezing and whistling. Sir Howland slept sitting up, his back against the gong post, a sword across his lap. He was hard, that old man.

Despite her consternation over her encounter with Ezu, Raika quickly fell asleep. She knew something was wrong, unnatural about him, but her fears melted away under surging waves of slumber.

As Ezu told her, she walked the beaches of Saifhum that night. Enjollah was by her side.

* * * * *

Warmth fled Nowhere during the night. The temperature fell, and as it departed it called forth a heavy mist from the soil. Howland awoke with a start as a firm hand clamped down on his wrist.

"It's Amergin."

He rubbed his eyes. The Kagonesti said, "We have fog."

Howland slowly stood. Fog, their friend when they escaped from Robann, was not welcome now. Ten thousand enemies could encircle the village under cover of fog, and no one in Nowhere would even know it until it was too late.

"Call everyone to arms!"

Amergin ran off to arouse the village. Howland climbed atop the well wall and tried to see through the murk. The fog was thready and dry, swirling around anything that moved. That was some help.

Shouts stirred the sleeping village. A clatter of arms and the thump of bare feet announced the rising of Nowhere. In short order Raika, Khorr, Carver, and Robien gathered at Howland's feet. The minotaur rubbed his eyes, yawning with enough force to stir the kender's unkempt hair. Robien looked a little befuddled, very unusual for him. Of all the hired fighters, Raika seemed the most relaxed. She stretched her long arms, bowed and flexed with languid grace. When Carver made some grumpy remark to her, she just smiled and ruffled his hair.

Unbidden, Ezu appeared from behind Howland. He stood patiently watching the commotion around him. He was neatly dressed for once—broadcloth tunic and wide-legged trousers, sash belt, and his usual sandals. No antlers, flowers, or fireflies.

In twos and threes and sixes, the villagers crowded around the assembled mercenaries. Faces swollen with sleep, they babbled to each other about the cause of the alarm.

"Is it Rakell? Is he here?" many asked. Howland waited a while, hands clasped behind his back, until the farmers settled down.

"People of Nowhere," he said, "I called this alarm because of the fog. Until we know better, we must assume the enemy is in the vicinity."

Groans and grumbles rose from the villagers.

"You scared us to death!" Bakar whined.

"There's no enemy?" asked Caeta.

Paul B. Thompson

"There's no one!" Bakar answered crossly.

"Silence!" Howland's commanding voice stifled dissent. "Do you think this is a game? This is war, or have you forgotten?"

With few further complaints, the villagers assembled into their respective fighting groups. Carver and the children were given the vital task of keeping lookout for signs of trouble outside the village. When everyone was at their appointed place, Howland called Robien to him.

"Collect six spearmen," he said. "We're going out for a look around."

Robien rounded up half a dozen of the more agile farmers.

Howland turned to Carver. "The watchword is 'Fangoth.' Understand? Anyone who comes near who doesn't say 'Fangoth' is the enemy! Spread the word!"

Perched on a hut roof, the kender gave a jaunty salute and passed Howland's message on to his young followers. "Fangoth! Fangoth!"

"Quiet, now," the Knight said as they crossed the trench. Below them, farmers huddled in the damp earth, clutching homemade spears and maces. Khorr walked up and down the length of the trench, bolstering his frightened troops' morale.

"Take up the planks behind us," Howland said. Khorr himself took hold of the bridge and heaved it behind the trench.

"You know the watchword?"

The minotaur said, "Yes, 'Fangoth.' Anyone who comes near who doesn't say the word will get hurt."

"We'll be back soon."

Howland led his little band out into the mist. It was deathly quiet. Two dozen paces from the trench,

172

Nowhere could not be seen at all. Small sounds carried through the fog: careless talk, the rattle of tools, weapons, and breakfast pots. Howland sighed. The enemy could get an earful this morning and at very little risk.

He arranged his party in arrow formation, with the experienced scout and hunter Robien on point. Howland was behind him on one side, trailed by three villagers. Three more were arrayed on the other side. They walked slowly through the barley stubble, straining their senses to detect what might lie ahead.

Wilf followed Howland. After walking some distance, he froze in mid-step. Dropping to one knee, he hissed a warning to the others.

Everyone stopped. "What is it?" Howland whispered.

"Horses!"

Howland turned to Robien. "I don't hear horses, do you?"

"Not hear, smell!" Born and raised a farmer, Wilf knew beasts equally well by sight, sound, or smell. Before anyone had time to dispute Wilf's claim, the soft clop-clop of horses' hooves were distinctly heard.

There was no cover but the mist. Like hares being stalked by hounds, Howland and his men held themselves motionless, not even drawing breath.

Two men on horseback appeared out of the fog, riding across a few yards ahead of Robien. They wore mismatched bits of armor, indifferently painted black.

"If you ask me, the boss is barkin' at shadows," one of the riders muttered. "These farmers ain't gonna fight us. They got no more backbone than a slug!"

Scouts! Rakell was out there, somewhere, groping in the fog!

Robien looked back at his leader. His face asked the question, do we attack?

Howland curtly shook his head. Let them pass.

When the mist closed around the pair of riders, Howland gestured for everyone to follow him. Hands on sword hilts to keep them from rattling, they ran in a crouch back the way they came.

A horse neighed behind them. One of the farmers looked away toward the sound. He promptly tripped on the barley stubble and fell flat on his face. To Howland and the rest, his fall sounded like a thunderclap.

Sure enough, hoofbeats came their way at a trot. While Wilf and another villager hauled the fallen man to his feet, Howland drew his sword and let the flat lie against his shoulder.

Robien, moving like a ghost, took his place beside him. Wilf and the farmers formed a small circle, as they had been trained to do, kneeling on one knee with their spears braced against the ground.

A man appeared on horseback, riding easily with the reins loosely in his hand. He still had his lance propped on his right boot. He spied Howland and turned his animal toward him.

"Steady," said the old Knight under his breath.

"Who goes there?" asked the rider. "Seen anything?" He evidently took the sword-armed Howland for one of his own band.

Too late he spotted Robien and the villagers behind Howland. The rider reined up and tried to bring his lance into position. Howland rushed him. Having no shield on his arm, the brigand had no way to fend off the attack but with his lance, a thick-shafted spear with an iron hand-guard and square, pointed head. Howland easily avoided the sweep of the heavy weapon and thrust upward at the bandit. His point took the rider in the armpit. Grunting, the bandit dropped his lance.

The horse whipped around, knocking Howland to the ground. The wounded rider tried to spur himself out of danger, but he hadn't reckoned on Robien's agility. The Kagonesti vaulted onto the horse's rump and landed astride behind the bleeding man. Planting a hand on the side of the man's helmet, he shoved him off. The bandit tried to get up, but Wilf and the farmers swarmed over him, battering him down, finishing him off with awkward spear thrusts.

Robien returned, riding the bandit's horse. Howland brushed himself off, saying, "Can you handle the beast?"

"I can ride," answered the elf.

Howland tossed him the dead bandit's lance. "Watch our backs, then."

The farmers had already stripped the fallen rider to his breechnap. Each man carried off some part of the dead warrior's belongings. Though disgusted by their greediness, Howland did not reproach them. They lived hard lives. It was their custom to take whatever goods fate put in their hands. There were high lords and generals of great repute who did the same, taking the choicest booty from the defeated for their own gain.

"Back to the village!" he said, keeping his voice low.

More horses galloped to and fro in the fog behind them. The hoofbeats grew louder, punctuated by the twang and hiss of a bow and arrow.

Someone cried out. Howland planted a foot and spun around. Three bandits, one armed with a bow, had caught up to the fleeing farmers. One villager was down, pierced by an arrow. Still burdened by their booty, the remaining farmers were sitting ducks for an accomplished archer.

"Hai! Over here!" Howland cried. The bowman ignored him and picked off another farmer. Howland snatched up a stone and hurled it at the bandits. A lancer, watching his comrade's fun, heard the stone and pointed at Howland.

The archer, armed with a short recurve bow, took deliberate aim at him. Howland stood still, arms folded across his chest.

He'd been shot at many times, and he knew how to handle a lone bowman. From a range of perhaps forty yards, he had just enough time to drop out of the way of the arrow once it was loosed—if his old limbs didn't fail him.

He heard rather than saw the release of the bowstring. The high twang was his cue. He could plainly see the dark-shafted arrow twisting in flight, coming straight at his chest. As soon as Howland could make out the fletching—goose feathers, gray—he threw himself hard to the left. The arrow passed right through where he'd been standing.

With a flurry of hooves, Robien galloped out of the mist, lance leveled. He spitted the archer in the ribs but lost his grip on the unfamiliar weapon when the man toppled from the saddle. The remaining two lancers spurred their mounts at him. Robien snapped the reins, for he wore no spurs. and rode hard to Howland.

"Give me your hand!" Robien cried.

Howland would not. He felt safer on foot in the fog than trying to out-ride experienced horsemen.

"Get back to Nowhere!" the old Knight ordered. He slapped the animal's rump. It bolted, and Robien was hard pressed to stay on.

Shouts and hoofbeats resounded in the mist. Running

hard, the old Knight soon saw the jagged line of sharpened stakes that delineated the trench. Robien, a few yards ahead, slid off the borrowed beast, shouted the watchword, and scampered across the narrow plank restored for the scouting party's return.

Howland dodged between two stakes. Below he saw the trench was crowded with wild-eyed, frightened farmers.

"Fangoth!" he growled, gasping from his sprint. Heel to toe, he threaded his way across the deep ditch. Wilf and the three remaining farmers came hard on his heels.

"They're coming! Stand to!" he cried, throwing himself down the opposite slope of the dirt mounded up behind the trench. Khorr repeated the order in his booming voice.

Fifteen riders galloped out of the fog. The small party were plainly astonished to find themselves charging a well-prepared defense instead of a wide open village. Reining in frantically, they managed to avoid impaling themselves on the stakes, but this left them open for a ferocious counterstroke.

Howland stood up on the ridge of the earthen mound, sword in hand. "Now! Give it back to them!" he roared.

The farmers in the trench poked and thrust at the milling horses. Pricked on the flanks or belly, a few horses reared, throwing their riders. Climbing out of the trench, Khorr and five village men swarmed on the fallen bandits, battering them with stone-headed maces.

Screaming at the top of their lungs, Raika and her spear carriers came running up behind Howland. They were out of range but howled and grimaced as threateningly as they could. From the rooftops nearest the north end of the trench, Carver flung darts with his whippik. He was fast, but his aim was off, and he hit no one.

Clearly shocked to meet such fierce resistance, the bandits quickly broke off battle and rode away. Watching them go, Howland wished he had four good archers. He could have picked them all off from the mound.

Swallowed by the fog, the bandits left four dead behind, in addition to those slain by Howland's patrol. Elated villagers whooped and hollered, some mounting the rampart in front of the trench and baring their bottoms in the direction of the fleeing enemy.

Howland swiftly stifled such foolishness. He strode up and down the mound, barking orders.

"Who's hurt? If you're hurt so much you can't fight, report to the camp for treatment!" The elderly women of Nowhere had been given the task of tending the village's wounded. "If you're not hurt, shut your mouths and take your places. Do you think you've won? They'll be back, and you'll get arrows in your arse if you keep up this stupid display!"

Raika was disappointed that she and her band had not been able to participate in the skirmish. Howland sent her away, growling, "You'll get your chance to fight!"

Whatever joy the villagers felt at their first repulse of the bandits quickly died when they heard the trumpets blow. First from the north, then the east, south, and west, brass horns blared through the fog, announcing the presence of Lord Rakell on every side. Nowhere was surrounded.

NOWHERE

Chapter Eleven

Test of Iron

All too soon the late morning sun scoured away the mist. What was revealed when the fog burned off made every heart in Nowhere skip a beat.

Arrayed on the plains around the village were scores of horsemen, many more than the thirty-odd riders who had originally swooped down on the farmers and carried off their people to slave in mines. From his perch atop the tallest house, Carver counted eighty-nine horsemen, ten ogres, and most ominously of all, a wheeled catapult drawn by six brawny oxen.

Standing on the stone wall surrounding the well, Howland, Raika, Robien, and Amergin watched the bandits as they galloped about They did not close on the village though, not yet. Howland had an idea why.

"Rakell isn't here yet," he surmised. "Look at them! All this to-ing and fro-ing! No decent commander would countenance such a waste of energy. Rakell must be delayed."

"You mean he may show up with more men?" said Raika.

"No more than a dozen, I'll wager—Rakell and his personal retinue."

"The odds are too much. I never bargained on this," Robien said.

"None of us did." Howland lowered his hands from his brow, where he'd shaded his eyes against the glare. "I hope none of you had any other plans for your life."

He jumped down, calling for Caeta, her father the Elder, and other prominent villagers. Old Calec tottered up to Howland wearing a rusty iron pot on his head. At first Howland took it to be a misused cooking pot, but on closer inspection he saw it was an old-style Solamnic helmet, of the kind worn by the yeoman infantry.

"Where did you get that?" he said sharply.

Calec touched the helmet absently. "Marren's house. When we cleared it out, we found many old armaments," he replied. "What do we do now, Sir Howland? The enemy is more numerous than we expected—"

Howland plucked the helmet off the aged man's head. Judging by the nicks and dents, it had seen hard use.

"Marren had this? Laila's father?"

"Aye, with some other martial goods." The elder gestured, and the villagers behind him displayed various soldierly items: a pair of leg guards, an armored skullcap, and a good war dagger with an iron blade a foot long. Howland examined these things closely. They were all of Solamnic workmanship, a style he knew well. He dated the arms to his youth, thirty to forty years ago. Thirty years ago Howland had been a proud and powerful young warrior, serving the gracious lord Harbard.

"Sir Howland!" Robien prodded him insistently. "Sir Howland, the enemy!"

The present returned like a slap in the face. Howland saw a squadron of lancers were trotting straight at the trench.

"Everyone to your places!" he cried. "They mean to test our mettle. Show them what we're made of!"

He hurried to Khorr with Robien at his heels. Raika mustered her little company of spearmen, and Amergin organized his slingers.

The bandits came on deliberately, sizing up the defenses as they came. Bodies of the men who'd fallen during the melee in the fog still lay in the newly mown field.

From atop the earthen bulwark Howland peered into the trench. Khorr had taken his place in the center of the ditch, flanked by an equal numbers of villagers on either side.

"Fight hard!" Howland said. "They're searching for weakness. Don't show them any!"

Arrows flickered into the dirt on either side of Howland's feet. The old Knight disregarded the danger until Robien pulled him down. How he wished the farmers had bows of their own!

"Get Amergin," he said quietly. "Tell Carver to hold the whippiks until the enemy presents a better target."

Robien raced away with Howland's orders. When the bandits were within lance-reach of the line of stakes, Howland stood and shouted, "Now, Khorr, now!"

The minotaur came roaring out of the trench, followed by screaming farmers brandishing spears, clubs, and axes.

They had strict orders not the leave the shelter of the stakes, but with the hated foe so near, some forgot what they'd been told and ran out too far. Two villagers were promptly trampled into the dirt. They might have perished had not Khorr stormed in, swinging a mace in each hand. He clubbed down two riders and dragged the impetuous farmers to safety.

Noting the frenzy of the villagers' resistance, the bandits broke and rode away. Howland guessed what was next. He glanced over his shoulder to make sure Amergin and his slingers were coming. They were, at a dead run, Robien with them. A quick check showed Carver and the children were in place on the rooftops.

Fifty yards from the stakes, the riders suddenly turned and spurred hard, charging back on Khorr's troops. As Khorr had been instructed, he kept his men out of the trench, seemingly confused and leaderless.

"Stand where you are!" the minotaur boomed. The farmers shifted nervously, fearful of the thundering horses and bright lance tips rushing at them. Above, Howland held his breath. He could have shouted instructions to Khorr and his men, but he wanted to see how they would perform without him.

"Spearmen, kneel!"

In ragged order, the farmers went down on one knee, extending their spears forward. They filled the gaps between the larger, heavier stakes.

Ten yards. Eight. Six . . . two of the villagers yelped and dropped their weapons, scampering frantically into the trench. Howland swore out loud. The rest held.

The bandits boldly charged home. They must have believed the villagers would break. All they had to do then was maneuver between the sharpened obstacles and massacre the farmers. The riders were brave, but their judgment poor. Most of the farmers stood fast, and the stakes were closer together than they appeared.

Horses screamed and reared as they collided with the sharp wooden points. Warriors fell heavily from the saddle. In moments the gallant charge became a mass of bloody confusion.

"Now, slingers! Now, whippiks!"

Around Howland, Amergin and his slingers loosed a storm of pellets on the trapped horsemen. Lacking enough metal stars, they had to use smooth stones, which while deadly against unarmored targets, were not so effective against iron helmets and breastplates. The storm of flying stones took their toll, however, and the whippik darts completed the rout. More than one rider, hearing the terrible sound of airborne projectiles, glanced upward to receive a stone or dart in the face.

One by one the bandits turned tail and galloped to safety. The last to fall was a hard-riding fellow at the rear of the formation. Amergin slipped one of his few remaining stars into his sling and let it fly. Sunlight flashed off the whirling, pointed disc until it buried itself in the small of the rider's back. He threw up his hands and slid lifelessly from his horse.

Khorr raised a cheer, which the villagers atop the mound echoed again and again. From the rooftops, the whippik corps jeered the retreating brigands with all the crude and cruel vigor that comes naturally to children.

"Enough!" Howland said gruffly. "We haven't won yet." To give weight to his words, a score of archers rode forward, out of range of slings or whippiks, and peppered the trench and mound with arrows. Everyone hastily took cover.

"I count eight," Robien said, sliding his sword back into its scabbard. "And six animals."

Howland peered over the trench. Eight new bodies littered the ground. He didn't bother to count slain horses.

"They won't attack here again," Howland said. "Next they'll try the houses." The perimeter of the tiny village suddenly seemed very wide and long. Where would the enemy strike?

He told Amergin, "Go to Raika. I'll join you after I have a word with Khorr. Robien, stay with me."

Amergin led his slingers away. Howland and the bounty hunter climbed over the rim of the mound and slid down into the trench. Wild-eyed farmers presented a hedge of spear points to him when they landed.

"Easy, lads. Don't you know your own commander?" said Robien.

"Beg pardon, sir!" said the nearest villager, a burly woman with stout arms and a childlike face.

"It's all right. You did well." Howland slipped among them, patting the sweating, trembling farmers on the back as he went. "You fought well. Be proud!"

"They're not so tough!" declared a young man in a leather apron, the village cobbler.

"They won't mess with us again!" said his companion. Howland let them brag. Soon enough events would deflate their buoyant spirits.

He found Khorr standing over the two men who'd run away from the bandits' attack. They huddled together miserably in the bottom of the trench. Though Khorr towered over them, looking very fierce, Howland could tell the minotaur poet was sorry for them.

"What am I to do with you?" Khorr said not very

forcefully. "Every hand is needed. I can't send you back to wait with the gray-haired grannies, can I?"

"Answer your commander!" Howland barked when the men said nothing.

"No, sir!" they chorused.

"They must stay," Howland said for all to hear. "No one is excused from fighting, not now. We can't spare anyone! Put these white-livered dastards among those who fought most bravely. Maybe their courage will rub off."

The unhappy pair slunk away. In private tones, Howland said, "Keep alert. I don't think they'll attack you again, not today, anyway." He pointed to the opposite end of Nowhere. "They'll try the east end next."

"How do you know, sir?" the minotaur asked.

"Rakell's not here yet. Some underling must be in command. I suspect he wants to impress his master and capture the village before Rakell arrives. I've watched the bandits. They're fine riders, but they know nothing of tactics. Their next move will be to attack as far away from the trench as they can, thinking they're being foxy." Howland grinned. "I'll teach them a thing or two."

"Yes, sir!"

Khorr boosted Robien and the old Knight out of the trench. As man and elf descended the earthen mound behind the trench, they heard the minotaur's deep voice proclaim,

Let us sing of wind and wave and wonder,
Shouting seven songs of wild wanderings!
Sea and sky, land and lie,
Ballads long and martial—!

"*Windwave Ballads*, first canto," Robien declared.

Howland smiled. Fighter or not, Khorr was an inspiration to his men. Many captains counted as greater warriors could not claim that.

As he crossed the village common, ignoring the cowering old women and weeping babies, Howland saw columns of dust rising outside the ring of huts. The air was still, so the dust gave an excellent indication of where the bandits were moving. Large numbers were riding hard from west to east, just as Howland predicted.

He bumped solidly into someone. He was about to shove the lout aside when he realized it was Ezu.

"The battle is joined?"

"Yes. Stay out of the way, will you?" Howland tried to slip by, but Ezu moved the same way, and they collided again.

"I beg your pardon!"

"Get out of my way!" Howland snapped. He stood stock still until Ezu stepped carefully to one side. The Knight strode on, leaving Robien to catch up.

"I hope you win!" Ezu called after him.

"I wouldn't give you two coppers for your life if we don't," Howland fumed to himself.

Movement at the edge of his vision caught the Knight's eye. Carver and his young cohorts were moving along the row of houses, the kender leaping over the gap between huts then catching each child as they followed. They chortled with delight, sounds that cheered and chilled Howland at the same time. He was glad they were not scared. He was appalled they were not terrified.

Raika paced back and forth in front of her recruits. They tried to look soldierly, but their drab, loose-fitting clothes and unkempt appearance spoiled any semblance of warriorlike demeanor. Their spears leaned this way and that. Trembling with excitement, Raika snatched the spear from Bakar's hands and rapped his skull with the shaft. He howled, clasping his head.

"You're a soldier, not a scarecrow!" she yelled. "Try to act like one!"

Amergin and the slingers stood in a loose half-circle, facing the arc of houses that enclosed the east end of the village. There was a small, rain-washed gully beyond the huts, deep enough to hide a man lying down but not deep enough to hinder a horse. On his own initiative, Amergin had sown this gully with strands of thorny creeper.

The houses, packed with dirt, were linked together by a series of disguised obstacles—chicken fences and animal pens, reinforced with stones and heavy layers of earth, cesspools with their plank roofs removed, nearly invisible lengths of horsehair twine strung between buildings at the precise height of a mounted man. When Howland and Robien arrived, everyone was tense but ready.

Smoke drifted over Nowhere. Raika stretched up on her toes to see what was burning.

"Did they set fire to the barley wisps?" she wondered.

Flames leaped up from the windmill. Outside the ring of houses, Howland had deemed it indefensible, so with heavy hearts the villagers had to abandon the only stone structure they had. Now they were paying for their temerity. Fire belched from the slit windows. The mill sails, woven from dry grass, blazed up furiously. Heavy wooden gears crashed through the burning main floor into the cellar.

Some of the farmers began to wail. A few left their places and started toward the mill. Raika stormed after them, catching them by the collar and cuffing their ears.

"Where do you think you're going?" she said, shaking a weeping farmer. "Rakell's boys would love it if you ran out there right now, wouldn't they? Pah!" She spat at their feet. "You'd be dead quicker than I can spit!"

"The mill . . . the mill . . ." they groaned.

Into the scene tottered the Elder, Calec, still wearing his battered Solamnic helmet. "Why do you weep?" he rasped. "It's only a pile of stones and logs! What are your lives compared to that? It's our mill, but it's my home, you know. Do you hear me crying?"

Gradually the lamentations faded. By the time the mill tower collapsed into the burning cellar, the villagers' eyes were dry.

"Get ready," Howland told his comrades. "The bandits have enjoyed easy vengeance on an empty building. Now they will want blood."

Horns blared around them. Anxious farmers turned from one signal to another, uncertain where the danger lay.

"Look to your front!" Raika said, shoving her spearmen into line. "They're trying to confuse you!"

Trumpet calls could not disguise the rumble of massed horses. Yellow dust rolled out behind the column of lancers. They were coming at the east end, just as Howland had predicted.

"Amergin! Choose your targets and loose at will!"

The elf let his sling drop from his fingers. "Load!" he shouted. His newly trained slingers put two flat stones in each pouch.

"Spin up!"

Ten slings whirled in fast circles.

Curses and shouting, joined by the squeals of unhappy horses, told the defenders the bandits had reached the thorn-lined gully. That was enough for the forester. The slingers slung, and the clang and clatter of missiles on armor resounded over the shouting.

Howland called to Carver, "What can you see?"

The kender cupped a hand to his mouth and called, "A saddle or two emptied, but they're coming on!"

"Ready your whippiks!"

"Aye, Sir Howland!"

Raika drew her sword. "Forward to the huts!"

The line of spearmen tramped ahead, five villagers in each gap, as Robien had taught them. The latter asked Howland's leave to join them.

"Go," said the Knight, "but don't get killed!"

Shrill screams rang from the rooftops as the children launched their darts at the enemy. Through the gaps in the huts, Howland saw the lancers were dismounting and walking forward. They couldn't use their lances on foot—they were too long—so they resorted to whatever hand weapons they had—swords, maces, flails, even daggers. Howland almost laughed aloud. How poorly led they were!

The brigands pushed through the gaps between the huts until they reached the chicken pens barring their way. They kicked at the flimsy-looking fences, only to discover they had been stiffened. As the village spearmen looked on, the raiders began to hack at the waist-high barriers with sword and axe.

Raika exploded. "What are you gawking at? Get at them!"

Rushing into the alley, she slashed down a bandit who'd gotten astride the fence. The enemy withdrew a few steps, uncertain, and the spear carriers moved up to support their captain. There followed a confused battle in which the farmers jabbed ineffectually with their long wooden spears and Rakell's dismounted warriors fended off clumsy attacks with their motley assortment of weapons.

Raika jumped over the barricade and advanced on the bandits. She dueled hard with a long-haired blond soldier, trading cuts and parries. He was skillful and might have beaten her had not a whippik dart lodged in the hollow of his neck. Distracted by the painful wound, he missed Raika as she lunged, catching him between his hip and lower edge of his cuirass.

Two houses over, Robien was battling two bandits at once. They spread apart, trying to flank him, but villagers swarmed down the alley and drove both men back over the overturned barrow Howland had put in place to block the way. Neither made it. Robien got the first as he clambered over the barricade, and the spearmen got the second when he stumbled. All five villagers crowded in, pinning the unfortunate man to the hut at his back.

Confounded on two fronts, the brigands tried filtering left and right into alleys, but they were held up by a line of wicker baskets loaded with dirt and stones. Led by Wilf, four spear-carriers charged the enemy. They impaled three bandits on their eight-foot spears before a second band, supported by a pair of archers, crossed the gully and began shooting down the brave farmers.

Wilf and his people could not stand against a pair of expert bowmen, so they darted down the alley into the common. Wilf cried, "Sir Howland! Help!"

He saw the danger immediately. Ordering the villagers to lie flat to avoid being picked off by arrows, Howland shouted for Carver to drive the archers away. The kender tried to comply, but he and the children had used up much of their ready supply of darts. The whippik fire faltered. The archers raised their sights and took aim at Nowhere's valiant children.

Something amazing happened.

A boy of twelve took an arrow in his leg. He collapsed, dropping his whippik, weeping with pain. He might have slid off the roof completely had not Carver and three other children grabbed him.

Cries of outrage filled the villagers' throats. Fathers and mothers alike rose up and charged the callous bandits with renewed fervor. Arrows dropped two, but the remainder swarmed over the astonished raiders, grappling with them bare-handed. Order was lost and discipline forgotten as the angry farmers bludgeoned, clawed, and kicked any bandit they laid hands on.

A single trumpet blared out on the dusty plain. Eagerly the bandits quit the melee and remounted their horses. By the time they were swallowed up by churning dust clouds, eight more of their number lay lifeless among the huts.

Nowhere had paid a price, too. Three villagers were dead, and six wounded to various degrees, including the boy hit by the arrow. So far the village had lost three killed and eleven injured.

Dead warriors were stripped of their weapons and armor, and these were distributed to the victors. Wilf found himself sporting a bronze helmet and short iron sword. Raika and Robien reorganized the tired villagers, passing out praise and criticism in equal measure.

"Bloody fools!" Raika raged. "Didn't you hear Sir Howland's order to keep down? Charging a pair of archers! Some of you weren't even armed!"

"We beat them, didn't we?" Caeta answered proudly.

The Saifhumi woman had to admit they had.

Water was fetched from the well. Everyone gulped down as much as they could, cutting the dust from their throats and soothing the fire in their breasts. They'd beaten off two attacks today. Small ones, to be sure, but they had done it!

Howland and Robien went back to the well and stood atop the wall. From there the Knight could see the bandit army had concentrated into three distinct groups, one south of the village, one northwest, and one due east. The aimless riding and horn blowing ceased.

Stillness fell over the plain. Dust settled. Howland got down. He leaned both hands on the well wall and sighed.

"What is it?" asked Robien, though he had an idea.

"The pointless demonstrations are over. Rakell has returned," Howland said. Dipping his hands into the bucket, he splashed cold water over his face. "Now the real battle begins."

* * * * *

By dusk, the stifling calm had held for half a day. Formations of bandit horsemen rode away, leaving smaller bands to pitch camp in plain sight of the village.

Wounds were washed and bound, and the evening meal was prepared. A kind of unnatural lethargy took hold of the farmers. The euphoria of fighting off their enemies had passed, leaving in its wake the numbing realization the fight would go on, tomorrow, the day after, maybe as long as anyone on either side remained alive.

Howland convened a council around the well before the first stars of night appeared. All his people were there along with the leaders of the village: Caeta, Wilf, the elder women and men, and old Calec, alone still full of fighting spirit.

Howland explained the situation. They'd driven off two haphazard attacks, undertaken, he believed, by some junior leader of the bandits. Now Lord Rakell was present, and things had settled down.

"Don't let the lull fool you," he told them. "When Rakell moves, things will be different. If he's any commander at all, he'll use every weapon in his arsenal against us."

"Will the ogres come too?" asked Caeta.

Howland nodded solemnly.

She shuddered.

"What can we do, then? Have we any chance of survival, let alone of winning?" Robien said.

Howland hooked his thumbs in his shirtfront and gazed at the fire. "We do."

Farmers and mercenaries alike exchanged looks of wonder.

"Ten days ago you believed we were doomed," the Elder rasped. "Why, now, do you think we can win?"

"A good general must understand his enemy," Howland replied. "Seeing them fight today, I understand them better now. Rakell rules them with an iron hand. His men must fear him. I'm counting on that. I myself will deal with Rakell."

"You can't hope to negotiate!" Raika said. "Not with murderers who shoot down children!"

"I will not negotiate."

Howland was silent for a long time, thinking. The others debated with increasing anger, as everyone proposed his own wild scheme to win.

Carver said, "If we can take a few prisoners alive, we can make them tell us where the gold mine is!"

"There's no gold mine!" Wilf retorted.

"If his warriors grow weary of Rakell's rule, perhaps we can turn them," Robien suggested. "If only a dozen desert, it will discourage the rest."

"The ogres—!" Caeta began once more.

"Be silent!" Howland said suddenly. His voice was like a thunderclap. Even Carver shut his mouth for once.

To Robien, Howland asked, "How does one kill a poisonous snake?"

"Strike off the head."

No sooner had the bounty hunter spoken, than he, Raika, Amergin, and Khorr all perceived Howland's plan.

"Strike off the head!" the minotaur repeated. "A classic notion. In *The Lay of the Blue Dragon*, the hero Zadza frees the minotaurs of the Scarlet Isle by beheading the vile beast Murmoroc."

"This is no time for poetry," Raika said.

"On the contrary, I would like to hear the tale of Zadza," said Howland, leaning back against the well. "In brief prose, if you please, Khorr."

The minotaur spread his big hands. "Your loss, friends! *The Lay of the Blue Dragon* is a wonderful piece, 1,629 septameters in five cantos . . ." Khorr sighed, sending a shower of sparks skyward from the campfire.

"The climax of the story is thus: Zadza, unable to defeat Murmoroc in open battle, stages his own death. The minotaur tribe of the Scarlet Isle send supplicants to the dragon, begging for mercy. Murmoroc agrees, if the minotaurs send ten females and ten males to him as sacrifices. Unable to offer resistance, they sadly agree.

"Twenty-one minotaurs show up at the dragon's lair—"

"Twenty-one?" said Caeta. "Why not twenty?"

"I can guess," Howland said, smiling. "Zadza was the twenty-first."

"Yes! You know the poem?" Khorr asked.

"No, but I recognize the tactics. Go on."

"Zadza comes disguised as a funerary priest. While he burns incense and sprinkles the water of death over the twenty sacrificial victims, he lulls Murmoroc into inattentiveness."

"And then?" said Carver, rapt.

"He cuts off the dragon's head with his axe," said Khorr.

The kender applauded.

Howland said, "Very good. That's just what I have in mind." He beamed at all the puzzled faces. Turning to the Elder Calec he added, "You're going to help me."

"Help you what?"

"Cut off the dragon's head."

NOWHERE

Chapter
Twelve
In Harm's Way

Night passed, tense but quiet. The black landscape outside the village was alive with glimmering campfires, tiny red flames winking like the eyes of a hundred wolves, patiently haunting a beleaguered herd. Howland and Robien checked the defenses constantly, keeping the farmers on guard awake with jokes, threats, and an occasional slap or kick. Howland did not rest until an hour or so before dawn when he sat down, back against the well, dozing until cock's crow.

He arose seemingly refreshed, and called his people together. Robien was never far from him now. Amergin, who wouldn't sleep in an artificial structure, slept under a spindly apple tree in the common. When Howland called, he rolled to his feet, coughed once, and came swiftly. Carver had to be called four times not because he was still asleep but because he was eating. He appeared before his commander munching a hot barley cake, two more tucked under his arms.

Khorr, clothes damp with mud from having spent the night in the trench, guzzled a bucket of water before he could speak. Hardest of all to rouse was Raika. She passed the night on her bedroll in the midst of her spear company, but when the sun rose, she was the last to stir. The busy cacophony of morning broke around her, and she never cracked an eye.

"I can wake her," Carver vowed. He held up a gray chicken feather.

Howland's brows climbed high. "You live dangerously, kender!"

"I don't think he wants to live at all," Khorr growled.

With a supercilious smirk, Carver strolled to the sleeping Raika. His band of village children gathered round the kender wherever he went. When they saw their leader, feather in hand, standing over Raika, they burst out in fits of giggling. Not even their shrill merriment disturbed the Saifhumi woman.

"Sir, about today's action—" Robien began.

Howland, watching Carver intently, held up a hand. "Wait."

The kender squatted down, looking over the sleeping woman for exposed skin. She had a blanket drawn up to her eyes, covering her nose, chin, ears, and neck. He moved to the other end. Three dusky toes protruded from the hem of the blanket. Carver gave his weapon a final flourish, and applied it to Raika's toes.

Her foot twitched, like a horse shrugging off a pesky fly. Carver waited until Raika stopped moving then swished the feather back and forth under her exposed toes. This time she brought her right foot over and violently scratched the tickled spot with her other big toe.

Carver frowned, gazing at the uncovered sole of Raika's right foot. He drew the feather down once, up, and down again, all the time watching for her eyes to open.

With the speed of a striking hawk, Raika's leg lashed out, catching Carver in the chest. He flew a good six feet before landing spreadeagled on his back. The chicken feather drifted slowly to the ground between them. The whippik company drew in a collective breath when they saw their fearless commander struck down, but their shock soon gave way to delight, and the children laughed uproariously.

So did Howland. He slapped Khorr on his broad back and laughed till tears slid down his mustache.

Amidst all the gaiety, Raika got up. Her eyes were screwed nearly shut, but she threw off the blanket and strode to the well, not speaking to anyone until she'd taken a dipper of water.

"Is the pest alive?" she said.

The village children hauled Carver to his feet. His eyes were rolled back. The older children marched him around to clear his scrambled head.

"Alive he is," said Khorr, "but not very happy, I'll wager."

"He plays any more tricks on me and I'll make him truly unhappy!"

"You were awake?" said Robien.

She waved at the tumult around them. "Who could sleep through this?"

Now that the morning comedy was done, Howland assembled his troops. In short, simple terms, he explained their situation as he saw it and what he proposed to do about it.

"The enemy outnumbers us, is better armed, and has more experience. They can move where they will and fight when they want to," he began.

"Maybe we should just surrender," Raika muttered.

"I don't advise it. If not massacred, we and all the villagers would likely end up slaves, working in Rakell's iron mine."

Raika said sourly, "I withdraw the suggestion!"

Howland continued. "We can fight until we do enough damage to Rakell's force that he decides to quit, but I don't think that's in his character."

"Why?" asked Khorr. "Surely a good commander knows when to leave a losing battle?"

"This is a wild band, an army of deserters and cutthroats. A man like Rakell rules by delivering success to his men. If he fails, his men will desert him in droves or might even murder him and elect a new, more ruthless leader." Howland looked at the bandit camp in plain sight south of the village. "On the other hand, as in Khorr's tale of Zadza, an outmatched opponent can sometimes win by striking off the head of the dragon, and in this case, we must try to kill Rakell and as many of his lieutenants as possible. Without leadership, the bandits may fly apart like dandelion blossoms in a spring breeze."

Baldly stated, Howland's plan sounded simple—but impossible.

"You say that awfully easily, old man!" Raika protested. "Do you expect us to cut our way through four score bandits and ask Rakell to stand still while we lop off his head?"

"A direct assault won't work. We wouldn't reach Rakell's tent, much less the man himself." Khorr asked, "How can it be done?"

"Three of us will go," Howland said. "We'll ask for a parley and present ourselves to the enemy. When the time is right, we'll draw daggers and slay Rakell where he stands."

"Is that honorable?" said Khorr.

"No," replied Howland quietly, "but it is necessary."

"The three'll be slaughtered!" Raika burst out.

Howland was silent.

"Count me out!" she said. "I'm not volunteering for a suicide mission! I prefer to take my chances here."

"I wasn't going to ask for volunteers," Howland said evenly. "I have three in mind already." All eyes were on him. "Myself, Amergin, and Ezu."

Amergin showed no surprise, no expression at all. The other misfit mercenaries were thunderstruck. Carver looked visibly relieved, fanning himself happily. Honorable or not, Khorr was clearly downcast that he had not been asked to go. Suicide missions were dangerous, yes, but the stuff of great poetry.

Raika, surprisingly, did not rant or rave. Instead, she asked, "Amergin I understand, but Ezu? He's not a warrior—he's not even one of us! No one knows where he is half the time!"

Indeed no one had seen the traveler since yesterday. They assumed he'd hidden during the fighting.

"Surely I would be a better choice, Sir Howland," Robien said quietly.

"No. You would be a better choice to command in my absence." The words 'when I'm dead' floated unspoken in the air.

"Why Ezu?" said Khorr, puzzled. "What good can he possibly do?"

The old Knight said. "Since we go pretending we want only to talk, Ezu's very appearance will serve to convince

Rakell we're up to no mischief. After all, who would attempt anything grave with so foolish-looking a companion?"

Robien folded his arms and said to his fellow Kagonesti, "What do you say, Amergin?"

"I am in debt to Sir Howland," the forester replied. "I said I would follow him till this fight was over. If he means to walk into the enemy commander's tent with a dagger in his hat, I will go too."

Raika clucked her tongue in disgust. She mumbled something about "throwing your life away."

"How and when will you propose this parley?" asked the minotaur.

"Late in the day. Twilight will help us, and the timing is important. It's best to approach the enemy after fighting off one of their attacks. That will make it seem more as if we're anxious to talk." Howland smiled ruefully. "If we fight hard, they'll be more willing to listen, too."

Horns resounded in the enemy camp. Dust billowed into the cloud-flecked sky.

"Find Ezu and bring him to me," Howland ordered the kender, who sprinted off.

The mercenaries dispersed to their waiting troops. Khorr's trench fighters cheered loudly when the towering bull-man returned. In contrast, Raika's spearmen cringed as she approached, shouting orders in her harsh, grating voice.

"Fire burns, no matter what the color," Robien said, observing the different ways his comrades led their contingents. Howland did not hear him. He was watching the enemy.

A body of horsemen rode out from the bandits southern camp, maybe fifty strong. They came within a two hundred yards of Nowhere and halted, dismounting. The bandits, now on foot, arrayed themselves in a long, single line. Each man had a good-sized basket on the ground in front of him. Howland guessed what they held.

"Send word all around the village!" Howland called, voice rising. "Expect arrows—lots of arrows!"

Robien ran to pass along the Knight's warning.

The archers stepped through their bows, stringing the powerful staves with the ease of long practice, as Robien returned.

Howland walked around the rim of the thick stone wall surrounding the well, scarcely looking where he put his feet. One misstep and he'd plunge sixty feet to the water.

"The attack will come from the north or east," he said. "The bowmen are only there to cover the main thrust—"

Telltale streams of dust rose in the north. "There!" said Howland. "Warn Raika! Have her bring her spearmen to the north side!"

Carver came jogging up, alone. "Can't find him!" he gasped between breaths.

"Ezu?"

"Yes! I've looked everywhere. I can't find him!"

"Never mind. Get your whippikers in position on the north side of the village. That's where the brigands will hit us."

Carver started to leave.

"And watch out for archers!"

He shrugged, smiled in his careless way, and went to round up his young charges.

"Sir Howland," Robien said. "What happens if the bandits choose to attack us on two sides at once? We don't have enough people to battle on two fronts."

"I know," was all the former Knight would say.

"What do we do?"

"Fight harder."

Howland jumped down. It wasn't far, but the landing staggered him. Robien stepped forward to brace his commander, but Howland pushed him away.

"It's nothing," he said brusquely. "Old bones. Fatigue." He pointed to the distant bowmen. "Stay here and watch them. If they start our way, or if other troops join them, fetch Khorr and his men from the trench."

"Yes, Sir Howland."

The bandits coming down from the north camp also got off their horses well out of sling and whippik range. There were between thirty and forty of them, armed with swords and shields. Their lances they left with their animals. Even more could have joined the attack, but every tenth man held the reins of the horses his comrades left behind. Seeing this gave Amergin an idea.

"Sir Howland," he said. "Horses . . . ?"

He saw at once what the forester meant. "How many will you need?"

The Kagonesti wrinkled his nose. "Four."

"Take six, young, strong ones."

Amergin nodded, and dashed away.

From behind, the defenders heard the twang of bowstrings, followed by the hum of arrows in flight. To a man, the farmers flung themselves on the ground, arms over their heads. The first volley of arrows landed outside the ring of huts. The second buried themselves in the thatched roofs.

"Get up, you worms!" Raika cried, kicking Bakar in the rump. He yowled and leaped to his feet, incensed. Raika folded her arms and stood nose to nose with the outraged farmer.

"You have something to say?"

"Yes!" he declared, not without a quaver.

The third volley of arrows sprouted along the edge of the common.

"Speak your mind," Raika said coldly.

"Stop kicking me!" the timid farmer declared.

"Then don't present your rump to the sky!" She said this pleasantly, and her scowl slowly turned into a smile.

A rush of wind, and the fourth volley probed farther into the village. One stray missile brought down a rooster, pinning the bird to the ground in a spray of gaudy feathers. Other arrows clinked off the well wall or stuck shivering in the windlass frame.

Sheepishly, the farmers got to their feet. They huddled against the walls of the north side huts, confident the dirt-packed dwellings would protect them.

Raika ran to Howland, standing alone near the center of the common. The sixth volley arrived in pieces, arrows dropping at wide intervals all over the village.

"They must be lofting them straight up," Raika said.

"Almost. The wind is breaking up the volleys," Howland replied.

"How far can they reach?"

"A good, dry short bow can send an arrow three hundred yards." He looked back unconcerned at the far-off line of bandit bowmen. "They seem to be having trouble reaching past two hundred."

"Good enough!" Raika stormed back to her troops, yelling at them to stand up.

The bandits' northern force was coming on at a steady pace but in no real formation. Howland relaxed a little. His band, backed by close to thirty villagers with long spears, ought to be able to hold off a similar number of brigands with swords. If Amergin's scheme came off, they'd give the bandits a surprise.

Twenty yards from the village, the attackers raised their swords high and screamed bloodthirsty war cries. Atop the huts, Carver and the village boys made obscene gestures back at them.

Arrows continued to fall out of the brilliantly blue sky behind them, randomly, like thunderbolts. Howland ignored them, even when one struck close by his right foot.

Whippiks swung high, and the bandits had to raise their shields to protect their faces from the darts. Unable to see forward, their charge slowed. Raika moved her spearmen into the gaps between the huts.

"C'mon, you murdering sons of dogs!" Raika shouted. "Come fight us, face to face!"

They did just that. Splitting into groups of three or four, the brigands leaped over fences and other obstacles in their path. Raika and the spearmen countercharged. Crude as they were, the wooden spears easily pierced the boiled leather jerkins most of the bandits wore. Drawing back, the invaders lowered their bronze shields to fend off the spears. When they did, Carver's whippiks scourged their heads and shoulders. Most of the whippik darts were made from dried cornstalks weighted with small stones in the hollow cores and tipped with two-inch long dragon-toe thorns. Though rarely lethal, the darts made painful wounds. Once a bandit had four or five of these nasty missiles in his neck or face, he lost all interest in further fighting.

Horses neighed loudly. Farmers and bandits alike paused their battle long enough to see what was disturbing the animals. What they saw delighted the villagers and dismayed Rakell's raiders.

Amergin and six hand-picked men had stolen out of Nowhere, circled wide of the scrap going on between Raika's troops and the bandits, and attacked the men left behind to guard the horses. There were eight of them, minding close to forty horses, and they could not let go the animals' reins to defend themselves without losing all their comrades' mounts. Amergin and his slingers had popped out of the grass ten yards away and swiftly struck down one guard after another. Freed, the high-strung horses broke away, inspired by stinging stones flung against their rumps. As the last bandit guard was struck down by Amergin, all the horses scattered to the winds.

Panicked by the sight of their precious mounts abandoning them, the bandits quickly ended the attack. Some even threw down sword and shield and ran full-tilt after their animals. Amergin and his slingers had a field day bouncing hard stones off the fleeing brigands. Their rout was so complete the defenders sallied forth to drag some of their fallen foes into the village, where their arms and armor were stripped off and distributed among the villagers.

Victory seemed total when Howland heard a shriek rise from the east end of Nowhere. The wounded and elderly had crept away from the barrage of arrows, sheltering in the curve of houses on the northeast border of the village. They were safe enough there, but when the bandits were repelled, some of the villagers came out to see the enemy's defeat. Among them was Calec, the ancient headman. As he hobbled across the common on stiff, aged legs, a stray arrow took him high in the thigh. He went down without a sound but his neighbors raised a wail.

Howland hurried to the old man's side. The cloth yard shaft had terrible force behind it, plummeting down from so high. It had passed through Calec's left thigh, and the broadhead was buried halfway through his right as well. The impact had virtually nailed the old man's legs together, piercing arteries in both limbs.

Caeta cradled her father's head. Howland knelt by the elder, ignoring the humming arrows that continued to fall.

"They're on the run?" whispered Calec.

"They're beat," Howland said.

The elder sighed, a long rattling exhalation. "Good. Hammer them like a gong—"

Caeta closed his eyes. "Good-bye, papa!"

More projectiles thudded around them. The archers could see villagers clustered around the fallen Calec and were concentrating on them. Gathering the old man's legs while his daughter took his arms, Howland and Caeta carried Calec to a safer spot.

Amergin and the slingers returned, laden with swords, shields, and good iron daggers. There was enough captured weaponry to equip every fighting villager with a metal blade of some kind.

Calec was the only one killed on their side during the battle, but he was more than just the eldest of the village elders. He was the fighting heart of Nowhere, and now that heart was stilled.

Yet there was little time to grieve. As soon as the bowmen returned to camp, a fresh party of riders issued forth. Unlike the previous bands of bandits the people of Nowhere had faced, this new force appeared well armored and mounted on fine-looking horses. They carried banners too, the color of faded gold, whipping from the tips of their tall lances.

Raika's and Amergin's contingents rushed across the common to the south side, stumbling through a thick hedge of buried arrows as they came. Carver and his followers got down from the roofs and fell to harvesting this strange crop. The kender yanked an arrow out and examined the keen iron head. It was a real war arrow, and with the shafts clipped, they would make deadly whippik missiles.

Robien counted the riders as they cantered in a double line, parallel to the village. To Howland he said, "I make it twenty-eight!"

"Rakell's elite," Howland called back. "We won't panic these men."

"Could be worse," said Raika, taking a deep breath.

Amergin inquired with a single raised eyebrow.

"Could be ogres."

A signal trumpet blared, to be answered by horns in the other bandit camps. Once the armored brigands were in place, they halted, facing Nowhere. Long, pointed banners flipped slowly in the light midday airs.

"Robien, go to Khorr. Have his men stand ready to reinforce us," Howland said. The bounty hunter departed on his mission. Wilf stepped up beside the old Knight, nudging him.

"What is it?"

Wilf held a cavalry helmet out to Howland, one taken from the recently beaten bandits. "For you, sir." Worn bright by years of use, it was real iron, with a peeling leather pad inside.

"Thank you." Howland slipped the helmet on. The cheek pieces were hot against his face. It fit perfectly. He buckled the strap under his chin.

Wilf made an awkward attempt to salute. Howland was touched, but the moment was broken by Raika's loud shout, "Wilf? Wilf? Where's that idiot gone off to now?"

The young farmer ran back to his place with the spearmen. Howland was waiting for Robien's return when someone else touched his elbow: It was Ezu. Maybe the helmet muffled his footsteps, but Howland had heard and seen nothing of the odd traveler until he appeared.

"Where have you been?" Howland demanded.

"Here and there," said Ezu. "You're busy? I'll come back—"

"You stay right by my side!" Howland thundered. "I need you—"

Out on the plain, the armored brigands started forward.

"Stay by me!"

"I'm no warrior," said Ezu mildly.

"You are now!"

The bandit elite kept their lines straight and came on, not at wasteful gallop but at a steady trot.

"Stand by to receive cavalry!"

Raika, Amergin, and all the villagers looked at Howland in surprise. Though they'd heard his shouted commands for a while now, there was something different about his last command. Maybe it was the helmet or the sight of enemy knights, but the years seemed to have fallen away from him. He stood straighter, and his voice carried across the dusty common with uncommon energy and clarity. This was Sir Howland as he once had been.

The villagers knelt in two staggered lines, spears wedged against the ground. No attempt would be made to meet the enemy in the gaps as before. Behind the spear carriers, Amergin placed his slingers. Carver and the oldest half-dozen boys occupied the rooftops, while the younger feverishly cut up arrows and passed bundles of remade darts up to their friends. Of Robien, curiously, there was no sign. Howland glanced around for him, frowning.

At forty yards the riders swung their lances down, first the front rank then the second. They increased their pace to a canter.

"What are you waiting for, kender? Let them have it!"

With a whoop, Carver flung the first dart. It caromed off the visor of one of the riders. Dismayed, he ordered his boys to try their luck. Even with iron-tipped darts, they could make no impression on the armored riders.

Reluctantly, for kender liked animals, Carver cried, "Aim for the horses!"

At ten yards the enemy burst forward in a sudden spurt. There was no room to achieve a gallop, but they put on speed and crashed bodily through the barriers between the huts. Darts and sling shot clattered off them like hail. One or two horses got tangled in the vines and thorns, but the riders lowered their lance tips to the ground and with a single upward swing, swept the tangle aside.

The farmers' line of spears stirred restlessly. Raika, standing behind Bakar, called out, "Those lances don't hurt at all, you know, going in."

"Really?" said Bakar, face streaming sweat.

"Yeah, it's the coming out that kills you."

Four armored riders broke through into the commons. One fell when Amergin put one of his precious metal stars through a slit in his visor. Howland drew his sword. "All right, then! Get them!"

Shouting and screaming, the farmers broke ranks and raced at the bandits. The rider nearest Howland calmly spitted first one, then another villager with his lance, flicking the impaled body of the first off before striking the second. Howland yelled to distract the deadly lancer, who promptly turned toward him. The black iron lance head cut through the air, driving toward Howland's chest. Fear and weakness he'd learned since leaving the trade of arms vanished, and all the old moves flowed back from the depths of Howland's memory. He struck the lance aside with the flat of his sword and got under his opponent's reach. Once you beat the tip, he thought, a lancer was at a disadvantage against a good swordsman. Howland gripped his hilt in both hands and thrust hard at the rider's belly. He twisted away, and the point of Howland's blade skidded off his iron cuirass. The old Knight spun around, ducking under the horse's head and coming up on the lancer's left. The horseman was clad in three-quarter armor, not full plate, so the back of his legs were vulnerable. Howland swung with all his might, and felt his old sword bite hard behind his enemy's knee. The bandit brought his heavy lance around, and the shaft connected solidly with Howland's head. His new helmet saved him, but he went down. Moments later the lancer fell too, bleeding heavily from his leg wound. He tried to rise, but Wilf ran up and struck the lancer on the head with his spear shaft, flattening the struggling rider. Howland rolled to his feet, snatching the dagger from his belt. He jammed the point through the joint between the lancer's gorget and helmet. Shuddering, the bandit went slack.

On his feet again, Howland looked for the gallant Wilf, but the melee had separated them again. More lancers had penetrated the line of huts, and though the farmers were fighting valiantly, giving as hard as they got, the enemy was too powerful to stand up to at close quarters. Howland was about to order his people to fall back to the well when one of the whippik boys screamed, "They're coming! They're coming this way!"

Between two houses Howland glimpsed another force of riders approaching. There was no way to stop them unless Khorr's men left the trench and helped them. Where was Robien? Why had he not returned?

"Fall back! Fall back to the well!" Howland cried. The defenders tried to obey, but they were thoroughly mixed in with the enemy. Bakar fell, lanced in the back when he dropped his broken spear and tried to run. Seeing him fall, Raika felt a surge of rage. She threw down her spear and sprang at the man who'd struck Bakar, vaulting onto the rump of his horse. The heavily armored bandit couldn't deal with Raika so close behind him. She twisted back and forth until she got a hand on his chin and wrenched him right out of the saddle, hurling him to the bloody earth.

Taking up the reins, she recovered a lance and used it to impale first one foe then another. The bandits shrank back, giving way before her.

Howland and Amergin gathered eleven villagers by the well. Cut, bleeding, and panting, they put their backs to the stone wall, ready to ward off another charge.

The elf felt something warm on his back. He was pressed against the Ancestor, and the fractured totem was warm to the touch, far warmer than the other stones in the wall. Yet there was no time to contemplate this mystery. The second wave of attackers were riding through the gaps created by the lancers.

"Time to sell our lives dearly," Howland shouted. Beside him, Amergin loaded his last bronze star.

Just as the bandits cleared the huts, a noise at the flank made them slow. Startled beyond measure, the defenders clustered around the well saw what looked like a two-wheeled cart come charging over the dirt mound behind the trench. In the cart were Robien and three farmers, armed with spears. Pushing the cart from behind was Khorr, head down and feet churning.

With a shout, the cart hit the horsemen, bowling them over like clay tankards in a bar fight. Having disrupted the second wave of attackers, Robien and the spearmen jumped down to join Howland by the well. Khorr backed up the cart and retreated to the trench.

"Where have you been?" said Howland.

"Preparing this surprise. I hope you don't mind. It was Khorr's idea."

"Where is he now?"

In answer, the cart reappeared atop the mound, brimming with more spearmen. This time Khorr ran hard down the hill into the center of the enemy. Coming to a stop after upsetting four armored lancers, the minotaur put down the poles of the cart and laid about with his stone mace. Not even the thick plate of the lancers was proof against a blow from a twenty-pound stone, and the bandits withdrew. Now, ten of Rakell's elite horsemen lay dead in the village, along with another eight rank-and-file bandits. Seven villagers were slain and many more wounded.

Raika rode up to where Bakar lay, unmoving. She lifted one leg over the saddle and dropped to the ground.

"Fool," she said bitterly. "Never turn your back on the enemy!"

She threw down her sword with disgust. It landed across Bakar's back. He groaned.

"What? Alive?" She rolled the farmer over. Bakar's face was white as milk, but he was breathing.

"You're hitting me again," he moaned.

"Shut up!" Raika stood. "Where are those healers? We have a wounded man here!"

Seeing the bandits ride sedately back to camp, Howland slowly let out the breath he was holding. Khorr presented himself with his men, saying, "We beat them again, Sir Howland!"

"So we did."

"Will they come again today?" Robien wondered.

"Yes."

Elf and minotaur looked crestfallen.

The Knight explained. "If Rakell keeps to the strategy he's been following, he'll mount spoiling attacks all day to keep us off guard and prevent us from repairing our defenses."

Robien uttered a Kagonesti curse. Khorr asked, "What can we do?"

"Carry on despite them. Any show of weakness will bring on an even more serious assault."

Suddenly Howland had a thought. "Where's Ezu?"

"Here."

Ezu was sitting cross-legged on the well wall right behind him.

"How long have you been there?"

"Since you said, 'Fall back to the well.' Am I not where you wish me to be?"

"Yes, fine. Don't budge from that spot!"

While weary farmers struggled to rebuild the broken-down barricades between the huts, others used Khorr's cart to clear away the enemy dead.

Raika, pleased with the fine horse she'd acquired, rode

out sixty yards from the village and in full view of the bandits' south camp thrust a broken lance deep into the dry turf. She propped a battered, blood-smeared helmet on the end of the lance, spat on the ground, and rode back to Nowhere.

Chapter Thirteen

The Dragon's Head

F our times more before sunset the bandits tested the defenders of Nowhere, pushing, probing, looking for any weakness that could be exploited. Before the sun was low and red in the west, the farmers were speechless with exhaustion, and Howland's fighters had survived from one crisis to the next, throwing the enemy back each time with skill, determination, guile, or sheer will.

After the last attack, everyone collapsed where they stood. Only Howland remained on his feet, endlessly circling the village, ever-vigilant for the enemy's next move.

Flat on her back Raika said, "How does he do it? How does that old man run and fight and command all day and not fall over dead from weariness?"

Seated nearby, Robien put his face in his hands and

mumbled, "He was bred to battle, like a hound to the hunt. He'll keep going as long as his heart beats."

Raika gazed at the sky, still blue overhead but streaked with feathery, scarlet clouds. It was indescribably beautiful, and Raika stared at the heavens as though she'd never seen them before. At sea, the sky was always laden with portents for good or ill, mostly ill. A bank of clouds in the wrong place, the color of the horizon at dawn or dusk held meaning for the success or failure of a long voyage. On land, the sky said nothing to her, but it was beautiful.

"Why am I here?" she mused aloud.

Lying on his belly a few feet away, Wilf stirred and raised his head. His freckled face was spattered with mud and blood.

"You're here to fight this fight," he said.

"What good will it do? Tomorrow, or the next day, we'll all die. The longer it takes, the harder we'll go . . ." Her voiced trailed off.

"Nonsense!"

Everyone around Raika sat up. Howland was standing over them, hands on hips. "We're doing well!" he declared.

Raika pushed herself up on her elbows. "Think so, old man?"

"I do. The worst attack was the second, and every one since then has been weaker and more tentative. Their last attack was positively feeble! Carver and the children could have driven it off by themselves!" He gestured to the growing heap of bandit dead laid out by the trench. "We've killed thirty of the enemy and lost only nine killed and eleven wounded. Now's the time to launch our stratagem. Before the sun sets completely, I will ask Rakell for a parley."

Robien got stiffly to his feet. "Do you really think the bandits will flee if their leaders are killed, Sir Howland?"

"I do. They've taken a hammering today."

Raika sank back with a sigh. "So have we!"

"Remember we're dealing with warriors who could not take the discipline of a true army. They chose banditry to have an easy life. Today they've learned that not everyone will bow down to them." He looked away to the brigands' north camp. "I'll wager some have deserted already."

Amergin walked up, looking wan but unflappable as ever. Howland gave him a message scrawled on a slip of goatskin, which the Kagonesti tucked into his belt. Next Howland asked for the frailest, most frightened-looking villager still capable of walking to Rakell's camp and back. Caeta offered to go herself, but Howland insisted on a less hardy representative. He finally chose a stooped old man named Tuwan, Bakar's uncle. He was scrawny to the point of emaciation, in part because of a long-standing illness. Tuwan had only two teeth in his head. When he smiled, he looked like Death walking.

Caeta supplied a swath of faded linen, which Howland tacked to the haft of the bandit's lance as a flag of truce. Amergin and Tuwan left the village by crossing the trench, then turned left and made for the bandits' southern camp, the biggest of the three.

"Afraid, old fellow?" asked Amergin as they crossed open ground.

Tuwan showed both teeth. "A poor man who's lived as long as me has seen everything awful there is," he replied. "Done a lot, too. One thing I ain't done is spit in the eye of a lord."

"Don't do it today unless you're tired of living," the elf said.

Tuwan cackled, sucking air through cracked lips.

From his place atop the well, Howland watched the Kagonesti forester and the gaunt old farmer slowly merge into the brown expanse that was once thick with growing barley. A quartet of riders galloped out from the camp, ringing Amergin and Tuwan with lance tips. For a few seconds Howland held his breath. If the bandits were too angry, they might slay his emissaries rather than listen to them.

Robien's eyes were keener than his. Howland asked him, "Can you see what's happening?"

The bounty hunter stood beside the Knight, shading his eyes from the scarlet rays with his hands. "Amergin is showing them your message," he said. "They're reading it. . . . What did you write, Sir Howland?"

"I told them a column of two hundred armed men was on its way to relieve us and that I expected them in two or three days."

Robien dropped his hands and gazed in awe at Howland's brazen lie.

"Even if Rakell doesn't believe it, some of the more faint-hearted bandits might bolt." He gave his second in command a wink. "I signed the message 'General Howland uth Ungen, Knight of Solamnia.' "

"Maybe they'll just surrender!"

Howland looked solemn. "Jesting aside, this is our last, best chance to come out of this with our hides—and honor—intact. While I'm gone, keep everyone on their toes. Rakell's just as capable of treachery as he ever was." He straightened his dusty clothes and removed the scarred helmet.

Distant movement drew Robien's attention. "The pickets are returning, and so are Amergin and Tuwan!"

Howland saw the two slight figures coming back to Nowhere. "Message delivered," he murmured. Now it was time to prepare.

Treat every mission as if it were your last, Lord Harbard used to say, because one day it will be.

* * * * *

From the detritus of battle, Howland scrounged the best possible outfit for a general and a Knight. Caeta and other village women sewed together a mantle from cloaks worn by slain bandits, while Wilf and some farmers polished armor for Howland to wear. They hammered out the dents and stoned away the sword cuts until the old Knight had a presentable set of three-quarter plate. With his old sword at his side, he looked every inch the seasoned commander.

Amergin did little other than wash the grime from his hands, face, and neck. Ezu, who had reluctantly agreed to join Howland on his mission, following the Knight around all day like a shadow, disappeared at the last moment to don his best clothes. When he returned from the darkened row of huts to the firelit common, he brought conversation to a standstill.

On his head he wore a tall, conical hat made of stiff white leather, the crown of which was cut in the shape of a forward-curling horn. His hands and face were powdered dead white, and two red circles were painted on his cheeks. Ezu's soft wraparound tunic had given way to a starched white version with wide, pointed shoulders and wide lapels. The lapels and back of the tunic were embroidered with colorful designs, stylized flowers in red, black, and gold. Ezu's belt was likewise broad and richly decorated, and his trousers' legs were wide and stiffened with wooden strips sewn into the fabric. On his feet he wore thick-soled wooden sandals.

"Sink me!" Raika exclaimed. "Is this how folk in your country dress?"

"Only for the highest ceremonial occasions," said Ezu. "It's a bit gaudy, I know, but Sir Howland told me to look my best."

Howland walked slowly around Ezu, appraising his ensemble. Hand cupped on his chin, he said, "It's better than I hoped. Rakell will be so dazzled he won't look twice at Amergin or me."

In the lull since the parley, Khorr had used his great strength to chisel out of captured bandit armor plate ten stars for Amergin's sling. Each four-pointed disk was made of forged iron, much harder than bronze, and hurled by the elf's expert hand, they could penetrate armor. Howland gave the stars to Ezu with instructions to hide them on his person.

"Where?" asked Ezu.

Raika made a rude suggestion. The farmers laughed until Howland silenced them with a scowl.

"Put them in your hat," said the Knight.

Ezu did better than that. The base of his headgear had a cuff, made when the leather was folded double to support the weight of the crown. He slipped the iron stars into the cuff. The upper half of each missile showed, but by evenly spacing them around the rim, Ezu made them look like decorations.

Howland knew the bandits would relieve him of his sword and dagger, but he wanted to retain his long scabbard. The finial ball, or drag, at the end of the sheath was actually the grip of a ten inch stiletto. It was meant to be a Knight's weapon of last resort. For Howland that was what it would be.

Raika, Wilf, and two farmers went a hundred yards onto the dark plain and set up two pairs of crossed torches, ten feet apart. After lighting them, they hastened back to Nowhere. Before long, a column of riders left the southern camp, each man bearing a burning brand. They arrived at the torches, formed a double line, and waited.

Seeing the horsemen, Howland said, "Time to go."

Amergin nodded silently. Ezu adjusted his hat (now much heavier, since it was loaded down with the forester's ammunition) and said, "Tell me again, Sir Howland—why have I been chosen to go with you?"

"You wanted to meet the folk of different lands? Well, here's your chance to meet some."

The traveler looked unconvinced.

"Then do it because I ask it of you. We saved your life, didn't we?"

Ezu nodded.

"Do this as payment on a debt of honor."

"What am I to do, exactly?"

"Say as little as possible to the enemy. Don't discuss our situation, our strength, or our weakness. Your task is to stand by, look exotic, and distract the bodyguards."

Plainly worried, Ezu took his place on Howland's left, while Amergin stood on his right. Robien ordered a hole opened in the barricade. Farmers pulled aside a tangle of casks and thorny vines.

"Farewell, Sir Howland, and good luck!" said Caeta.

"Give 'em the point!" Raika said.

"Bring back any gold or jewels you happen to find lying about!" urged Carver.

Robien clasped hands with Howland and said to his

fellow Kagonesti, "Don't get yourself killed. I need the Brotherhood's bounty."

Some indeterminable emotion flashed across Amergin face. Whether it was amusement, affection, or anger, no one but the laconic forester could say.

The minotaur was the only one to bid good-bye to Ezu. "Return to us if you can! I want to hear some of the poetry of your native land," said Khorr genially.

"Come," said Howland simply. He strode between the earth-filled huts, firelight glinting on his borrowed armor.

They walked in silence half the distance to the waiting escort. Amergin finally broke the silence by saying, "How will I know when you want to strike?"

Howland considered this and replied, "I'll take off my sword belt. When you see me reverse my scabbard, you'll know the time is near. At that moment, watch me."

Ezu, his stiff trousers creaking and scraping with every step, seemed to have lost his usual poise. "Strike?" he asked. "What is your plan? I haven't been consulted, and I certainly hope this situation can be resolved without violence."

"Don't talk, traveler," Amergin said. "Walk."

The southern horizon was darkening from rose to purple. A slim silver crescent of the lone moon floated near the edge of the sky. Against this backdrop the horsemen sat waiting, horses' heads bobbing.

"Halt!" called one of the near riders. Howland and Amergin stopped. Ezu bumped into the Knight from behind. Flustered, he stepped back, muttering apologies.

The rider at the head of the right line of riders seemed to be in charge. "Are you Howland uth Ungen?"

Head high, the Knight answered loudly, "I am."

"Who are these with you?"

"Amergin, my chief scout, and Lord Ezu, my—" Howland struggled for properly impressive titles— "my personal advisor, soothsayer, and sage."

"Looks like a marketplace puppet," said another bandit. Rough laughter rippled through the ranks.

"Shut up!" The laughter died. "You will come with us. Lord Rakell awaits." The cloaked and helmeted bandit leaned down, hand out. "Your sword."

"This is a truce. My sword shall stay in its scabbard," Howland said loftily.

"Your sword, sir! It is the order of my Lord Rakell that you surrender your weapons, or there will be no parley!"

With a show of great reluctance, Howland pulled his sword out by the hilt and handed it pommel first to the bandit leader. Without prompting, he also gave up his war dagger. Amergin yielded his knife.

"What about him?" said the bandit, indicating Ezu.

"I do not carry weapons," Ezu replied calmly.

The bandits did not press the point.

"You will walk between our horses, single file, leaving a gap of five paces between you. No talking."

"Are we prisoners, or honorable opponents?" asked Howland. The bandit leader did not answer but turned his horse around. His men did likewise, and Howland was bidden to walk on. He did, followed a few paces behind by Ezu. Amergin came last.

As they approached the bandits' camp, Howland tried to absorb as much information about the enemy as he could. The horsemen around him were mostly young men, between twenty and thirty. Their leader was a little older, perhaps thirty-five. All sorts of nationalities were present, judging by their coloring, clothing, and accents— Ergoth, Nordmaar, Abanasinia . . . lands from all points of the compass. The only common thread he saw among them all was the rough black armor of Nerakan light cavalry. How fitting that all these disparate and desperate characters should turn up at a village called Nowhere.

On closer inspection, the camp revealed much, too. It had no defenses—no palisade, no trench, no sharpened stakes to foil enemy horsemen. It was a hodgepodge of tents great and small, arranged in no order. Bonfires blazed at intervals between the patched canvas shelters.

That was too bad, Amergin thought. For the deed they were contemplating, darkness would have been better.

It was not a disciplined camp. Bandits strolled about, gobbling stew off tin plates and drinking from clay bottles. Seeing Howland and his companions, they stopped eating long enough to glare balefully at the cause of their grief. A few of the harder-looking brigands fingered blades as Howland passed. The back of Amergin's neck tingled from all the hostile eyes raking over him. He was grateful for Rakell's escort now.

Catcalls and rude remarks greeted Ezu's entry into the camp. Playing his part, he acknowledged every greeting with a seemingly good-natured nod or a wave, as if they were the kindest good wishes.

The riders led them through a labyrinth of tents to the center of the camp. There a high-walled tent was pitched, with many lesser appendages attached to it. The leader of the escort reined in his mount and called Howland forward. Seven bandits emerged from the tent and took charged of the village delegation.

"Are you the general?" asked one of the men on foot. He was a much older man, almost Howland's age, with a grizzled red-gray beard and a massive scar where his left eye had once been.

"I am Howland uth Ungen."

"Huh. Right." He barked orders to the younger men with him, and the trio was roughly and thoroughly searched for weapons. Amergin kept his face impassive. Would they find his sling? The stars in Ezu's hat? The stiletto in Howland's scabbard?

A bandit with fresh cuts on his arms and face grabbed Howland's scabbard. Rattling it, he saw it was empty and left it dangling from the Knight's hip. Nor did they find Amergin's sling, which was merely a length of braided twine and a leather tab. When it came to searching Ezu, though, the bandits were in for a surprise.

One snatched the hat from Ezu's head. He peered into it, saw nothing, and flung it on the ground. Before Ezu could stoop to retrieve it, a small brown rabbit hopped out of it into the firelit night.

"Hey!"

The veteran bandit grabbed the rabbit by the scruff of the neck and shook it under the younger man's nose. "Didn't you see he had a *rabbit* in his hat?"

"But he didn't, Taylo!"

"Then where did this come from?"

"Oh my," said Ezu, squeezing between the two raw-boned bandits. "He shouldn't have been there, the rascal." He took the rabbit from Taylo's hand and inserted it back into his hat. Once on his head, Ezu smiled benignly. "Settle down, Brownie!"

"Gimme that!" The grizzled bandit took the curled headpiece off Ezu. He shoved his hand into it, expecting to find a handful of soft fur. Instead, his blue eyes widened in alarm. When Taylo withdrew his hand, he was clutching not a rabbit, but a thick, coiling snake with iridescent copper scales. With a shout, he tried to hurl the serpent to the ground, but the reptile was too tightly wound around his hand.

"Get it off!" he cried to all and sundry. His young subordinates remained rooted where they were.

Howland shot a glance at Amergin. The elf was watching the ridiculous scene with great amusement. When Howland caught his eye, they exchanged a knowing look. Ezu's ability to befuddle onlookers was truly a great asset to their cause.

The snake was halfway up Taylo's arm when he drew his sword, apparently to hack off his own arm, snake and all. Ezu made soft shushing noises and gently pried the serpent loose.

"Now, Brownie," he said soothingly, "behave, will you?"

"You said the rabbit was Brownie," said one of the young guards.

"Sometimes," said Ezu. He carefully fitted the bulky reptile into his hat.

"Sometimes?"

"Sometimes Brownie's a rabbit. Other times he's a snake."

The bandits were incredulous.

"That's nothing!" Ezu assured them. "Once he came out a full grown bear. I had no end of trouble getting him back into the hat then!"

The guards stepped back warily. A tall man with a black forked beard, dressed in a burgundy velvet robe, appeared in the tent door. "What in thunder is going on here?" he demanded. The bandits fell into line, white-faced. "Are these the ones from the village?"

"Yes, my lord!" said Taylo.

"Did you search them for weapons?"

"Yes, my lord. That is—"

"Well, did you?" the well-dressed brigand roared.

Taylo weighed whether or not he should describe Ezu's hat and its peculiar occupant to his superior and evidently decided against it.

"All is in order, my lord!" he declared with a stammer.

"Bring them in!"

Howland and Amergin were chivvied inside. The bandits ushered Ezu in with considerably more circumspection.

Inside, the tent had a gaudy splendor. The ground was covered with thick carpet runners, brocaded in Nordmaar style. Brass and pewter lanterns, every one a different shape and size, hung at intervals overhead. Racks of spears and unstrung bows were sited at every turn, and the air was heavy with the smell of incense, spilled wine, and roasted meat.

After three turns, Howland and his companions found themselves in the great room in the center of the tent. He quickly counted fourteen people in the room: nine men, four women, and a dwarf in a deep blue robe. The dwarf had a scale set up, and was weighing a smooth metal ingot. Since it was the wrong color for gold, Howland assumed it was iron from Rakell's mine.

Noticing the arrival of visitors, one man in the crowd stood. He was stocky and broad-shouldered, with prominent black brows and a nose pressed flat by too many years in a helmet. His black hair was salted with a little gray. Howland took him to be fifteen years his junior. Draped in black silk, he wore a heavy silver chain around his neck, and his fingers glittered with many rings. There was something about this man, though, that Howland almost recognized. . . .

"General uth Ungen?" said the man, voice laden with irony.

Howland did not respond immediately. The black-garbed man separated himself from his comrades and came to face Howland and the others.

"I am Rakell," he said. "You've put me to a great deal of trouble, do you know that?"

"That is why I am here," Howland returned.

Rakell studied the old Knight's face closely. "You don't remember me, do you?"

Brow furrowed, Howland said, "Have we met?"

Rakell laughed loudly, displaying fine white teeth. "We once served the same master, Burnond Everride!"

Howland shuddered as if struck. Recognition came to him in a flood. "You rode with Lord Burnond's host!"

"So did you. I was not known as Rakell then, nor were you a general."

Ezu, plainly curious, spoke up. "Sir Howland was a Knight of some repute."

"Quiet, popinjay! You've heard the tale 'Sir Howland' spun for you, no doubt." Rakell turned to his minions. "See here what time and tide has accomplished, my friends!" He swept back to an ornate wooden chair and sat down. "I, who was once a prince of my Order, am now a prince of thieves, while Howland here, a sergeant in Lord Burnond's guard, has become a general of farmers!"

Amergin looked to his leader. Sergeant?

"Sergeant was his highest rank. Did you think a true Knight of the Rose would deign to serve the Dark Order so readily?" Rakell laughed again. "When they brought me the note you wrote, I almost believed it. I knew someone with martial skills was directing the farmers! But a Knight? I consulted the rolls of the ancients orders and found no Howland uth Ungen."

Howland unbuckled his sword belt, saying nothing. He

wrapped the leather strap around the scabbard and turned it over. The finial, a brass ball kept bright by constant rubbing, gleamed by lantern light.

"So," whispered Howland, "you know me. Then you did not ask us here to parley?"

"Negotiate with a sergeant, a turncoat to his own people? Not hardly!" At Rakell's nod, guards rose in a body, swords in hand. "You've made things difficult here, and I have troubles enough! A damnable red dragon holds me up for tribute . . . the mine needs workers, and there aren't enough villages in the region to provide a full corps of diggers. However, once you're dead, the farmers will lose heart and give in. All will be as it was."

Rakell's captains seized Howland, Ezu, and Amergin. Howland tried to free the stiletto, but he was easily wrestled to the carpet by four younger, stronger warriors.

"What are you waiting for? Kill him now," Rakell said harshly.

A blade touched the back of Howland's neck.

"Wait, my lord."

The new voice came from the far right of the room, where a man sat motionless in a high-backed chair. As thin as Tuwan, the old man in the chair had a wreath of fine, white hair and a lined, leathery countenance. He was richly outfitted, like the other bandits, in finery stolen from some noble house. His most striking feature was his sunken, useless eyes.

"What is it, Marren?" said Rakell.

"Why kill such an unexpected asset?"

"Asset? A broken-down old soldier with delusions of knighthood?"

"Deluded or not, he's held your band off for how many days?"

Rakell frowned. "Get to your point, Marren!"

The blind man held out his hand. One of the women present, a striking maiden with hair the color of clover honey, moved to assist him. There was enough resemblance between her and the old man to see they were of the same blood. She helped Marren stand and guided him to Rakell.

"He wouldn't come here unthinking," said the blind man. "I daresay he reckoned on some treachery of his own. Isn't that so, sergeant?"

Amergin and Ezu said nothing, and Howland's words were growled into the carpet. At Rakell's command, he was dragged to his feet.

"Tell me, what happens if you don't return?" asked Marren. "You must have reckoned on some plan."

"My second will carry on the fight," said Howland. Blood ran down his nose and over his lips.

"So there are no troops coming to relieve the village. That was a lie, too."

Howland gazed at the floor.

"He knows everything about their defenses," said Marren. "Question him first, kill him later."

"I won't talk!" Howland cried.

"Of course you won't," Rakell said, sneering. "You came here to die. I intend to oblige you."

Again the blade went to the old soldier's throat. Again Marren said, "Wait!"

Sighing, Rakell said, "Are you sure you know whose side you're on, Marren, or did you live in that dust-hole village too long?"

"My exile was no less bitter than this man's," Marren replied, indicating Howland. "If you hadn't found me, I would've died in Nowhere, forgotten by the order and all my comrades."

"Touching," said Rakell, "but what do you care whether this old fraud lives or dies?"

"You gave me a chance to join you. Why not give him the same chance? From what you say, he is accustomed to switching sides."

"You were my old commander, Marren uth Aegar. I learnt the fine art of war from you, and for that I owe you. I bow to your wisdom, but not in this instance. I owe 'Sir Howland' nothing better than a swift stroke through the heart, and killing him will hasten the end of the siege of Nowhere."

Ignoring Rakell, Marren pointed a finger unerringly at Howland's face. "Will you consent to join Lord Rakell's band?" he demanded sharply.

"Never. Better a dead general of farmers than a live traitor!"

Marren's hand dropped to his side. He shrugged and turned away. His young kinswoman guided him back to his chair.

"Enough delay. Take him outside and shorten him by a head," Rakell said. "Killing him here will only dirty the carpet."

"What of the other two, my lord?"

"Put them in chains. They look strong enough. They can dig ore like the others."

Amergin tensed to fight, even though he was boxed in by a a pair of naked sword points. Sensing the oddly dressed human was less trouble, two of Rakell's lieutenants sought to manacle Ezu first.

"Hold out your hands!"

Ezu complied without demurral. When the bandit tried to clap the iron bands around his wrists, they closed on air, falling to the rug with a loud clank. Ezu's hands hadn't moved.

"Fool, on his wrists!" Rakell said.

The bandit tried again as Howland was being marched out. Again the manacles seemed to pass through the traveler as though he were made of smoke.

"Be of good cheer, Sir Howland," Ezu called out to his leader. "It's not our time to die."

"Somebody gag that fool!" barked Rakell.

Howland and his guards reached the door. Ezu tilted his head back. His nose wrinkled, and he opened his mouth wide, making gasping noises. The bandits around Ezu drew back.

"What's he doing now?" Rakell got out of his chair. "Subdue that man, at once!"

"I think he's having a fit!"

Ezu snorted. "Going—going—to sneeze!"

He did, magnificently. At once all light in the room went out.

Chapter Fourteen

Who Sows Embers . . .

When darkness claimed the tent, the room exploded. Everywhere there was the scrape of iron blades and shouts of alarm. One of the guards still held a sword point firmly at the back of Howland's neck.

"Stand still! Be quiet!" Rakell bellowed. "Keep your heads!"

Someone screamed, a blood-chilling sound. Howland heard a soft whirring, then a thud, and the blade at his back shifted abruptly and fell lengthwise across his back, landing on the carpet beside him. He bent and seized the short sword, peering ahead in the darkness.

There was a clash of iron, punctuated by more grunts and curses.

"Stop it, fools!" Rakell cried. "You're fighting each other!"

Howland crawled forward on his hands and knees, finding himself against a wall where it seemed safe to stand. The whirring sounded again, and something sharp clipped his ear. Touching his stinging earlobe, Howland realized he was bleeding. Amergin! He was using his sling in total darkness. He crouched down, anxious to avoid being slain by his own confederate.

He didn't dare say a word. If he spoke, he might give himself away to the enemy.

"Can't someone make light?"

"Oh, mercy, I'm stabbed!"

"Let go! Let go of me, I'm one of you!"

Howland felt a light tug on his sleeve. He whirled, sword ready at his side.

"Who's there?" he muttered.

"Marren."

He reached out his left hand and grabbed a fistful of the blind man's robe. Guided by his grip, Howland pressed the sword against Marren's jaw.

"Traitor!" he hissed. "You would see your neighbors enslaved! Why shouldn't I kill you?"

Marren leaned forward, confident in his mastery of darkness. "Because Malek is here. His brother too. Now I will lead you to them. Quiet yourself."

Some large heavy object crashed behind them. A pungent, smoky smell filled the room.

"Who knocked over the censer?"

"Not me . . . why can't I see the flames?"

"Because it's out, idiot!"

"If it's out, why is it still fuming—?"

New screams shattered the air.

"I'm burning! I'm burning!"

Marren calmly pushed the blade away from his face

and pulled Howland's hand from his robe. Taking the old
soldier by the wrist, he led the way. Howland pulled
against the old man.

"Amergin? Ezu?"

"Come away," Marren insisted in a harsh whisper.
"Come away, or all with be lost!"

Reluctantly, Howland let the blind man guide him out
of the room. They entered a cool, breezy passage as dark
as the previous room. There were no lights anywhere.
Even the bonfires outside, which had cast such lurid
shadows on the tent walls on their way in, seemed to have
gone out. What was happening?

Unerringly, Marren led Howland to open air. Once outside—he knew this by the sound and smell—Howland
was shocked to realize he couldn't see any better! The
darkness was everywhere. Even the stars were gone. The
sky and land were as black as an onyx box.

"I can't see!" Howland exclaimed. He planted his feet
and refused to advance farther.

Marren touched his face lightly. "I thought so," he said.
"Rakell's boys were too confused to be just nightblind."

"How did this happen?"

"Your friend in the funny pants—what's his name? He
did it."

"How could he? How do you know he wears odd
pants?"

"Though blind, I hear well. Rakell's men made many
comments about his clothes. Darkness fell when your
companion sneezed, so it must be his doing."

Howland shook his head. Ezu *had* sneezed. At the time
Howland imagined the strange traveler had somehow blown
out the lanterns. How could his sneeze have the power to
extinguish the campfires outside and the stars as well?

Marren resumed his fast walk. Howland let himself be led. More than once he felt heat on his face and believed he must be passing a still-blazing campfire. No one interfered with them. Whatever force had stricken Howland must have blinded every bandit in camp. All around them men floundered in the sudden darkness, cursing or calling piteously for help.

Canvas brushed against Howland's forehead. Marren was taking him into a tent.

"Let me borrow this," the old man said, plucking the sword from Howland's hand. Ahead, two male voices were disputing loudly about the cause of the sudden, all-encompassing darkness.

"It must be an eclipse!" argued one. "The shadow of the moon has fallen across the world—"

"Moon? Don't be a dolt! The moon is bright, it don't have a shadow!"

Howland heard two dull clangs, and the disputatious guards fell silent. Marren returned and clasped his hand again. He put the hilt of the sword in Howland's other hand.

"Thank you for the loan."

They ducked between two heavy flaps. The room beyond was hot and close and felt very small. Howland could smell sweat, hear breathing.

"Malek? Nils?" Marren called softly.

Something stirred vigorously at their feet, yelping incoherently. Howland went down on one knee and found the brothers lying back to back, gagged, with their hands and feet bound. Working by touch alone, he untied the closest farmer's gag.

"What's happening? What's happening?" sputtered Malek.

"Ssh, quiet!"

"Sir Howland! You've come to rescue us! Are you alone?"

"Marren uth Aegar is with me."

Malek writhed against his bonds. "Where is he? I'll kill him! Tell me where he is, the vile traitor!"

"Be still, will you? Marren brought me here. I had no idea Rakell's men had taken you."

"We were captured three days after we left home," Malek said. He heaved against the cords around his wrists. "I saw Marren riding next to Rakell, wearing a velvet robe and golden chain! He has sold out his own people!"

There was no reasoning with him, so Howland untied Nils first. The older farmer moved slowly, grunting from obvious pain.

"I looked at a guard wrong," he said, "and got a beating for my trouble."

Horses galloped by, and the riders careened from the saddle, crashing to the ground just outside the tent. Everyone inside went stiff and silent. Whoever fell outside showed no sign of rising again anytime soon.

Whispering, Howland said, "I'll free you, Malek, if you control yourself."

"Where's Laila?" he asked too loudly.

"I removed her from the room first," said Marren calmly, "then came back for Sir Howland."

"Don't call me that," Howland said quickly and harshly. "You know I don't deserve it."

"What do you mean? You're a great warrior, a leader! A worthless turncoat like Marren should kiss your dirty shoe!" Malek hissed.

There was no time for explanations, so Howland let the matter drop. Nils and Malek could walk, the former with difficulty, and Marren said he could lead them back to Nowhere.

"What about Amergin and Ezu?" asked Howland.

"The forest elf is better off than all of us. He can see in darkness," said Marren. "As for your strangely dressed companion, as the author of this confusion I assume he is safely gone."

"What are you talking about?"

"I heard the elf moving easily in the darkness. He even used his sling to fell the bandit standing over you. Whatever the spell was your friend used, it affected only humans, not the elf."

"Ezu a wizard!" exclaimed Nils. "Huh!"

"I won't go back to the village without Laila!" said Malek.

"Malek, be sensible! How can we find her now? None of us can see," his brother said.

"Her blind father could find her! Can't you, Marren?"

Howland had a vague impression of the withered, white-haired old man nodding.

"I can find her, but I'll guide you to the north side of the camp then go back for her myself. It's safer for you that way, and Rakell does not yet suspect that I have done anything against him. Besides, my life matters little. Soon the disease in my bones will finish me, and I don't want to be remembered as the tool of bandits."

"Why were you treating with Rakell?" Howland demanded.

"He and I were comrades-in-arms once in the Dark Order. He thought he could enlist me in his new cause, and for comfort's sake, I let him think so. I acted selfishly, I can't deny. That's over now, and I have a chance to pay back the good people who took me in when I arrived here, a sickly exile, twenty-seven years ago." He moved to the door. "We must hurry."

Supporting Nils between them, Howland and Malek followed the blind man out. There tiny embers glimmered in the night, though they knew they were really raging bonfires. Overhead, a few fuzzy points of light were growing visible in the sky again.

"Hurry!"

Marren led them haltingly through the maze of tents. The camp had grown quiet in the hour since darkness claimed their sight. Now and then they heard shouts or groans and heard horses snort as they grazed among the unconscious forms of their masters. In the unnatural dark, Marren found his way to the northern side of the camp. When the tall, untrammeled grass of the plain brushed against their knees, they knew the party was nearing freedom.

"Here you are. Can you see better yet?" Marren asked.

Howland could make out murky shapes but could not judge size or distance. Malek saw the stars and little else. Nils, for some reason, saw the best of any of them.

"I can make out the ground a few feet in front of me," he said. "I can guide us back to the village.

"Good luck," said Marren. "If you don't encounter riders from the other camps, you'll make it."

"What about Laila?" Malek demanded.

"I'll restore her to you. I swear it, on my forgotten honor as a Knight." The old blind man smiled thinly, enjoying the irony of his words. He turned to Howland.

"Sergeant?"

Howland responded reflexively. "Yes, sir?"

"I seem to have lost my sword. Will you lend me yours?"

Howland weighed the purloined blade in his hand. His own sword had been taken away. This was the only weapon he and the brothers had between them. Nevertheless, he found Marren's outstretched hand and pressed the pommel into it.

"Thank you," Marren said. "I'll try to do some damage with it."

"Put half its length in Rakell if you want to do some real good!" said Malek bitterly.

They heard rather than saw Marren slip away. Hobbled by Nils' injuries, the three men made slow progress across the field. Every time a loud noise erupted behind them, they stopped and looked around, but as far as they could tell, they weren't being pursued.

By the time they reached the spot where Howland, Ezu, and Amergin had met their escort at the beginning of the night's adventures, the vision of all three men was nearly fully restored. They circled wide and came upon the trench, with its fearful hedge of stakes and earthen rampart.

"Who goes there?" called a voice tentatively from the darkened defenses.

"Fangoth!" Howland replied.

"Is that you, Sir Howland?"

At his clipped affirmation, a plank wobbled over the rampart and fell across the trench. Malek and Nils tottered across. Howland came last.

Khorr, backed by wide-eyed farmers clutching cut-down lances, greeted Howland heartily. They were likewise delighted to see Nils and Malek again. The happy reunion palled, however, when Khorr looked behind them and asked, "Where's Amergin and Ezu?"

"We got separated," Howland answered grimly. "Keep a sharp lookout for them."

On Nowhere common, nervous villagers crowded around to hear Howland's account of the mission.

"Rakell lives," he said heavily. Groans followed. "He never had any intention of parleying with us. He only agreed to the meeting so he could capture and decide our fates first."

Raika asked about Amergin and Ezu. Howland told them everything, from Ezu's powerful "sneeze" to their rescue by Marren uth Aegar.

"Ezu a true wizard? I don't believe it!" Robien said.

The other hired fighters were not so skeptical. Raika, remembering her special gifts and the uncanny way Ezu came and went, found it easy to believe the strange foreigner had hidden powers.

As for Marren, older folk like Caeta recalled when he first came to Nowhere. Weak and wounded, his clothing and horse had marked him as a man once of substance in spite of his diminished circumstances. Nilea, a village woman, had nursed him to health. She subsequently became his mate and the mother of Laila. Marren survived but never prospered. The wasting sickness took hold of him, and he spent twenty years dying a hair's breadth every day.

"So Marren was a Knight," Nils mused. "If Laila becomes your wife, will that make you noble, too?"

Malek saw no humor in the question and glared fiercely at his older brother.

"One more thing you should all know," Howland said in a low, shamed voice. "Just as Marren and Rakell were old comrades in arms, so too were Rakell and I."

No one responded until Malek said, "You spoke of your service to the Dark Order. You were forced to do what you did. It was not of your choosing."

"No, I was a sergeant in the army of Lord Burnond Everride. I was never a Knight, much less a general. I lied about that. I've misled you all this time. You should have an honest commander, not someone like me, and I recommend you choose Robien."

"Nonsense!" said the bounty hunter. "No one here could have commanded as well. No one has more experience of war than you. You are our commander, Knight or not."

Caeta agreed. "We don't care what you were before you came to us. Since the battle began, you've proven again and again you deserve our trust. If you are not a Knight, so be it, but we have made you our general. No one else."

Howland looked away, ashamed to let anyone see the color in his face. If ever there was a time for a blindness spell, this was it.

* * * * *

Just before dawn, Amergin returned. He rose up from the uncut grass and ran to the barricades on the northeast side of the village. Easily vaulting the tangle of fences and vines, he stole up on the two farmers on guard there. Both were sleeping.

He tapped one on the shoulder. The scruffy, yellow-bearded man awoke with a yell and grabbed the spear leaning against his shoulder. His shout aroused his comrade, who dropped his spear, tried to pick it up, and promptly tripped over the shaft of the other man's weapon.

Amergin clamped a slim brown hand over the yelping farmer's mouth. Eyes wide, he saw he was facing the Kagonesti forester, not a bandit sneak attack.

"Know me?"

The farmer nodded, slowly.

"Don't shout. Yes?"

Again a nod.

Amergin took his hand away.

"Happy day!" exclaimed the not-so watchful watchman. "We feared you were taken by the enemy!"

The fallen guard got up and likewise expressed delight upon seeing Amergin. "Howland returned with Malek and Nils," he said. "Did you know Sir Howland was not a real Knight? They say he used to be Rakell's bootblack, or something—"

"No, stupid, he used to groom Marren's horse!" He added for Amergin's benefit, "Our Marren was a *real* Knight—"

The elf left them arguing. Beyond the line of huts, Amergin came upon Raika's spearmen, deployed to intercept anyone who emerged. They'd heard the guards' cries and taken up positions without waiting to rouse their captain from her bedroll. Some deeds were more dangerous than others.

The forester quickly found himself surrounded by a bristling ring of spears. The farmers knew Amergin, of course, but they were so shaken by their ordeal that the elf had to calm them before they lowered their weapons.

Robien arrived. Howland was still resting after his busy night, so the bounty hunter was in charge.

In Elvish, he said to Amergin, "Glad to see my bounty is still safe."

Amergin did not deign to respond to this sally. In the common tongue he said, "So Howland is safe." With rare emotion, he added, "What of Ezu?"

"There's been no sign of him," Robien answered. Nor had Marren or his daughter Laila turned up.

When the sun was well up, a shout of dismay went up from Carver's lookouts, posted on the hut roofs. Their cries awoke Howland, who left the shadow of the old well and asked what it was the young sentinels saw.

"The bandits! They've staked someone out!"

Howland, Robien, and Malek clambered onto the nearest hut to get a look. Sure enough, the bandits had erected two poles on the plain, out of whippik range. Between the poles was the dark outline of a man, tied to them and hanging limply.

"Is it Ezu?" called Carver from his perch.

Robien shaded his eyes. "I don't think so. Whoever it is has white hair—"

"Marren!"

Malek asked, "What about Laila? Where is she?"

Howland had no comforting reply. The general of Nowhere slid down the thatch and dropped to the ground. Robien and Malek followed., "I wonder what did happen to Ezu?" the old soldier mused. "I don't think normal bonds can hold our friend the traveler."

Malek broke away, running to a stand of captured arms. He sorted through a pile of swords, trying to find one straight and sharp. Each blade that failed to measure up he tossed aside violently. The others followed him, exchanging looks.

"Going somewhere?" asked Howland mildly. The angry youth ignored him.

"You escaped once by the fortunate intervention of a wandering wizard. You won't be so lucky a second time."

"Talk about luck!" Malek said, eyes blazing. "You went to kill Rakell and failed. Then you got lucky and escaped. I will not fail, and I do not care about your brand of luck!"

He found the best of the hard-used blades and shoved

it through the rough sash tied around his waist. Howland and Robien did nothing to stop Malek as he stormed to the south barricade and started climbing over it.

"You won't get to Rakell, you know," Howland said.

"I don't care about Rakell or my life! I must save the woman I love!"

"If you're killed, what good will your sacrifice do?"

Malek faltered. Howland pressed on. "If you'll stay here and put that fury to good use, defending your neighbors, I'll make you a pledge," he said.

Malek halted atop an old rail fence. "What do you mean? Speak plainly!"

"Just this: If you remain here and fight like a soldier instead of a love-struck berserker, I pledge that I myself will kill Rakell and do my best to free Laila. She hasn't been punished like her father. I'll wager she is safe for the time being. The coming battle will decide everything, and I pledge to you that I will trade Rakell's life for my own. Is that plain enough?"

Malek snorted contemptuously, but Howland waved aside the young farmer's disdain.

"On my honor—" he almost said "as a Knight"—"On my honor as a soldier. Good enough?"

Malek jumped down. He went to Howland and put out his hand. Before he could grasp it, Malek drew the nicked edge of the blade over his own palm, drawing blood. Never taking his eyes off Malek, Howland drew his dagger and scored a cut on his hand too. Old soldier and young farmer pressed their bleeding palms together, wordlessly sealing their pact.

"Good enough," said Malek.

NOWHERE

Chapter Fifteen

. . . Shall Reap Fire

All night long every living soul in Nowhere labored. When Howland's plan to cut off the dragon's head failed, there seemed no hope of staving off a final, destructive attack. However, the general of Nowhere had one last stratagem. Everyone's help was required to make it work. Almost a quarter of their strength had been killed or wounded, but the remaining defenders strove mightily through the night. The night took on a chill, the first hint of autumn, and the clarity of the cool air brought out every one of the myriad stars salting the heavens.

Looking up from his labors, Howland felt for the first time that there were no gods looking down on them. Live or die, their fate was in their own hands. Such notions used to worry him. Now, faced with imminent destruction,

247

he found the spiritual solitude strangely comforting. If there were no good gods to come to their aid, there were also no evil ones to persecute them.

Dawn arrived in a light mist. Unlike the ponderous fogs they'd experienced before, this mist clung low to the ground, running in thin streams before the south wind. Day broke dark, with heavy clouds rising in the east and south. The bellies of the clouds were gray as slate, heavy with rain.

Villagers were still hauling baskets of earth to an earthen redoubt backed up against the rampart behind the trench. A simple triangle with sides eight feet high, the redoubt was constructed all in one night, using all the dirt formerly packed into the farmers' huts. Howland wanted to dismantle the roofs and use the rafters to make a palisade atop the mound, but the villagers ran out of dirt—and time.

A very tired Raika was overseeing the dumping of earth when she heard a low rumbling, combined with a high-pitched squeaking. Standing on the highest part of the dirt pile, she looked for the source of the sound. It originated from the bandits' eastern camp. A large, indistinct object was rolling through the barley stubs, propelled by more than a dozen grunting warriors.

"Sir Howland!" she cried. "They're coming from the east!"

Howland, Malek, and Robien climbed the loose earthen mound and spied what Raika had seen.

"A siege engine?" asked the elf.

"I can't tell. It isn't tall enough to be a fighting tower," Howland said.

Even as they tried to evaluate this new threat, the bandits ceased their shoving and stopped. Distant shouted commands reached the defenders, the words indistinct.

"Hey! Hey!" Carver was standing on one of the huts. "They're forming up to the south!"

A quick glance confirmed the kender's alarming report. Lines of horsemen had filed out of the south camp and taken up places along the low rise, facing the village. Their ranks had been thinned, but they still represented a daunting force for the depleted defenders.

Amergin, out of the village on reconnaissance, came running back, chased by three lancers. He vaulted neatly over the chest-high barricade on the north side of Nowhere, leaving his pursuers frantically trying to rein in. Carver's boys pelted them with whippik darts, but the riders fended off the missiles with their shields before galloping away.

Out of breath, Amergin presented himself to his commander.

"They're coming," he panted. "All that remain."

"From the east and south, too." Howland looked down from the mound at the hard-pressed Kagonesti. "Thank you for your efforts."

Amergin dismissed his gratitude with a slight toss of his head.

"They mean to come at us from all sides this time," Raika muttered.

"It was bound to happen," Robien said. "Could we—?"

He never got the chance to finish. There was a loud crash from the east, followed by a soft whistling. The next thing the people of Nowhere knew, a sixty-pound boulder landed just inside the ring of houses. Screaming children and old folks scattered as the rock, chiseled round to fly true, bounced on the hard soil and sailed on. It ricocheted twice more, finally burying itself in the soft slope of the new redoubt.

"So, they've brought out the catapult," said Howland.

"Can they knock down our defenses?" asked Raika.

"They can smash up the huts, but their stones won't have much effect on a pile of earth." Howland pointed to the hysterical villagers cowering by their homes. "Get them inside," he said. "There'll be more stones, ten or more an hour if the catapult crew is good."

Malek, who'd stayed at Howland's side most of the night, wondered where the bandits were getting their projectiles. "You don't find stones like that lying about, not in this country."

Howland agreed, looking a bit relieved. "They must have brought a store of boulders with them. That'll limit their fire." He gave orders to recover any loose catapult stones and haul them to the top of the earthen mound.

"What for?" asked Raika.

"I mean to return them to their owners."

Wounded villagers as well as those too old or too young to fight clambered up the sides of the mound. Inside, the dirt walls were held back by stakes, planks, and matting, leaving a tight sheltered zone inside, roughly twenty-four feet by twelve at the widest point. The villagers not fighting crowded in, huddling close together. Babies wailed. At one point a catapult stone hit the edge of the rampart sending a shower of dirt over the cowering families. Panic broke out, as one wounded villager cried out that they were being buried alive.

At this juncture Khorr appeared above them, brandishing a battle-axe taken from a fallen bandit. With all the power of his considerable voice, he boomed,

Take heart, hopeless, helpless ones!
Heroes of thy own hearth help thee!
Spilling the blood of the invader!

It was as much from the force of the minotaur's delivery as the words he recited that the terrified villagers were calmed. Khorr's band of spearmen raised their weapons high and cheered. Not to be outdone, Raika bullied her contingent into a battle cry, too. The result was not as stirring as Raika wanted.

"Milksops!" she shouted. "My one-legged granny can shout better than you!"

"Why does your granny have one leg?" asked Bakar.

"Shut up! Now yell like you mean it!"

From out on the plain, the bandits raised a cheer of their own. To Howland it sounded forced. This was not the fight they had joined Rakell's band for. Easy pickings and plunder, that's what they preferred. Brawling with fear-maddened peasants was not the sweet life they'd been promised.

Carver came running. The usually unflappable kender was genuinely agitated, though it was impossible to say if he was frightened or thrilled by the news he bore.

He tugged Howland's shirt sleeve, and when the old soldier bent near, the kender said (quite loudly) in his ear, "Ogres!"

Howland paled. Raika uttered one of her favorite expletives. Robien wiped his smooth chin and lips with one hand, drawing air in through his teeth with a sharp hiss.

"How many?" asked Howland.

Carver counted to ten on his fingers and said, "Six!"

"Khorr!"

The minotaur circled around the mound. "Yes, Sir Howland?"

"I have an especially dangerous task for you." He relayed Carver's news. "It's your job to try to stop the ogres."

Khorr tapped the head of his axe against the palm of his large hand. "Do you think it is possible?"

"You must try. Our survival depends on breaking every element of Rakell's attack. No matter how well we fend off his human warriors, everything will be for nought if the ogres can break through at will."

The minotaur nodded his massive, horned head thoughtfully.

Howland clapped Khorr on the arm. "Good. You can do it. A minotaur is worth any number of ogres, after all!"

"But is a poet worth six trained warriors, I wonder?" Khorr replied.

"Good stuff for your epic," said Raika encouragingly.

"If I live to compose it."

The sixth boulder launched at the village demolished a hut on the north side, sending up a plume of yellow dust. Because the huts had been emptied of dirt, they fell easy victims to the plunging stones. The catapult crew shouted with joy at their success, but Howland sent Malek and four farmers to recover the rock.

The bombardment continued until the mist evaporated. A hot, humid wind scoured the scene, driving dust in the bandits' faces. The wind died. The turgid clouds, which had been crawling from east to west like a school of malignant jellyfish, stopped with the wind. For a moment, calm reigned.

Trumpets blared on three sides. Howland shook hands with everyone close by—Khorr, Raika, Carver, Amergin, Caeta, Malek, and Robien.

"Good luck," he told them all.

Everyone ran to their place. The outer line of defense,

the huts and barricade, would be defended until the enemy broke through, which Howland conceded would eventually occur. When that happened, everyone was to fall back to the redoubt. Once there, there was no place left to retreat.

A few fat droplets of rain landed in the dust. As the bandit army started forward, a light shower began. Howland looked up at the sky.

"This is good," he mused to Robien. "Rain will slacken their bowstrings and weaken their catapult skein."

"Blade to blade, then," said the bounty hunter.

Howland grunted.

The three bandit contingents were not well-coordinated. The southern band, presumably under Rakell's command, started forward early. The eastern segment, where the ogres were stationed, got moving next, but the slow-walking creatures held their human allies back, and Rakell's mounted troops moved farther ahead of them. Lastly came the northern contingent, mostly men on foot, marching in loose order toward the little ring of huts.

A horse neighed close by. Howland turned to see Raika mounted on the animal. Bakar handed her a brigand's lance, which she couched inexpertly under her arm.

"Bend your arm more!" Howland called to her.

Raika acknowledged his advice with a wave. She turned her horse around and trotted to the east end of the village to await the ogres.

Forty yards from Nowhere, Rakell's southern force lowered their lances and charged. Howland couldn't believe an experienced commander would allow his cavalry to charge huts and fences. He ordered Amergin and his slingers forward to empty as many saddles as they could.

"Save one iron star for Rakell!" Howland said.

Amergin held out his hand, displaying the missile he was keeping for just that purpose.

At ten yards the slingers hurled, felling six bandits at once. Two tangled their feet in their stirrups and were dragged by their charging mounts. Amergin drew his group back a few steps and hurled again. Four bandits went down as well as two horses, then the enemy was upon them. The lead riders leaped their horses over the low barricade, coming down amidst the slingers. Amergin and the rest drew swords, but they were scattered and intimidated by the bandits' lances.

"Come on, they need help!" Howland cried. With Robien and ten farmers with spears, they ran to the slingers' rescue.

The second line of horsemen reached the barricade, dismounted, and rushed the barriers with their swords. Carver led in his young whippikers. Leap-frogging from roof to roof, they got above the enemy and scourged them with darts made from the bandits' own arrows. Furious, some of the bandits abandoned the barricade and tried climbing the huts to get at the dart-throwers.

"Go back, all of you!" Carver shouted, pulling boys and girls away. Foolishly brave, some children were willing to go toe to toe with the bandits, but they wouldn't stand a chance.

Two bandits stood unsteadily on one roof. The thatch, which supported the diminutive kender and children well enough, had been softened by rain and now sagged uncertainly under the armored warriors. Stung by days of frustration and defeat, their faces contorted, the bandits gingerly crossed the conical roof, slashing at the fleeing children.

Carver let out a yell and drew his sword, a brigand's curved saber he'd ground down to suit his reach. Scrambling over the tight thatch, he drew off one bandit, and they traded cuts. Carver parried clumsily, holding the ungainly weapon in both hands. The bandit wasn't much better off. After a third blow, his left foot plunged through the roof, and he fell, losing his sword. Carver darted in and plunged his short blade into the bandit's ribs, behind his iron breastplate.

He had no time to celebrate his victory. The second bandit dealt Carver a smashing blow to the head with the crossguard of his sword, sending the kender stumbling backward. His new opponent raised his blade high for the killing blow. Carver tried to deflect it, but the thatch gave way under them both. Kender and bandit plunged through and vanished.

Howland saw Carver fall, but he was deeply engaged with enemy horsemen. He and the farmers had rushed to attack, jabbing their spears at the faces of bandits and horses alike. They danced backwards when the puffing steeds stormed at them then advanced again when horse and rider turned away to face other threats. In this way they managed to bring down three or four bandits, who were promptly dispatched as they rolled helplessly on the ground.

One after another, Amergin's slingers had been lanced or ridden down until only the elf and two village women remained. They retreated to an alley between huts. There they held off several onslaughts until bandits swarmed at them from the other direction. Amergin and his surviving slingers were swallowed up in a wave of flashing armor and snorting horses.

Seeing Amergin beset, Howland forgot the sword in his hand and snatched up a loose stone, which he hurled at a near rider. It clanged off his helmet, dazing him, and in the confusion that followed he was speared from three directions by desperate farmers. Raika swooped in, trailed by her spear company. She might have known next to nothing about wielding a lance, but even a tyro can stick a sharp point into a target. The brave woman aimed her weapon at a well-turned out bandit with saffron plumes on his helmet. Her lance head skittered across his ribbed cuirass and caught on the brace on his shoulder. The brigand and Saifhumi sailor went flying off their respective horses. Raika bounced up, full of fight, but the bandit rolled over dead, pierced through the throat.

Howland fought his way to her side. "What of the ogres?" he yelled.

"Still coming, but slow! My one-legged granny—"

He missed the rest, as he dodged an enemy lance. The southern attack had disintegrated. Remnants of the enemy force were streaming the gaps, however. Panting hard, Howland watched them as light rain flecked his face, stinging from many small cuts and scratches.

"Reform your people," he told Raika. "Where's Khorr?"

"I left him to watch the ogres."

"All right. Go back and wait with him. He will need your help."

The villagers carried off their own dead and wounded, secreting them inside the redoubt. Howland tried to look for Amergin, but men and horses lay in heaps in the narrow lane, and arrows were raining down on the battle scene from enemy archers on the plains.

He and Robien then tried to push their way inside the hut where Carver had vanished, but the weakened structure began to collapse the moment they yanked at the door.

"Lookout! Catapult!"

Howland and Robien threw themselves down. A smooth sphere of sandstone hurtled through the air with deceptive slowness. It hit a few yards from Robien and dug in, caught by the thin layer of mud made by the rain.

Howland rounded up the closest available villagers. Only six were still fit to fight, three women and three men. Howland's little army was thinning every hour.

With their kender leader gone, the young boys and girls also left the rooftops and presented themselves to Howland. The old soldier was deeply moved by their gallantry. They were too young to stand and fight armored horsemen, but the situation was so grave he had little choice. He ordered the young folk to take up positions atop the redoubt, guarding the salvaged catapult stones.

"Stand ready to roll them down when I give the signal," Howland said. "Not before! We'll be fighting with our backs to you, so we won't see them coming until the last moment. Wait for my command."

Carver's whippikers responded unanimously, "Yes, Sir Howland!"

At the far end of the village, Khorr bellowed a warning. The ogres squad, six strong as Carver had reported, had almost reached the first huts. The minotaur and his loyal spearmen formed a wedge. Behind them were arrayed Raika's band in loose formation.

Khorr stood at the front, waiting, his axe laid on his shoulder. No one saw his lips moving soundlessly as he recited the fourteenth *Windwave Ballad* under his breath. It was the *Song of the Shipwrecked Sailor* about a minotaur who fights off a tribe of ferocious cannibals single-handed then persishes when the battle is over from the prick of a poisoned arrow.

The leading ogres put aside their weapons and tore at the barricade with their bare hands. Great nobby knuckles flexed, and timbers snapped like straw. Seeing this, Khorr launched himself at the ogres. His men, full of pride in their stand in the trench days ago, followed close behind.

The first ogre had just broken through the flimsy barrier of fencing and vines when the burly minotaur appeared before him. Used to dealing with puny human, elf, or dwarf foes, the ogre was taken aback to see such a large creature rushing at him. He stepped back and groped for his battle-axe, hanging by a lanyard from his waist. Khorr charged in, kicking and swinging his broad blade. Khorr's axe severed the ogre's hands at his wrists. They hit the ground still gripping the axe handle.

Sweeping his axe up, Khorr ripped the ogre from belt to chin. Mortally wounded, the creature dropped but too slowly for the minotaur, who planted a foot on the ogre's chest and kicked him aside and continued on.

Consternation reigned among the remaining ogres. No one had told them they would have to face a battle-mad minotaur, the only creature in the world ogres regarded with a degree of awe. They abandoned their attempt to tear down the barricade, backing away from Nowhere to regroup.

Raika slipped in behind Khorr in time to see the ogres beating a retreat. Spotting the thoroughly dead ogre Khorr killed lying in heap six yards away, Raika whistled excitedly.

"Now yell," she advised her towering friend. "Brandish your axe!"

Khorr threw back his head and roared so loudly that even Raika felt a thrill of fear. He made chopping motions with his bloodstained blade, cleaving the air in all directions.

"How's that?" he muttered over his shoulder to her.

"I'm convinced," Raika said.

The ogres were made of stern stuff, however. Overcoming their surprise, they stood shoulder to shoulder and screamed defiance back. In unison, they raised their axes and started for Khorr at a dead run.

"I could use your help," Khorr called. Crouching behind what remained of the barrier, the farmers extended their spears and braced themselves.

"What, no poetry?" Raika said, licking her dry lips. No amount of rain seemed to moisten them.

Khorr blinked his limpid brown eyes. For once he couldn't think of an appropriate stanza to quote. Maybe the old legends of heroes who fought with a never-ending stream of verse on their lips were just that, tired old legends—

Only one word came to mind, Raika's favorite obscenity. Khorr said it flatly. Behind him, the Saifhumi woman laughed long and loud.

"Now *that's* poetry!"

The ogres hit the defenders like a landslide. One of them literally burst through the shell of an empty hut, scattering wattle and daub everywhere. Khorr caught the lead ogre's thrust with the flat of his axe and tried to turn the creature's blade away, but the ogre was powerful. Khorr's bronze muscles coiled, writhing under his skin like snakes in a sack. Slowly, then with increasing speed, he turned the ogre's axe, despite the fact his hulking foe was using both thick arms to resist Khorr.

Raika popped up under the minotaur's arm. She ran her iron-tipped spear into the ogre's armpit. Dark blood gushed forth. He tried to bat the woman's spear away, but when he let go of his axe with one hand, Khorr overpowered him.

The ogre's right arm flew back, and in the next instant the minotaur cleaved his skull.

Behind the first ogre was another, this one armed with a pair of cleaverlike swords called falchions. He came at Khorr with both blades flailing, and the minotaur had to give ground. Raika jabbed at the ogre, who chopped the head off her spear. She dropped the useless pole and whipped out her sword. She felt as if she were facing a bear with a dirk.

With a screech, one of the ogre's falchions slashed across Khorr's chest. His banded armor stopped much of the blow, but bright lines of blood appeared. If the minotaur felt any pain, Khorr didn't show it. He chopped hard, not at the ogre's hands but at his weapons. Catching the left falchion on its flat edge, Khorr's axe cracked the wrought-iron blade. Khorr brought his right foot back and parried the ogre's next attack. Weakened by the minotaur's blow, the ogre's left blade snapped off. He threw down the stump of the broken weapon and lunged point-first with the remaining one. Khorr was taken completely off-guard. Six inches of iron pierced his belly.

He grunted in surprise. His grotesque foe exposed yellow tusks in a ferocious snarl of triumph. Khorr shook his head and backed off the ogre's blade then drove the upper point of his axe into his opponent's chest. Driven by the minotaur's mighty muscles, it went through a quarter inch of bronze cuirass like a nail through a pewter plate. Khorr gave the axe a hard twist, cracking the ogre's ribs apart. The monster fell dead at his feet.

The minotaur poet staggered backward, blood seeping from his wound. Raika sheathed her sword and tried to shore up her great companion.

"Stand up! You'll be all right!" she cried.

"Who can be all right with a hole in his belly?" said Khorr. He dropped to one knee.

Three ogres were dead, slain by the minotaur. Now the other three crashed through the defenses on either side, scattering the farmers who tried to oppose them. Seeing their mighty leader falter, Khorr's men linked arms and threw themselves at the closest ogre. Eight men, each armed with a metal-tipped spear, impaled the ogre and drove him backwards into a still-standing hut. Ogre and hut collapsed together. Shouting Khorr's name, the villagers rallied behind him.

The last pair of ogres reached the village common, opposed only by Raika's scattered band. They encircled the ogres, keeping a safe distance while jabbing ineffectively at them.

Bolstered by the sight, Khorr rose to join the circle around the ogres. In as harsh and commanding a voice as he could muster, the minotaur said, "Lay down your arms and you shall be spared!"

The creature facing Khorr spat yellow phlegm. His meaning was clear.

Raika claimed a lost spear and urged her timid followers forward. Stabbing at the ogres' faces or feet, they kept them off balance long enough for Khorr to land a telling blow on the arm of the leader. This ogre sagged to the ground, and Khorr's men quickly finished him off, impaling him again and again.

Alone, the last ogre threw down his axe. The farmers, thinking he meant to give up, lowered their guard.

"Look out!" Raika screamed.

Drawing a dagger the size of Carver's sword, the last ogre took a great leap and landed on Khorr. Locked together, the giants toppled into the mud. Raika tried to rush in and stab the ogre in the back, but she was knocked down by a flying fist. The blow almost broke her jaw.

The dagger flashed once, twice, covered in blood as it rose. Khorr had lost his axe when the ogre tackled him. All he had left were his enormous hands. Despite his wounds, he got his foe in a headlock. Over and over they rolled, right to the center of Nowhere. At last Khorr got hold of the ogre's great flapping ear and with a supreme heave wrung his enemy's neck. It cracked like a flash of lightning. The ogre let out a final grunt, and his limbs went slack.

Raika was there. She and two farmers levered the ogre's stinking carcass off Khorr.

"Hey, poet!" she cried, "don't die yet!"

"Death is not the end," the minotaur said faintly. "Every epic closes with an epitaph."

His hand slowly opened. Into the mud fell his most prized possession, the *ronto*, the memory book Ezu had given to him.

Raika picked up the rain-spattered book. Howland, Robien, and the villagers from the redoubt came running up.

"In all my life I've never seen such a fight!" Howland exclaimed. "Did Khorr kill all the ogres single-handed?"

Raika looked up at Howland. She was glad of the rain coursing down her face.

"Yes. Yes, he did." She knew it wasn't true, but it would make a better story that way.

NOWHERE

Chapter Sixteen

Nowhere Again

Rain fell harder, changing the dusty common into a bowl of mud. Both sides used the downpour as an excuse to draw apart. When Rakell's hired ogres were repulsed, the bandits on the east side of Nowhere retreated hastily. Unsupported, the northern prong of the attack also withdrew without closing with the defenders.

If the bandits were hard-pressed, the defenders of Nowhere were bereft. Only a few adults escaped any injures, and these carried Khorr's body back to the redoubt, struggling through the mud all the way. Wrapped in the best blankets the farmers had, Khorr was laid to rest in the trench he had so ably defended.

Atop the earthen wall, Howland looked out over the somber scene, sorely troubled. In a single engagement he'd

lost half his remaining people. Brave Khorr was dead.
Carver was still missing. They'd not been able to dig out
the collapsed hut where he'd plunged through the roof
fighting his bandit foe. Amergin had disappeared. During
the fight with the ogres, Rakell's men had cleared the field
of their dead and wounded, horses included, and of the
Kagonesti forester there was no sign. Dead or captured, he
was lost to Howland either way.

Caeta came to him with a steaming bowl of broth. She
draped a hairy cowhide cape over his shoulders to keep
the rain off.

"What word?" she said.

"A few riders passing between camps. That's all."
Howland sipped the broth. It was chicken, hot and salty.

"Why don't they give up? Haven't we cost them far
more than the worth of one little village?"

Howland pulled the cape up closer to his neck. "That
may be the problem," he replied. "We've hurt them
greatly. Now Rakell may be fighting for the sake of pride,
not profit."

She didn't ask what he thought their chances were.
Everyone knew there was no escape.

The rain persisted. Late in the afternoon a lookout
cried out for Howland. He climbed the slippery slope of
the redoubt and immediately beheld what had alarmed the
farmer.

Walking uncertainly across the harvest-bared south
plain came a lone figure, cloaked and cowled against the
weather. There was nothing special about him, save that
he was alone and on foot. He had no visible weapons, nor
did he carry a flag of truce.

Howland called for Robien. The bounty hunter hastened to Howland's side.

"Water's getting deep inside," the elf said, indicating the interior of the redoubt. Rainwater had collected to the point that the wounded and aged villagers had to abandon the redoubt for drier positions atop the earthen wall. A few even went back to their homes, saying it was better to die under their own roof than to cower in the mud.

"Never mind the water," Howland said. "We have a visitor."

Robien spotted the solitary figure. "Who can it be?"

"We'll know soon. In the mean time, keep a sharp watch on other fronts. This may be a trick to draw our attention away from another spot."

The loner on foot moved deliberately, but before long he was near the outer ring of huts. Howland, Raika, and Malek went to the same gap in the houses the bandits had broken down earlier. As soon as Howland entered the narrow lane, he saw the stranger had stopped. He stood outside the former barricade, unmoving, as rain streamed off his smoke-colored cowl.

Raika bared her blade. "Doesn't feel right!"

Howland nodded but moved forward. Malek caught his arm and stopped him.

"Remember Khorr's tale?" he said. "Don't you become the dragon who loses his head!"

Howland certainly didn't want to be assassinated, but someone had to meet the stranger. To mollify his companions, he turned back the flaps of his cowhide cape, leaving his hands free to take sword in hand.

They picked their way through the trampled fence, broken weapons, and smell of blood. Six yards from the newcomer, Howland halted. Malek and Raika stood on either hand, ready for signs of treachery.

"Who goes there?"

Gloved hands rose and pushed back the cowl.

"Ezu!"

"Right-right! It is I, friends! May this one enter?"

Howland and Raika stood aside, making way for their odd companion. Ezu glided past, saying, "I had to wait until someone came to greet me. This one didn't want to be taken for a bandit!"

"How did you get here?" asked Raika.

"I walked."

"Didn't Rakell hold you or question you?" said Howland sharply.

"Oh, we had a few chats," Ezu replied. "I must say, I prefer your company to his. Such a difficult man."

Raika laughed harshly. "Difficult? It's a miracle he didn't separate your head from your shoulders!"

Ezu smiled. "He mentioned doing just that, but he could not harm me."

Howland caught Raika's eye. *Could* not harm?

"Laila—did you see Laila, my betrothed?" Malek asked desperately, clutching the traveler's arm.

"The blind man's daughter? I saw her. She is well."

They returned to the muddy common. Seeing the sea of muck, Ezu sighed gustily. "This is too much rain," he said to no one in particular.

"Why don't you make it stop?" said Raika sarcastically.

The day-long downpour slackened then ceased.

Wide-eyed, Malek said, "What *are* you?"

Ezu unclasped the frog at his neck and let the heavy woolen cloak slide from his shoulders. "Who controls the rain?" he asked. "Not I. I'm just a traveler."

Beams of sunshine slanted in low from the west. Ezu pointed to the nearest standing hut, saying, "I have been ordered to bring a private message to you, Sir Howland."

Raika and Malek returned to the redoubt, while Howland and Ezu entered the small hut alone. There was nothing inside but lumps of dirt leftover from when the house had been filled. A few errant rays of late afternoon sun filtered through the dripping thatch.

Howland folded his arms across his chest. "Well?"

"I carry a message from Lord Rakell," said Ezu. His costume seemed much the worse for wear, torn and spattered with mud. "He bade me tell you that you may leave the village with your people, and no one will harm you. How did he put it? 'Tell the sergeant he's acquitted himself well. He may take his honor and go.' "

"What happens to Nowhere once we're gone?"

Ezu shrugged.

"I see. Did Rakell say anything else?"

"No, but there are things you should know."

Ezu lowered his voice and glanced around conspiratorially. "Half the remaining bandits have abandoned him. When you killed his ogre mercenaries, many jumped on their horses and rode away."

Howland felt a surge of hope. "How many are left?"

"Hard to say. Twelve? Or twenty? I didn't see them altogether."

Twenty! That greatly improved the odds. Howland wrung the eccentric foreigner's hand.

"We may live through this yet!" he declared.

More soberly, he related the loss of Khorr, Amergin, and Carver. Ezu frowned and clasped a hand over his mouth.

"So many deaths! The poet, did you say? What a pity!"

A single trumpet blared outside. Howland jumped at the sound.

"How long did you have to deliver the message and for me to reply?"

"Not long enough, I think!"

They dashed outside. Defenders gathered on the redoubt shouted and gestured to the south plain. Howland darted around the hut and saw a small body of horsemen coming toward them.

"Rakell must have sent you go to distract us. It doesn't matter." Howland shucked off the cape and drew his sword. "Let's get to a safer spot."

As they made their way through the village he said, "You cast some kind of spell in Rakell's tent to prevent my death. Will you do as much now to save us all?"

The mud squelched with every step. For a moment Ezu said nothing, then he replied, "I cannot interfere. I'm only an observer here."

"Will you observe us dying? Will you stand by and allow yourself to be killed?" Howland demanded.

"No one will harm me," Ezu said.

Again, such bland confidence. Who was Ezu, that no one dared raise a weapon to him? Filled with sudden anger, Howland raised his sword over Ezu's head. Instead of thirty-two inches of tempered steel he was holding a bundle of five white lilies!

"What?" he said, dropping the flowers. Ezu clucked his tongue and retrieved Howland's sword from the mud.

"Careful," he said, handing over the bare blade. "You'll still need this."

Howland and Ezu scaled the redoubt, taking their place amid the remaining defenders. Raika handed him his helmet. The old soldier declined.

"I will fight without it," he said.

The oblique rays shining under the clouds cast odd highlights on the scene. Everything seemed tinted gold, down to the muddiest, dirtiest farmer clutching a battered spear. By the gilding light, Howland could see Ezu's news was true—the bandit camps north and east of the village looked empty and abandoned. A few scrappy tents still stood billowing in the breeze, but no men or horses were in sight.

Riding toward them at a modest trot was the last of Rakell's bandit horde. No more than twenty, each rider bore a pennant on his lance tip.

With water standing in the trench and the bottom of the redoubt, everyone left in Nowhere stood atop the triangular wall. Babes in arms, elders too bent to stand up, sick, wounded, and dying filled out the ranks of the hale. Glancing left and right, Howland estimated his effective strength at sixteen.

"No one's to leave the wall!" he shouted. "Let the enemy come to us! Make ready the catapult stones. If they ride within ten yards of the foot of the mound, roll a stone down on them!"

The bandits entered the village at three points previously breached in the barricade. No one contested their entry. Once inside, they reformed on the common. Dressing their ranks, the horsemen waited silently.

A single horse and rider moved out from the line. He came within a dozen yards of the redoubt and stopped.

"Howland uth Ungen!"

Leaning on a well-worn spear, the old soldier yelled back, "What do you want, Deyamon?"

The bandit chief known as Lord Rakell folded his arms across the pommel of his saddle.

"So, you remember me now?"

"I do. Deyamon uth Kayr, a minor Knight in the army of Lord Burnond Everride. Why did you leave his service? Weren't his slaughters enough for you?"

"Any man, even a battle-tested warrior like Lord Burnond, craves peace once he reaches a certain age," the bandit said tersely. "Burnond put up his sword, but I cannot. I was not born to collect taxes or drill goblin infantry. I came here to make a kingdom of my own!"

"Then you've failed." Howland waved to the farmers and their families around him. "These people have seen to that."

"Yes, I underestimated you, sergeant. I was wrong. Now I say for the last time, come down from there, and join with me. Together we'll carve out a realm and rule it side by side!"

"Rule on the backs of the poor and helpless? No thank you." He held up his sword. "Come and take us, or ride away, Deyamon. Those are your only choices."

Rakell angrily snapped the visor of his helmet shut. His reply, if any, was lost when he did so, but he turned his horse back and rode quickly to his men. For a brief moment Howland thought the bandits might depart. He was wrong.

Hurrahing, the front row of horsemen spurred forward. Their lances were just long enough to reach the top of the redoubt wall.

"Lie down!" Howland called to his followers.

The sides of the earthen mound were too soft and steep for the horses to climb, so the bandits were left with no option but to ride up and down, poking at any hostile face that appeared on the rampart.

"Give 'em the stones!" Raika said. She and four village children rolled a sixty pound catapult shot to the edge and let go. Slowed a bit by the mud, the boulder still cut down a pair of horses, throwing the riders down as well. Cheering, the villagers rolled three more stones, but the bandits knew they were coming now and easily guided their mounts around them.

"Enough!" Howland said. "Save them for later!"

Rakell's second and last line of bandits dismounted, drawing swords and fixing shields on their arms. They tramped through the muck past their floundering comrades.

Some of the boys peppered them with whippik darts, and those slingers taught by Amergin thickened the hail with stones and stars. The armored warriors shrugged off the bombardment and started up the slope.

"Line up here! Shoulder to shoulder, that's right!" Howland and Raika pushed spear-armed villagers into a tight line while Robien cleared the non-combatants out of harm's way.

"Lower your spears! Lean into them!"

Rakell's men advanced into the spiny hedge of spear points. They beat the sharp tips aside with the swords and warded off thrusts with their shields. It was hard, fighting uphill, but their superior strength and training gradually overcame the other obstacles. Some farmers pulled back with shattered shafts and headless spears. Raika grabbed anyone retreating and forced them into line again.

"I've got no head!" wailed one farmer, waving his decapitated spear.

"I can see that!" Raika snapped, slapping the back of the poor man's skull, "but you've got six feet of hardwood. Keep the enemy off with it!"

The first wave of attackers, seeing their comrades advancing, got off their horses and joined the fight. Many slipped and rolled down the soft earthen mound, but spurred on by Rakell's example they rose and tried again.

The first bandits neared the rampart. Howland and Robien stepped up, swords ready. At the opposite end of the defender's line, Raika drew her sword, too.

Howland saw Rakell in the midst of his men, struggling up the slope. He deliberately stepped back from the edge to allow the bandits room enough to stand on equal footing. The line of spears pivoted away, forming a new line at right angles to the first.

Rakell's etched helmet bobbed into view. Howland waited. Robien moved in beside him.

"Leave him to me," Howland said calmly. The bounty hunter acknowledged his words with a curt nod.

Robien sprang forward, taking on the first bandit to reach the top. He kicked mud in the man's face, blinding him. Scrubbing desperately with his mailed hand, the lead bandit failed to parry Robien's long lunge. The elf's slim sword found a gap and slid in. Robien had to use his foot to free his blade when the bandit went face down in the mud.

Rakell reached the top and found a clear space. Howland was waiting for him.

He opened his visor. "So, it is single combat with you, sergeant? You're not gentle-born."

"Noble is as noble does," Howland barked. "I may be a disgraced man-at-arms, but you're a thief and a murderer, so we can fight as equals, don't you think?"

In answer, Rakell hurled himself at Howland. Fifteen years younger and five inches taller, he moved with surprising speed. Howland found the bandit chief's blade flashed close indeed. Only by yielding ground did he keep off Rakell's point.

He countered with short swings to keep Rakell off-balance. Once Howland's blade skidded off the chief's curved breastplate, and Rakell rewarded him with a heavy blow on the jaw. Howland staggered back, almost losing his grip on his sword. Stunned, he moved too slowly to counter the headlong thrust Rakell aimed at his chest. Howland brought his sword up, too late, too slowly.

Something gray and brown flashed between them. Howland saw Malek had leaped in front of him. The farmer hacked at Rakell with amateurish fury, enough so to force the former Knight back. Rakell countered with his shield, driving the boss into Malek's gut. The valiant young farmer fell to his knees, all air gone from his lungs. Rakell stood over him, his blade poised to run Malek through.

With a clang, Howland interposed his sword. Angry to the point of foolhardiness, the old soldier punched Rakell through his open visor. Blood coursed from the bandit chief's nose. Howland hit him again and kicked Malek until the latter crawled out of the way, collapsing out of Rakell's reach.

On they dueled. Rakell scored a cut on Howland's left forearm, and Howland beat a thrust and knocked the helmet off Rakell's head. They drew apart, panting heavily. Rakell's lip and chin were stained with blood, and Howland's eye was swelling shut.

They exchanged four fast cuts, neither man budging, then Rakell evaded Howland's blade with a viciously timed upthrust. It caught Howland in the hand. His sword spun away. He stepped back and drew his dagger, though an eight-inch weapon was meagre defense against Rakell's long sword.

They both lunged, Howland turning under the taller man's attack, trying to find a weakness in Rakell's armor. They struggled and heaved until Howland suddenly felt

Rakell stiffen in his grasp. Their eyes met. What Howland saw was not shock or fear but hatred—bitter, deep-rooted hatred.

Rakell's knees folded, but Howland saw no obvious wounds on the man. No one was near enough to have stabbed the bandit, and he saw no arrow in Rakell either.

Still clutching Howland's tattered sleeve, Rakell fell on his back, eyes wide and staring. He clung to life, shuddering, trying to bring his sword up for one last swing. In mercy, Howland finished his foe with a dagger thrust.

Finding Rakell's helmet, he raised it on the stump of a spear shaft, crying, "Rakell is dead! Rakell is dead!"

Robien and Raika, still fighting, saw the bandit chief's helmet and raised the cry themselves.

All along the line, the bandits turned their backs and fled. A few were struck down as they ran, but for the most part the farmers fell to their knees and gratefully watched the brigands leave. Before Rakell's blood cooled on the churned earth, not a living bandit remained in Nowhere. Alone or in small groups, they rode pell-mell for the horizon, taking nothing with them but the blades in their hands and the armor on their backs.

A curious quiet fell over the village. Howland let the pole and helmet fall and sat down hard beside Rakell's lifeless body. Next thing he knew, Robien was shaking him, saying, "Howland! Howland, can you speak?"

"Yes."

"We did it, Sir Howland, we did it!"

Raika stalked over and dropped heavily by her commander. She voiced a few choice curses, but she hadn't the strength to make them ring. She leaned against Howland's back and groaned, "Is there any strong drink left in this forsaken hole?"

A jug appeared under her chin. Surprised, Raika looked up to see who held it.

"Drink," said Caeta. "All we have is yours."

Malek got to his feet and ran down the hill. Everyone knew where he was going. He dashed out of the village, straight for the bandits' southern camp, crying "Laila!"

"You know, my family traces their line back to Kith-Kanan," Robien said, grinning, "but I've never seen or heard of anything like the duel you had with Rakell! Bards will sing about it for a hundred years!"

Raika leaned forward to examine Rakell. She only meant to close his lifeless eyes, but as she turned his head away, she noticed something. Blinking once or twice, she settled back and drank deep from Caeta's jug. It wasn't fruit wine, or farmer's barley dew either—it was brown rum, and it seared Raika's throat all the way down.

She held out the jug to Howland, gasping, "To you, sir!"

He had a modest sip, then passed it to Robien. The Kagonesti, without drinking, handed it off to the wounded Nils. While elf and farmer exchanged happy greetings, Raika turned to Howland.

"Quiet a fight you had," she said.

"I didn't win," he said slowly.

"I know."

With her toe, she pushed Rakell's head to one side, exposing the back of his neck. There, almost hidden by the bandit chief's thick hair, was a sharp, angular bit of metal, well coated with the dead man's blood. It took Howland a few moments to realize what it was: an iron star.

"Amergin!"

"Keep your voice down," Raika muttered. "Our friend lives—but things will go more easily for him if Robien believes him slain."

Howland agreed. The bounty hunter could truthfully tell the Brotherhood of Quen back in Robann that his quarry had perished in battle. Thus Amergin would be spared further trouble, and Robien too. Howland would have hated to see the two Kagonesti fight—not after all they'd been through together.

Robien returned with the rum. "Do you see, Sir Howland? Do you see?" he said excitedly.

Far out on the plain, a small group of people were wearily returning to Nowhere on foot. Leading the freed hostages were two figures, a few yards ahead of the rest. Even from this distance it was easy to see they were holding hands.

NOWHERE

Chapter Seventeen
Truth of Victory

With peace restored, the farmers worked hard to reclaim their lives. Hardly had the clash of arms faded into silence when they began tearing down the redoubt, using the earth to refill the trench. All the fallen were laid to rest there—old Calec, the village elder, Marren, who lost his soul and found it again even without his eyes, the children who had fought from the rooftops with Carver, and everyone else who perished fighting for the future of Nowhere—including the nameless bandits. Even they were given proper burial, lest their restless spirits remain bound to the scene of their violent deaths.

Last to be covered in the grave was Khorr. The farmers surrounded the minotaur's body with bound sheaves of barley straw, an honor usually reserved for their wisest, most respected elders.

277

In just a few days the redoubt was gone. Only a few damp clods of earth remained. The trench was filled in and trampled smooth, and all the barricades and barriers were pulled down. After that, the farmers turned to clearing out and repairing their homes.

Howland and his surviving fighters passed these days in deserved idleness, resting their aching limbs and nursing their hurts large and small. No one spoke of leaving yet or what they planned to do next. Their fatigue was too profound. In contrast, the villagers seemed to work ceaselessly. The hired warriors observed in wonder how quickly the farmers returned to their timeless tasks.

One morning, Malek and Laila entered her father Marren's old hut and did not reappear for some time. This did not seem too strange for long-separated lovers, but when they did emerge again their arms were full of unexpected treasures: pots of sweet oil, pressed fruit, barley flour in clay urns, cloth-wrapped cheeses and haunches of smoked game. Raika, asleep in the shade of a hut across the common, smelled the tang of cured venison and sat up, tossing aside the straw hat she'd been wearing to shade her face.

"Howland?" she called.

He was dozing too, sitting up as was his wont, his back against the daub wall of the hut. He cracked an eye when called.

"Eh?"

"Robien!"

The bounty hunter was already on his feet. "I see," he said slowly.

Together the hired warriors converged on Marren's house. They watched as Malek and Laila piled up stores outside the hut's only door. Malek greeted them cheerfully, but none of them responded.

"Where did all this come from?" said Howland.

"Why, the storage pit under the floor," Malek said, as if stating the obvious.

"Do all the huts have them?"

Laila shrugged. "Most do. It's where we store our reserves for winter."

Raika turned on one heel and marched to the next house. Nils, his wife Sai, and his son Larem were doing the very same thing as Malek and Laila, removing hidden goods from the hut. Raika snatched a pottery jug from Larem's hands. She yanked out the plug and sniffed the spout.

Howland and Robien arrived. She held out the jug to them. "Rum!" she cried.

"We also have beer," said Sai, a long-faced woman with frizzy red hair.

"Cold and parched as we've been these past days, and they have rum!" Raika threw back her head and took a long drink from the jug. After four swallows, she dashed the clay pot to the ground, shattering it.

Nils came out of his home. "What's this, Raika?"

"Miserable cheats!" She seized the injured Nils by his baggy shirt. "We ate barley cake for twenty-two days when you had venison?" She shoved him against the hut and reached for her sword. "After we shed our blood for you! We faced an army of bandits and ogres—for you! And this is our payment? I ought to kill you! I ought to kill you all!"

Her sword never came out. All at once Ezu was there, his hand over hers, clutching the hilt. She tried to pull free of him but found she couldn't.

"Don't interfere, wizard!" she snarled. "I won't be used this way!"

Ezu withdrew his hand, but Raika still couldn't draw her blade. It felt as if it were welded into the scabbard.

"So they lied to you," Ezu said blandly. "Are you surprised? A farmer has no one to rely on but himself. Their children learn at their parent's knee that the world is a hard, unforgiving place, willing to take everything the farmer nurtures in a single fire, flood, or raid. They're taught to hide everything valuable they have. This isn't just food or drink to them, it's life itself. Under the floors of each house you'll find all kinds of secret supplies: victuals of every kind, tools, weapons, even gold. They hide their meager wealth underground to protect it from catastrophe, but most of all to keep it from the rapacious ones with swords."

He stood aside. "Go ahead, demolish the house. Wreck the whole village until you get what you think is due you." Ezu put on the most solemn expression anyone had ever seen him assume. "Do that, then tell me how you are any different from Rakell."

A few steps behind Raika, Howland felt his outrage recede upon hearing Ezu's words.

Frustrated at her inability to draw her sword, Raika tore the whole thing off her hip, belt, scabbard and all. Wrapped in brass and leather, her sword was still a dangerous bludgeon, and Nils and his family scattered as she swung it hard against the door post. It made a deep gouge in the wood and put a dent in the scabbard, but Raika's rage dissipated with the blow.

"I've been here too long," she said to Nils. "I've shed too much blood. I would have killed you for a slab of venison and a bottle of rum."

She walked away, head hanging. Howland let her go.

Ezu said, "And you, Sir Howland? What will you do now?"

The soldier stooped to pick up a pot of pressed fruit Sai had dropped in her haste to avoid Raika's wild swing. The beeswax seal had broken, and sticky syrup oozed from the opening. Howland dabbed at the glistening syrup. Sweet berries. He handed the cracked pot to Sai.

"We've all been here too long. It's time to go." He rubbed his sunburnt brow. "If Robien and Raika agree to accompany me, we'll leave the village before sundown."

"My home is in the forest," the elf said, "but I will follow you one last time, Sir Howland."

"Please, call me just Howland. I've had enough of titles. The worst men I've ever known all had titles, so leave me apart from them."

The farmers had rounded a good number of bandit horses, and Howland was offered his pick of the herd. He took three for himself, Robien, and Raika, and a fourth to serve as a pack animal. He chose four stocky, sturdy beasts, each an indifferent color. They were not handsome, but they would walk all day with considerable burdens.

While the warriors packed their sparse gear, villagers prepared food and drink for their journey. By the time Howland, Raika, and Robien rode forth, their pack animal was well laden.

The surviving population of Nowhere gathered at the east end of the village. The setting sun was in their faces. Riding abreast with Howland in the center, the defenders stopped before the assembled villagers. Not a few of the farmers still clutched their spears, but most had abandoned warlike tools in favor of rakes, pitchforks, and spades.

Caeta raised her hand high. "We can never truly repay you for what you've done," she said. "Our loved ones are free, and our homes preserved. How can we tell you what that means to us?"

"You can't," Raika said flatly.

Howland was more diplomatic. "For myself, you owe me nothing. I regained something vital here, somthing I thought I'd lost." He considered his next words carefully. "Don't forget how to fight," he said. "Next time, when wolves are baying outside your door, take up swords and spears yourselves and defend what's yours. It's your right. Don't forget that."

He leaned down and clasped hands with Caeta, as did Raika and Robien after him. Malek and Laila, arms about each other's waists, waved and smiled. Nils, bolstered by Sai and Larem, added a hearty good-bye.

As she rode by, Raika spotted Bakar, one of the few survivors from her spear company. She turned her horse around, rode up to him, and dismounted. The young farmer, bearing his wounds without complaint, sidled away as Raika approached.

"You," she said roughly. "Come here."

He stayed where he was. "You're not going to hit me one last time, are you?"

"No, fool." Stalking over, she unbuckled her sword belt and handed it to Bakar. "This is for you. It's a good blade, if you can get it out of the scabbard. Think of it as a gift," she added, smiling. She swung up on her horse and cantered away to catch up to Howland and Robien.

Some of Bakar's neighbors surrounded him, curious about the Saifhumi woman's gift.

Bakar wrapped his fingers around the sword handle and pulled. The oiled steel blade slid easily out of its sheath. Whatever spell Ezu had cast on it was gone.

* * * * *

Three men, led by Wilf, took it on themselves to repair the cracked Ancestor in the well wall. They pried apart the stones from the top down, slowly isolating the long block of red sandstone. With reverence, two villagers gently lifted the broken top of the Ancestor free of the wall. Setting it down, they turned to freeing the lower half. Caeta happened by, and as she passed the rounded upper portion of the ancient totem rolled on its side, exposing its interior face to the sky. Caeta looked at it and gasped.

"It is them!"

Wilf and his helpers ceased tugging on the lower half of the Ancestor. "It's who?" he asked.

Caeta could only point mutely.

Wilf knelt by the red stone. The inside face was carved with a number of small faces, each about the size of a man's thumb, one below the other, from the rounded peak down to the break. The carvings had been turned inside when the wall was built, so no one living in Nowhere had ever seen the markings before.

Brow furrowed, Wilf ran dry, callussed fingers over the images. The bottom face was the smallest, but it had a pointed chin and long ears, like a kender. Above it was a human face, beardless . . . a woman's perhaps. Was that a turban on her head?

Lichen encrusted the next two faces. Wilf scratched it away with his thumbnail as his companions crouched behind him, peering over his shoulder. Caeta's startled cry had drawn others to the scene. They stood around, gazing at the broken totem, murmuring in low, amazed voices.

Under the gray lichen were a pair of similar faces, one facing up the other down, so it appeared they were staring into each other's eyes. One was depicted with a hood on, almond shaped eyes, and peaked ears. His compatriot was bare-headed, with cropped hair and identical ears. Two elves . . .

"Carver," Wilf said slowly, touching the lowest image. "Raika, Amergin, Robien—"

The next carved face had horns. Above it was a mature bearded man wearing a warrior's helmet.

"What does it mean?" asked the young farmer at Wilf's shoulder. He had no answer. He put the question to Caeta.

"It's an omen," she decided. "A promise from the past we did not see till now."

Bakar scratched his scruffy cheek. "What good is an omen if you find it too late?" he said, bewildered.

"Think of it as a token from the departed gods," the old woman replied. "A mark of favor from the great spirits to our humble village."

With considerable excitement, the men pried loose the lower half of the Ancestor stone, eager to see what it might show. Some prediction of the future, perhaps?

There was another image on the lower portion of the bloc: a full figure in profile, as long as Wilf's palm, striding vigorously. The relief was low, and the carving worn by years of rain, hot days, and cold nights. But two features were clear: the striding figure wore wide, billowing trousers, festooned with flowers, and on his head sprouted a fine set of deer antlers.

"So that's who he was," said Caeta.

Among the people of the plains there was an ancient legend. A legend of a stranger who came to their isolated settlements, spreading new ideas and new knowledge, teaching Nowhere's ancestors what crops to plant and sharing the secrets of fire and metal. The Wanderer, he was called.

Or, as Ezu always insisted, the Traveler.

* * * * *

The family of a farmer named Vank were clearing their hut by firelight. Vank had fallen in battle, fighting as one of Amergin's slingers. His hut was on the south side of the village, where the fighting had been the most intense. The roof had been smashed when an armor-clad bandit fell through it. Inside was a rat's nest of broken rafters and thatch, which Vank's wife and children patiently pulled apart and removed.

When the floor was clear, Vank's wife dug down a few inches to the open their storage pit. Where there should have been a plank lid, she found only loose dirt. Surprised, she called for her children to help her.

Digging furiously with their hands, they finally dragged out the broken planks, and Vank's wife thrust a burning brand into the hole.

A pale, dazed face looked up at her.

"Did we win?" asked Carver.

Vank's wife swooned. Her daughter ran for help, and soon half a dozen armed farmers came running, thinking a live bandit had been found in Vank's cellar. Malek was among them. He recognized the kender at once.

"Pull him out!" he shouted. A rope was lowered, and

Carver was hauled up. He was covered with fine dust, and one eye was black and swollen shut. He'd spent almost a week in the pit, but he was in remarkably good spirits, considering.

"I tried to dig my way out, but every time I touched the roof, more dirt fell in, so I quit. I figured Sir Howland would get me out eventually," he explained. "There was plenty to eat and drink down there."

"Howland is gone," Malek said.

Carver stepped out of the ring of curious villagers. He looked up and down the length of the common and saw none of his comrades.

"The bounty hunter elf and Raika too?" he said, already knowing the answer. The farmers nodded mutely.

"They left me!"

"We thought you were dead," said Malek.

The kender thrust out his small chest. "Takes more than an army of bandits to kill Carver Reedwhistle!"

A bucket of water was brought, and Carver set to washing. When his hands and face were clean, he clapped his small hands together, rubbing them briskly.

"Now that we're alone, just us friends," he said, grinning. "Tell me about the treasure."

* * * * *

Neither Raika nor Robien questioned Howland about their destination until they were well away from Nowhere. Once they were alone on the open plain, Raika said, "Where are we bound, captain?"

"Sergeant," he corrected. "I mean to find the iron mine Rakell was operating and free any slaves still working there."

"What about the Throtian Mining Guild?" asked the elf.

His tone was grim, unbending. "They'll see reason once I tell them Rakell is dead and his band dispersed."

"And the red dragon—what's his name?" Raika said.

Howland did not answer. His plan for dealing with the powerful guild and the even more powerful Overlord was the same: Creep in quietly, do what needs to be done, and don't attract too much unfriendly attention.

They were only three against unknown odds. A month past Raika would have called the enterprise mad, but after their amazing victory, she counted nothing Howland said impossible. She shrugged. It sounded like a worthwhile adventure.

On they rode. Howland didn't offer to stop or make camp. His companions stayed by him, unwilling to disappoint him by asking for rest.

Under a patchwork quilt of stars and wisps of cloud, they reached the high range, the last of the plains before the mountains rose in the east. Raika nodded in the saddle, letting her bandit-trained horse follow Howland's mount as she dozed. Robien might have napped too, but some hours past midnight he reined up.

"Whoa . . . what is it?" Howland said. Raika's horse fell to cropping the coarse broom straw at their feet.

"Someone's following us," the Kagonesti said.

Howland rode back to him. "How many?"

"Just one, on foot."

A glimmer of recognition lit up Howland's tired countenance. "One, eh? Why do I think I know who it is?"

If Robien knew, he didn't say. With Raika's horse still obediently following, Howland and the elf sauntered back the way they'd come. In less than a mile they spied a single figure wading up the center of the trail they'd made in the grass.

"How can you sense someone trailing us by half a mile?" asked Howland.

"The grass is dry. I heard his footfalls."

Howland wasn't sure if the Kagonesti was pulling his leg or not. They waited, reins slack, until the person on their trail was within easy earshot.

"Ezu! Is that you?" called Howland. Raika snorted and woke up when he shouted.

"Greetings, Sir Howland!" answered the familiar, cheerful voice.

He was wearing another one of his bizarre outfits—a short kilt made of some dark, checkered cloth, leggings, and a hip-length wraparound robe in red and gold. He had on a wide, stiff-brimmed felt hat and a pair of saffron-tinted spectacles. An enormous bundle was slung on his shoulders, and he balanced his load by leaning on a long hardwood staff.

"What are you doing here?" asked Howland.

"Still traveling—"

"Seems to me you're following us."

"We happen to be going in the same direction. I am circling the world by traveling east."

"You're welcome to come with us," the old soldier said. "You're a man who makes things happen."

They put Ezu's bag on the packhorse, and he rode double with Robien, the lightest of the three.

"Why do you wear those glasses?" asked Raika.

Without answering, Ezu unhooked the gold wire frames from his ears and offered the spectacles to her. She put them on.

"Sink me! It's daylight!"

Robien said, "What do you mean?

She gave the glasses to him. "Try 'em yourself!"

The elf slipped the springy wire hooks around his ears. When he raised his gaze to the horizon, he was startled to see the landscape of the high plain was bright as day. He could see Howland riding a few steps ahead, Raika, everything, as clearly as if it were noon.

He removed the dark yellow lenses and gave them back to Ezu.

With a smile, Ezu tucked the spectacles into his robe.

As the night wore on, Ezu told them stories of his travels, such as his visit to the island of Kernaf.

"Kernaf is inhabited entirely by pirates," he said. "They elect a chief to rule over them from a conclave of ships' captains. The current chief is a fellow named Gramdene, widely reputed to be the handsomest man in the world."

"A handsome pirate? Not likely!" Raika said. "Buccaneers lead too rough a life to be pretty."

"Well, I met him, and while I don't claim much taste in such matters, he was a most striking fellow," Ezu remarked.

Gramdene, he said, was not yet thirty, with olive skin, bronze colored hair, and eyes of different colors.

"How's that possible?" asked Robien.

"I cannot say, but I can vouch for them. One is darkest brown, like Raika's, and the other pale gray."

From plundered ships Gramdene acquired a rich wardrobe and never went out without being garbed in the finest silks, velvets, and brocades. He had a personal entourage of five fierce female pirates, whom he called his "Hand," who'd sworn blood oaths to defend Gramdene at the cost of their own lives.

"His wives?" Howland asked.

"No, indeed! The Hand are also sworn to chastity, lest jealousy of each other lead them to shirk their duty to protect Captain Gramdene."

Raika smirked. "Has this handsome fiend no lovers, then?"

Ezu shrugged. "It's a subject of much speculation. While I was on Kernaf, he was said to be paying court to a female captain named Artalai, granddaughter of pirate queen Artavash."

Raika twisted in the saddle to face him. "Does her line still exist? She was from Saifhum!"

Howland said, "I never heard of her."

"She was a bold and wicked woman, with hair like flame and a temper to match. The ruler of Saifhum, the Grand Mariner, obtains office by buying it. Whoever pays the largest sum to the inhabitants of the island wins the title for life. She tried to become ruler of Saifhum by pledging the greatest sum to the people but was outbid in the end by a moneylender, Pertinex.

"When Artavash lost, she led her fleet of sixty galleys away, sowing fire and destruction all along the north coast until her rage abated. Still hankering for a kingdom, she tried to capture the great city of Palanthas but was defeated. Eventually she reached Kernaf with her fleet. She massacred the natives living there, peaceful fishing folk, and proclaimed herself queen."

"A proper monster," said Howland. "Was she ever brought to justice?"

Raika shook her head. "Not in the way you mean, but she did meet a hard fate. She grew older and infirm, but she was still a hard-driving taskmaster. When the War of the Lance broke out, Artavash led her fleet against the

draconian invaders. She perished along with most of her
ships, but the draconians had to abandon the conquest of
Kernaf."

"They still revere her there," Ezu added. "There is a
colossal copper statue of her in the harbor, bright red
metal despite years of weather and sea spray."

"How can that be?" asked Robien. "Copper usually
turns green when exposed to sun and rain."

"The pirates set their prisoners to polishing it,"
explained Ezu.

"When I get home, I'll ask about this Gramdene,"
Raika said. "Handsomest man in the world, ha! Everyone
knows the best-looking men come from Saifhum!"

"Like Enjollah?" Ezu teased.

"Enjollah is a fine figure of a man but not handsome."
Raika looked thoughtful. "He has other qualities."

The three men raised their eyebrows.

"He's an excellent . . . navigator," Raika said stiffly.

The men said nothing.

By dawn the gray peaks of the mountains were in
sight. Howland and company encountered more traffic
here: wagons laden with iron ingots, escorted by rough-
looking hired cavalry. When asked, they denied working
for the Throtian Guild. Most of them were independent
workmen, they said, hauling iron to dealers in Sanction
and Neraka. Listening between the wagoneers' words,
Howland deduced the Throtian Mining Guild was an
outlaw operation, despised by legitimate miners and
merchants.

The western slopes of the mountains were dotted
with pits and tunnels of iron mines. The party rode
south, working their way along the foothills, inquiring
after Rakell and the Throtian concern. No one had any

information more substantial than "they're south of here" or "try farther south." Two days passed until they got their first serious lead—a burned-out caravan of six ore carts. Bodies littered the ravine, and they'd not been dead long. Some were laborers in coarse woolens, while others were lean, rangy men in mismatched armor, just like the ones who filled the ranks of Rakell's bandit army.

"What happened here?" Raika wondered. "Was it the dragon?"

Robien looked over the scene. "Not a dragon or rival bandits—rebellion. The slaves rose up and attacked their captors."

"How do you know that?" she asked.

The bounty hunter's practiced eye roved over the scene. "The horses are gone, but not the arms."

Desperate slaves attacked their guards, took their horses and the ones pulling the carts, and rode hard for freedom. A red dragon would have slaughtered men and beasts indiscrimately. Victorious robbers would have stripped the fallen riders of all their arms and armor. Had the guards taken matters into their own hands, they would not have left their dead comrades by the trail.

It was a simple matter to backtrack the caravan to its source. The trail led up a narrow, winding canyon, penetrating deep into the foothills. As darkness fell, Howland halted his comrades short of the mine.

"Better to enter by day," he said. "Tonight, rest. I'll go ahead and scout around."

Robien gave his reins to Ezu and slid off to the ground. "Let me go. This is my sort of job."

Howland agreed, and Robien went ahead on foot. The others withdrew up the hillside a hundred yards, camping behind a hedge of boulders. Since they couldn't afford to light a fire and give away their position, they ate cold rations. Raika, unaccustomed to the mountain chill, wrapped herself in one of Caeta's homemade blankets and went to sleep.

Howland sat with a naked sword on his lap. As he did most nights, he half-slept, resting but alert to any stray sign or sound. Long after Raika had begun snoring and he'd closed his eyes, he heard Ezu rise.

Opening one eye, he saw the traveler had changed clothes. Draped head to toe in charcoal-colored robes, Ezu was almost invisible against the rocky hillside.

"Going somewhere?" Howland rumbled.

Ezu seemed genuinely surprised, turning to peer at the old soldier through his tinted spectacles.

"I thought you were asleep!"

"It's an old trick that kept me alive on many a campaign." He shifted the sword off his knees, laying it on the ground by his right hand. "Where are you going this time of night?"

Ezu tapped his special glasses. "Darkness is no barrier to me," he said, smiling.

He moved toward the gap in the boulders that led down the hill to the trail. Howland was up in a flash, blocking the traveler's way.

"I've been thinking a lot about you since leaving Nowhere," Howland said quietly. "You have an astonishing ability to appear and disappear just when you're needed most. How is that, Ezu?"

"Travel is not easy. The world is full of cruel and dangerous people, you know. This one has cultivated many ways of getting by."

"When we first found you, you were trussed up, waiting

to be rescued. How is it no one since has been able to hold you?"

"I learn from my experiences."

Howland frowned. "Old Marren said you blinded everyone in Rakell's camp the night we were there. How? You were separated from us, taken by Rakell, but he didn't harm a hair on your head. He murdered Marren. Why didn't he hurt you?"

"This one removed himself from Rakell's presence."

"But not for more than a day." Howland presented the point of his sword to Ezu's chest. "I've figured it out, partly. The lynching party was right all along. You are a spy."

"How can you say that, after I've helped you?" Ezu asked.

Howland stepped closer, keeping his sword point over Ezu's heart. "Yes, that threw me for a time, then I realized the truth. Rakell wasn't the real master of this scheme. There's a mastermind behind everything, a lord whom you serve, too. Rakell blundered when he chose to remain at the village, fighting. It furthered your master's scheme, which was to get rid of Rakell."

Ezu held up both hands, like a petty thief caught by a shopkeeper. "You're a wise man, Howland. This guise of mine, Ezu the traveler, is a pretense—but you're wrong about one thing. I am not a spy."

Howland pushed his blade forward, pricking Ezu ever so slightly. The strange foreigner grimaced but held his ground.

"What lies at the end of this trail?" Howland demanded, voice rising.

"Just another pebble on the path of life, my friend."

Howland leaned on his blade. He only meant to cut Ezu

a little, to wipe the smug tone from his answers. Instead of flesh and blood resistance, Howland found himself blundering forward, passing through thin air where Ezu had been standing. His sword clanged loudly against a rock. Raika awakened, grasping for the weapon she no longer carried.

"Howland?" she said, bleary with sleep.

"I regret parting this way." Ezu's voice came from behind. Whirling, Howland saw the traveler's silhouette against the stars. He was standing atop a boulder a good twenty feet high. No one could have climbed up there so quickly.

"I would have liked to have seen your journey through to its end," Ezu continued, "but I cannot be fending off swords every time I chose to go wandering. Farewell, Howland uth Ungen." He bowed his head. "And to you, lady. When you meet Gramdene of Kernaf, remember it was I who first told you his name."

"Ezu!" Howland rushed to the foot of the boulder. Before he reached it, the traveler's black outline had merged into the night.

Raika got up, scratching her matted hair. "What just happened?" she said, spicing her question with a few favorite expletives.

Howland explained his suspicions and his theory that Ezu had been working for the same boss as Rakell.

"Do you really think so?" she asked.

He was no longer sure. Indeed he felt a little foolish and ashamed of having driven Ezu off.

Raika went to the boulder where Ezu vanished. She'd seen him do amazing things, but he had never disappeared in plain sight before.

"Will he return, do you think?

"I take him at his word. He won't be back," Howland said.

They leaned their backs against the boulder and gazed at their quiet, empty campsite. It suddenly seemed much darker and colder than before. Like a ghostly mask, the single moon peered between the mountain peaks. Howland felt suddenly and strangely bereft.

"I wronged him."

Raika shook her head. "Your reasoning was sound. I would have agreed with you had I been awake." She folded her arms. "Who was he, really? A wizard? A spirit? A god?"

"There are no gods," Howland said firmly. "They abandoned us."

They returned to their respective blankets. Before Raika lay down again, she saw something glinting in the moonlight. Curious, she groped in the shadows and found Ezu's saffron spectacles.

"Look here! Did he forget these?"

"I don't think so." Howland took the glasses and tried them on. "However silly he acts, I don't think Ezu does anything by accident." He drew in his breath sharply when he saw the mountain around them as clearly as if it were day. Removing the spectacles carefully he said, "These must be his parting gift for Robien."

"Why him?"

"I need nothing now, and he's already given you a present."

"What?"

"He named your future husband for you, didn't he?"

"Who?" Raika said incredulously.

"The pirate king of Kernaf, Gramdene— 'the handsomest man in the world'."

Raika tried to laugh Howland's assertion aside, but the

forced merriment expired in her throat. Could it be true? Was she destined to be Gramdene's wife?

Howland put the spectacles in his saddlebag. He would give them to Robien when he returned. As for Raika, thoughts of her future mate kept her awake for almost an hour.

NOWHERE

Chapter
Eighteen
Spoils

A t first light, Howland and Raika resumed their ride up the narrow val-
ley. Howland expected Robien back by dawn, but the sun
was over the mountain, and the elf was still gone. Yet the
valley was remarkably quiet and calm. Raika was the nervous one. She rode alongside Howland with spear in hand,
warily watching the heights above them.

As they ascended into the cleft of the mountain, they
noticed signs of recent violence. They came across wrecked
carts, abandoned equipment, and dead bodies, both slave
and bandit. Not all were human. A pair of ogres, overcome
by scores of small wounds, lay side by side atop a flat boulder. Evidently they'd made a stand against a large number
of opponents before succumbing. More curious were the
slain dwarves they found in overturned wagons. They

were prosperously turned out, but no one had bothered to plunder them. Judging by their injuries, they were felled when a hail of stones knocked them senseless. Their horses had gone wild, turning over the conveyances. If the impact had not killed the dwarves, their cargo had. Every wheeled vehicle was laden with scores of bright metal ingots. Several hundred lay scattered on the trail for more than a mile.

"Iron or steel?" Raika wondered.

Howland dismounted and picked up a hefty bar. He rapped the ingot with a handy stone, and it made a dull sound.

"Pig iron. Why would fleeing dwarves fill their carts with pig iron?" he mused.

Three plumes of smoke rose from the plateau ahead. As they rounded the bend, Raika spotted someone on the path. She pulled back on her reins and warned Howland.

He drew up beside her. "No, it's all right. It's Robien."

The Kagonesti was standing in the cart path, gazing at the scene. Raika and Howland rode slowly ahead until they reached him. Robien did not look up when they stopped on either side of him.

"Good morning," he said. "Sorry I didn't come back, but I thought I'd better keep watch here. I knew you'd come eventually." He lowered the sword from his shoulder and shoved it into its scabbard.

Raika and Howland got down, tying their mounts to a convenient sapling. Howland gave Raika a spare sword from the bundle on the pack horse. She buckled it around her hips. With Robien leading the way, they entered the silent camp.

A rough stockade of pine logs had been erected around the mine works, but many of the sharpened timbers had been toppled. They had been broken down from the inside, as every one lay with their crowns pointing outward. Inside the fence, all was chaos. Great heaps of cinders and slag, still smoldering, lay alongside the central path. The air stank of coke and sulfur.

"Is there anyone alive here?" Howland wondered.

"Someone's stirring. I heard him last night," said Robien. "I never caught up with them, and I decided to wait until you arrived."

A second dirt road crossed the first at right angles. They stood at the crossroads, taking in the scene. On their right was a massive furnace house made of local timber and stone. Two tall chimneys, one broken off to half the height of the other, still gave off smoke. The upper half of the broken chimney had come down on the roof of the furnace house, smashing it wide open. The wooden part of the structure had been reduced to charred wood, and the stone walls were blackened on the inside. Outside the furnace house were scores of abandoned wheelbarrows, some empty, some full and lying on their sides, spilling coal or dull red ore on the ash-covered ground.

To the left stood a number of plank and canvas huts, the kind used by an army on campaign. Most were trampled and torn. A few had been torched. Beyond them was a rail-fence stockade full of conical hide tents. The front of the stockade lay flat on the ground, facing outward.

The newcomers walked through the ruined camp. Now and then one or the other would stop to examine some trace, some relic, or some body. By the time they reached the shattered stockade, it was clear what had happened.

"The slaves must have revolted," Howland said, pointing to the conical tents. "They were housed here. At some point they rushed the stockade and broke it down. They rampaged out, demolishing the outer camp where their captors lived."

"Interested only in flight, they stole every animal they could find and fled," Robien added.

"Who brought down the chimney, I wonder?" Raika said.

"Who knows?" Howland said. "Maybe the black gang did it as part of the rebellion."

Everywhere they found signs of struggle, destruction, and a hasty departure. Near the mouth of the mine they found a sturdier, more finished building, built in the fashion of a dwarven mountain hall. Every window was shuttered with thick, seasoned planks, but they had been breached nonetheless. The big, iron-strapped door was off its hinges, stove in by a salvaged timber used as a makeshift battering ram.

Raika hesitated at the open door. "Hello?" she called. "Anyone there?"

No one answered, but they heard a scuffling from within. Out came three swords.

Robien whispered, "Guard the door, Sergeant. Raika and I will go in and flush out whatever's here."

Inside the hall was dim, with only the light from shattered shutters leaking in. Robien went right, Raika left.

She was sure she was standing in the sacked headquarters of the Throtian Mining Guild. Several rooms were filled with broken furniture and scattered sheets of parchment. Raika knelt to examine a random page. It was covered with columns of tiny, precisely written figures.

A thick, hairy hand protruded from under an upsidedown table. She kicked it aside and found the body of a dwarf. He'd been battered to death, but his rings and silver gorget were still in place. Raika pondered relieving him of his jewelry. He didn't need his finery any more, and the price of it might get her home to Saifhum.

Underneath the dead dwarf was a dark brown leather bag. It clinked when Raika nudged it. Sweat beaded on her lip. She opened the flap and poured the contents out.

Gold! Big Thorbardin double-hammer coins rang and rolled across the floor. Raika yelped with delight. She quickly counted forty-six double-hammers, which were twice the weight of a standard gold piece. Now she could get home in style!

She swept the thick golden disks back into the bag and quit the room without disturbing the dead dwarf's jewelry. The gold was ample reward, and taking it was less likely to anger the dead dwarf's spirit.

Raika emerged into the hallway as something darted across her field of view, passing from a room three doors down.

"Hey!" Raika fumbled for her sword. "Stand where you are!"

She darted into the doorway where the mysterious stranger had gone. No sooner had she done so when her danger-honed senses forced her to leap back. A heavy, black-bladed axe whistled by, missing the tip of Raika's nose by a hair. It crashed to the floor, burying its edge in the planking.

Raika promptly stamped her foot on the axe head, pinning it to the floor. She presented the point of her sword to her attacker's chin. He was an unusually short, rotund dwarf with wild yellow hair and a wide-eyed expression.

"Don't kill me!" he cried shrilly, throwing up his hands.

"Strange words from an axe-wielding ambusher!" Raika said. Flushed with anger, she stepped forward, forcing her captive back. "Give me a good reason not to cut your gullet here and now!"

"Take what you will, but spare me, gracious lady!"

Lip curled, she lowered her sword and grabbed the little man by the collar. He was a young fellow, with only peach-fuzz on his chin. Yanking him up so high he was on tip-toes, Raika propelled her prisoner into the hall.

"Robien! Howland! It's all right—I caught a little rat!"

Howland sidled cautiously through the open doors. "What have you got there?"

"The last of the mining guild, I reckon." She shook the unhappy dwarf. "What's your name?"

"Banngur, if you please, lady." He shrank from her fearsome glare. "I'm not of the guild."

"Who are you, then?" asked Howland.

"A scribe, honorable sir. A bookkeeper. I keep—I kept—the tallies for the Mining Guild."

Robien appeared behind them. "You'd better come see this!" he said urgently. Without waiting for a reply, he dashed out again.

Howland and Raika followed, the Saifhumi woman holding onto Banngur's collar all the way. Robien led them deep into the hall, into a large open room. Judging from the stone walls, the dwarves had built their headquarters into the side of the mountain itself.

From one side of the room to the other, and from the entrance to the rear wall, the place was filled with waist-high piles, covered with tarpaulins. Howland estimated there were more than a hundred piles.

Robien lifted the corner of the nearest tarp and flung it back. Bright metal gleamed.

"Iron?" said Howland.

Robien shook his head. "I tried to score it with my knife blade. It's steel."

Raika loosed her grip on Banngur. The pudgy book-keeper tried to flee, but she easily tripped him. Planting a foot on his squirming backside, she whispered hoarsely, "Is *all* of it steel?"

"Probably." Howland swallowed, hand holding his own throat. "This was the treasure Rakell was defending. There must be tons of steel here—"

"Eleven tons and forty-two hundredweight," said Banngur. "Property of the Throtian Mining Guild, Limited."

Raika kicked him. "Property of us!"

"Wait," said Howland. "Let the dwarf up."

She let Banngur stand. Howland bade the little man come closer.

"Tell us what happened here," he said.

Banngur looked from one face to the other. Deciding Howland's was the most trustworthy, he moved away from Raika and Robien.

"The dragon came," he quavered.

"The red dragon? He did this?"

"He flew by and knocked down our chimney, that's all." said the dwarf. "When that happened, the workers revolted."

"You mean, the slaves rebelled and regained their freedom?"

Banngur nodded.

"How many slaves?"

Numbers were Banngur's business. "Two hundred twenty-nine, all told," he said.

"How many guards were there when the rebellion broke out?"

The dwarf thought a moment, silently moving his lips. "Eighteen humans, and three ogres."

"How many dwarves?" said Raika.

"Eleven, but none were soldiers. Guild members supervised mining and smelting the ore, but discipline was left to Lord Rakell's men."

Howland caught his comrades' eyes. Almost casually, he asked, "What happened to Rakell?"

"He rode off to gather more workers," Banngur said, "but he never came back. When the workers—"

Raika narrowed her eyes at him, and the dwarf corrected himself.

"When the slaves realized Rakell was overdue, they grew restive. The dragon toppling the foundry stack was the last straw. They refused to fight the fire and attacked the few remaining guards."

"Who killed the dwarves—the prisoners or the guards?"

Banngur looked downcast. "The guards. Guild Master Tharmon would not ransom us, so the guards struck him down and looted the camp, looking for gold."

"Speaking of which . . ." Raika hefted the bag she'd found. She tossed it to Howland. He glanced inside. It was a handsome sum, but compared to the lake of steel before them, it was a pittance.

Robien hefted a bright ingot. "Why didn't your master buy off the remaining guards with steel?"

Banngur had no answer.

"Pride, wasn't it?" said Howland. "That, and steel is too bulky to move without draft animals, and they were all gone, weren't they?"

Banngur nodded again.

"How long ago did all this occur?"

Banngur said several days—on about the same day that Rakell perished in Nowhere.

"Get out," Howland said.

Banngur blinked a few times, uncertain what the human meant.

"Begone!" the soldier shouted. "You're free, get out!"

Banngur shuffled backward a few steps then said, "I have nothing. How will I get to civilized parts?"

Howland tossed the bag of gold coins at him. "That'll get you anywhere you want to go."

"If some rascal doesn't gut you first and take it away from you," Raika said cheerfully.

White-faced, Banngur ran from the room.

Raika ran to the center of the storeroom, whipping off tarps right and left. "We're rich, sergeant! We're stinking rich! By thunder, with a third of this haul I could buy the office of Grand Mariner of Saifhum myself!"

"I've never seen so much steel," Howland agreed.

It fell to Robien to voice the unhappy truth. "But we'll never get it all down the mountain."

He held up an ingot in each hand. "These weigh twenty pounds apiece. There must be thousands of them. How can we move them? We only have four horses between us."

Raika clutched at a pile with both hands. "We could repair some of those wagons—!"

"No time," said Howland.

"What do you mean?"

"Too many people know about this hoard. Every slave who escaped, every hired blade who took part in the slaughter of the guildmasters knows this steel is here. How long do you think it will be before one of them comes back with enough help to claim the steel?"

"So we'll take what we can! Maybe two or three piles each?" Raika said desperately.

"We'd kill the horses trying to haul so much, and if we took a few wagon loads, how would three of us defend our cargo against every wandering mercenary gang and brigand band on the plain between here and the sea?"

Raika's joyous expression shattered like a cheap pot. "Can't we take *something*?"

"No more than you can safely carry." Howland stacked four ingots in the crook of his arm. "This is enough for me."

Robien took none. "Steel means little in the forest, my home. When I need money, I collect the bounty on a wanted criminal. Beyond that, my needs are few."

"Well, carry some steel for me then!" Raika protested. She tried to manage five bars, but one slipped out of her arms and fell ringing on the floor.

In the end she loaded her horse and the pack animal with ten ingots, two hundred pounds of steel. Each bar bore the stamp of the mining guild, certifying its purity and hardness. When Raika returned to her island home, she wouldn't have enough to buy the office of Grand Mariner, but she would have enough to purchase and outfit her own ship. She would be a captain at last.

By early afternoon they were back on the trail, riding down the ravine to the plain. Robien, who hadn't asked before, queried Howland about Ezu.

"He left. You know Ezu," he said. "He did leave you a parting gift." Reaching into his saddlebag, Howland brought out the saffron spectacles. "Ezu wanted you to have these."

The elf would not take them. "I must rely on my own skills, the ancient ways of my people, and not a conjurer's tricks."

Howland shook his head. "They're a tool, like any

other. You carry a steel sword, which your forebears did not know. Would you give up steel to be more like your ancestors?"

They argued good-naturedly for some time, and Robien finally accepted Ezu's spectacles.

On level ground, Howland stopped his horse. Already Robien had turned his mount south, toward the forest lands of his birth, while Raika faced north, toward the distant sea. Howland faced dead ahead, due west.

"This is where we part," he said.

"Come to Saifhum," Raika urged. "A man of courage and wits can do well there."

"Ride south, if you wish," countered Robien. "In the forest, all are free."

Howland thanked them, but declined both offers. "The time is right for me to return to Solamnia, the land of my long-ago youth. I've cleansed my soul of the stain of collaboration. The steel in my saddlebags will buy me a small homestead, and there I will live out my remaining years. I shall till my own field," he said, "and raise the food I eat."

"You, sergeant? A farmer?" asked Raika ironically.

"It's an honest life."

He shook hands with Robien and wished the elf success. Robien managed a cryptic smile, saying, "Only one bounty has ever escaped me."

"Amergin?" Howland said.

"He died in the battle," Raika added unnecessarily.

"Yes. The Brotherhood of Quen will be very disappointed."

The old soldier said, "Everyone needs one failure in their life. It keeps you humble."

With a final wave, Robien galloped away. Following the

lowest contour of the land, he soon disappeared in the distance.

"Farewell, old man," Raika said. She put a strong hand behind his neck and pulled him roughly to her. She kissed him on his stubbled cheek.

"Farewell, sailor. I didn't think we could do it, but we did."

She wrapped the reins of her mount and the pack horse around her fist. Patting the bars of steel in her saddlebags, Raika said, "Next time you go recruiting, leave me out, will you? The pay was good, but the hours were terrible!"

She moved off at a stately walk, unwilling to tired her burdened animals. It took a long time for the Saifhumi woman to pass out of view, but Howland remained where he was until he was alone on the plain.

The setting sun stabbed at his eyes. Hitching the brim of his old felt hat down low, Howland started for home.

The Minotaur Wars

From *New York Times* best-selling author Richard A. Knaak comes a powerful new chapter in the DRAGONLANCE® saga.

The continent of Ansalon, reeling from the destruction of the War of Souls, slowly crawls from beneath the rubble to rebuild – but the fires of war, once stirred, are difficult to quench. Another war comes to Ansalon, one that will change the balance of power throughout Krynn.

NIGHT OF BLOOD
Volume I

Change comes violently to the land of the minotaurs. Usurpers overthrow the emperor, murder all rivals, and dishonor minotaur tradition. The new emperor's wife presides over a cult of the dead, while the new government makes a secret pact with a deadly enemy. But betrayal is never easy, and rebellion lurks in the shadows.

The Minotaur Wars begin June 2003.

Strife throughout the land of Krynn

CITY OF THE LOST
The Linsha Trilogy, Volume One
Mary H. Herbert

After the near-disaster chronicled in *The Clandestine Circle*, the Knights of Solamnia send Linsha Majere to an outpost in the backend of nowhere. But trouble seems to run in her family, and Linsha soon finds herself involved in a war between two dragon overlords, the Knights of Solamnia, the Legion of Steel, and invaders from across the sea.

August 2003

DARK THANE
The Age of Mortals
Jeff Crook

Beneath Thorbardin, a spellbinding fanatic preaches revolution, turning the hearts of those who are caught up in the cause. The ancient dwarven nation is bloodily divided, and the true leadership banished.

November 2003

Tales of
Ansalon's ancient past

WINTERHEIM
The Icewall Trilogy, Volume Three
Douglas Niles

Inside the forbidding confines of Winterheim, a royal captive is
scheduled for execution. A do-or-die assault on the ogre fortress comes
from without, but rebellion is spurred from within.

January 2003

A WARRIOR'S JOURNEY
The Ergoth Trilogy, Volume One
Paul B. Thompson & Tonya C. Cook

The mighty Ergothian empire is gripped by civil war. Centuries before the
first Cataclysm sunders Ansalon, two imperial dynasts struggle for suprem
power. Amid this chaos and upheaval, a brave young peasant shakes the
towers of the mighty as his fate and the destiny of Krynn collide.

May 2003

SACRED FIRE
The Kingpriest Trilogy, Volume Three
Chris Pierson

At long last, the Kingpriest has overstepped his power. His chief
opponent is the warrior who was once his most faithful disciple,
but even that does not sway the visions of a fanatic.
Because of his blindness, all Istar will suffer.

October 2003

Before the War of the Lance, there were other adventures.

Check out these new editions of the popular Preludes series!

DARKNESS & LIGHT
Sturm Brightblade and Kitiara are on their way to Solamnia
when they run into a band of gnomes in jeopardy.

February 2003

KENDERMORE
Tasslehoff Burrfoot is arrested for violating the kender laws of
prearranged marriage – but his bride pulls a disappearing act of her own.

April 2003

BROTHERS MAJERE
Desperate for money, Raistlin and Caramon Majere agree to take
on a job in the backwater village of Mereklar, but they soon discover
they may be in over their heads.

June 2003

RIVERWIND THE PLAINSMAN
A barbarian princess and her beloved walked into the Inn of the
Last Home, and thus began the DRAGONLANCE® Saga.
This is the adventure that led to that fateful moment.

October 2003

FLINT THE KING
Flint Fireforge's comfortable life turns to chaos
when he travels to his ancestral home.

November 2003

TANIS: THE SHADOW YEARS
When an old dwarf offers Tanis Halfelven the chance to find his father,
he embarks on an adventure that will change him forever.

December 2003

The original Chronicles

From *New York Times* best-selling authors
Margaret Weis & Tracy Hickman

These classics of modern fantasy literature – the three titles that
started it all – are available for the very first time in individual
hardcover volumes. All three titles feature stunning cover art
from award-winning artist Matt Stawicki.

DRAGONS OF AUTUMN TWILIGHT
Volume I
Friends meet amid a growing shadow of fear and rumors of war.
Out of their story, an epic saga is born.

January 2003

DRAGONS OF WINTER NIGHT
Volume II
Dragons return to Krynn as the Queen of Darkness launches her assault.
Against her stands a small band of heroes bearing a new weapon:
the DRAGONLANCE.

July 2003

DRAGONS OF SPRING DAWNING
Volume III
As the War of the Lance reaches its height, old friends clash amid
gallantry and betrayal. Yet their greatest battles lie within each of them.

November 2003